JOY

CARLA HARTE

First Printing: June 2021

ISBN: 9798521122202

Carla Harte
www.carlaharte.com
carlahartewriting@gmail.com
Facebook @MrsHarteWrites
Twitter @carlaharteauth1

The beauty of a woman is seen in her eyes,

because that is the doorway to her heart.

The place where love resides.

Audrey Hepburn

Chapter 1

Once upon a time, in a land far, far away, lived a girl. But not just any girl. She had the fairest, wrinkle-free skin, the bluest brightest eyes and the reddest, plumpest lips.

Because it always is, isn't it? It's never now, and it's never nearby and it's never ever anyone who's just like we are.

They're never a bit tubby, or a bit old, they don't have one boob bigger than the other or a lazy eye or a dodgy back that takes 20 minutes to straighten up every morning.

Nope, fairy tales only happen for those who have the good fortune to be alive way back when and way back where and who have the vital statistics of a plank.

They wouldn't want any middle aged, halfway up the hill and out of breath types to be thinking that these things could happen to them. Fairy tales are for the young, right?

Sod that.

So . . . .

Once upon last Wednesday, in a house, just around the corner, lived a woman. A forty-two year young, four child bearing, grown ass adult who can think for herself and who ....

Wait . . . .

Maybe, as a grown ass adult, its absolutely fine that happily ever after only ever happens a long time ago and very far away. At least then, the reason life hasn't panned out quite as planned is purely a matter of logistics. We were simply born in the wrong place, at the wrong time.

But it's still ok to dream though isn't it, to have that little innocent hope that one day we can take a little day trip to far far away and that once upon a time might, after all, be just a day away. We are all, ultimately, the author of our own fairy tales and crafter of our own happily ever after, and for that we can be whatever the fuck we want to be.

So let's start from the top.

Once upon a time, in a land not *too* far, far away, lived a princess. A grown ass forty-two year old princess who talks too much, sleeps too little, survives primarily on cake and coffee and who lives on a housing estate somewhere between Manchester and Birmingham.

She's not there right now though. She's at the hospital where she's worked tirelessly for almost a fifth of a century. Half her life.

But tonight, she's not on shift. Tonight, she doesn't even know she's there.

Her uniform is torn and grubby, the tubes protruding awkwardly from each nostril are not standard staff issue and she's in a deep, deep sleep. But not the type that true loves kiss can rouse. This isn't an evil curse or a magic spell gone awry, this is just good old fashioned drug-induced sedation which will begin to wear off soon enough, all on its own, and slowly, hopefully, she'll be stirred by the rhythmic beep of the machinery that surrounds her bed and the faint chatter from the nurses station out in the corridor.

They sound worried though, as they potter in and out of the ward, biting their nails and checking out of the window as they fuss about needing to move her off the bay and to a side room in-case someone tries to get in again.

And, eventually, *if* she wakes up, she'll find out where she is and what happened.

But for that, we need to go back to the beginning. Right back to once upon a time . . . .

Chapter 2

C an we go yet?" moaned Elliot, Joy Lane's fifteen-year-old son, who was already on his bike and halfway out of the front door.

"Dad'll be home any minute." She pleaded.

"You know he won't be," he said, edging his back wheel further out of the door.

"He will, he promised," she snapped back.

"He promised last time, too. He promises every time," said Owen, Elliot's younger-by twelve-minutes brother, who was sat at the tiny kitchen table scrolling through his phone.

"Come back," yelled Joy, spotting Elliot's bike slipping slowly backwards out of the door.

Stomping down the hall and grabbing it by its handle bars, she yanked it back into the house. "Five minutes," she said, holding her palmed hand up in front of the scrunched-up face poking out from beneath a battered old baseball cap that reeked of wet grass and cigarette smoke. Joy turned to walk away, and he flipped his middle finger up.

Owen shot him a look and joined him by the door, his face darting to his feet and causing his muddy locks to dangle into his eyes, presumably so that she couldn't see them.

She still could though, as she turned and eyeballed the pair suspiciously.

So alike, yet so different, they were near identical in face, Owen's eyes were a little further apart and Elliot's brows tilted slightly lower and he wore a near constant pout, yet while Elliot was full of hot air and mischief, Owen was mostly full of guilt purely for knowing what his brother was up to most of the time.

"Just five more minutes. He knows how important this is," she said, reaching in between them both and locking the door from the inside.

Picking her mobile phone up from the kitchen countertop, she went to swipe the screen, but it was still unlocked and already open on his number from the last time she'd tried to call. So she hit the green button and lifted the slim black handset to her ear.

"You are through to the voicemail of 075267896. The person you are calling is unavailable," Joy hit end call and slat the phone back down onto the fake granite laminate.

'No, he fucking isn't,' she hissed under her breath.

"It's ten to, Mum. We're supposed to be there for seven," said Owen, "Maybe we should *all* just go."

Joy shook her head. "No, we can't take Zach . . . "

"But the school know what he's like, they won't mind," protested Elliot.

"But I will," she shot back, "This is about you two," she said, slumping down onto the hard wooden bench at the kitchen table and glancing through into the living room. Zachary, who at six years old was the youngest Lane, was currently sat butt naked in the window, wiping his hands around in the condensation even though she'd only dressed him in his favourite dinosaur pyjamas less than fifteen minutes earlier.

"I'll watch him while we're there, Mum," said Owen.

"You said that last time," she seethed. "It took us over an hour to get him down."

The truth was, she was still embarrassed about their last meeting at the school. In what should have been a simple ten-minute discussion, Zachary, having evaded Owen's grip, had managed to rip down three student exhibitions, empty every tub of hand soap from the toilets and had finally scaled the floor-to-ceiling multi gym in the boy's games barn. He was good at climbing, and he was quick, but he was only good at going up, coming down, he had a tendency just to let go, in which case any descent was always face first and usually resulted in a trip to A&E. She had vowed never again. Unfortunately, without anyone to stay at home with him, that meant not going at all.

"Then why can't Mischa have him," asked Elliot, making a covert grab for the key that Joy had left hanging from the lock.

"Your sister's at work, besides, she's already had him twice this week," she yelled, storming into the living room and plucking Zachary from the front window before sitting him down on the sofa. His dark chestnut hair was still damp from the bath and his big blue eyes, wide and excited, without the mere threat of sleep. He didn't look at her. He never did, he just stared blankly back towards the window, giggling. "Jammies stay on, Buddy, OK," she said as she chased after the discarded garments that were now being dragged around the room by Pelé, their dog. She managed to whip them off him before he vanished behind the sofa, and wrestled the crumpled pyjama top over Zachary's head.

Joy didn't really know if Mischa was at work or not, she just didn't want to ask her. She had already lied to her and told her that everything was better now. She simply hadn't been able to cope with the look of dutiful pity that her daughter had every time she had to ask her once again for help.

From the hall, Joy heard the front door slam and glancing over to the window, she spotted the rear wheels of Elliot's bike disappear up the path through the crack in the curtains, followed by Owen's legs perched on the top of his skateboard.

Giving up her fight with the nightwear, she slat it to the floor and rushed to the front door, swinging it open to find

Elliot already out of sight, while Owen was stood shrugging apologetically at the top of the path.

"It's too late now, Mum. We're going down the park with Jay," he said sheepishly.

Jay Bowler lived five doors down and was like a cross between the two of them. Not quite as bold as Elliot and not as studious as Owen, he was a good kid with a smart mouth and his own sleeping bag in the airing cupboard upstairs.

"Back by ten," she said, conceding defeat.

"We'll probably still be home before dad," he said before jumping atop the scuffed skateboard and speeding off down the street towards the park.

It wasn't really a park, more just open scrubland at the bottom of the estate where it backed onto the woods. Back in the day, before the boys had been born, there had been houses there and a play area with a big yellow roundabout and a metal death slide that, in the slightest sunshine, would burn your legs and graze your arse as you shot off the bottom onto rough concrete. But subsidence from local mines had rendered the area unsafe, and the whole lot had been ripped down by the council, leaving the kids with just one small playground at the top of the hill where the road into the estate met with the main thoroughfare into the village. Joy still had nightmare's about that slide, and the scars.

Checking inside that Zachary was still sat on the sofa, Joy stepped outside into the fine spring rain and paced to the end of the short path and out of the wonky gate. Crossing her arms against the cooling air, she stared out into the street. Twilight was creeping in, curtains had quickly closed and the smell of boiled veg lingered in the air like a bad fart in a hot room.

Joy and her family lived about halfway down the hill, or up it depending on which way you were coming. The plots were almost all the same, Small blocks of post-war semi's crammed in so close to each other that you could barely fit a push bike down the narrow pathway to the gardens behind. The houses weren't really semi's either, more like one average-sized house that had been split down the middle and divided into two, leaving those who lived in them with two small bedrooms and a third that might be big enough for a child, so long as they never grew tall enough to need a full-size bed or a wardrobe.

Twenty years ago, she'd thought herself lucky when, as a soon to be single mother in the late 90's, the Council had finally offered her a house on the corner of a cul-de-sac that had a decent sized garden but no drive, and even more so when she was given the option to buy it dirt cheap. And so, having had Mischa at twenty, she studied day and night to get into nursing school, so that by the time the tot started primary school, Joy was a qualified nurse with a mortgage offer, thanks to a full-time job at the local infirmary.

It was there that she had met him. Robin Lane.

He had been wheeled in one night when, after indulging in one too many at a family barbeque, he had accidentally shot himself in the foot with a crossbow. At twenty-three, he was younger than Joy by two full years, and she took pity on him when at the end of her shift, she found him sitting outside the hospital after no one had come to collect him and he didn't have enough for a taxi.

Within a month, he had moved in, and Mischa had taken an instant shine to him, no doubt for the fact that he always came home with chocolate and a new toy, and to a newly five-year-old, they were the only things that mattered.

The following Christmas, he proposed, and when they had found out they were expecting twins, they had put the house on the market in the hope of moving somewhere bigger, but as the boys were born, and the wedding came and went without so much as a sniff from an interested buyer, they took the house off the market and made the most of what they had, eventually extending up into the loft when Joy found herself unexpectedly expecting Zachary almost a decade later.

"Zach." she gasped, startling herself as she turned back to her own window to find him once again, butt naked on the wrong side of the curtains. Dashing back into the house, she slammed the door behind her as she plucked him from the sill, pulled the curtains to, and wrestled him into his pyjamas.

No sooner had Zachary had fallen asleep over an hour later, Pelé started barking, desperate for a wee and presumable eager on waking him back up again. Pelé was technically Elliot's dog, he had turned up with the little scruff some five years earlier after finding him wandering the estate, and after several weeks of looking for an owner who either didn't exist or wouldn't admit to him, none of them had found the heart to take him to the pound. About the size of a small pig, he was a cross, mixed with a cross, he had odd-sized ears, wonky eye's, his back legs were too long for his front and was he part longhair and part shorthair in uneven patches. Joy often thought that if you took a little bit of every other dog on the estate and stitched them all together, you'd get a Pelé.

As he scurried back in from the garden, she retreated upstairs and changed out of her good dress, the only one she had that was far too frumpy for the pub but was the perfect length to cover her lumpy knees and looked respectable enough to fool teachers or care workers into thinking that she wasn't actually in the middle of a breakdown.

She tied her long auburn hair up into a pony and changed into her trusty old joggers and a thick bobbled jumper before settling down with a cup of tea and a packet of custard creams to herself.

Now and then, she'd get up and poke a stubby thumb through the curtains and check to see if she could see headlights approaching or Robin's car pull up outside. This wasn't helped by Pelé, who jumped to attention at every little noise, and which would send her rushing back to check if it was him every single time.

It wasn't. Not yet.

Chapter 3

Joy sat on the sofa, arms crossed, jaw clenched, just waiting. She hated waiting, she hated herself *for* waiting. She hated him for leaving her waiting. She didn't fully understand why she was waiting.

Their house had always been so full of love.

Laughter at the dinner table, sud monsters in the tub, funny stories at bedtime, and then at night, once everyone else was sleeping, they'd curl up on the sofa and snuggle. Snuggling would almost always lead to canoodling, and canoodling often led to shenanigans on the sofa so as not to wake the boys given that the walls upstairs were as thin as crisps.

But then everything had changed. Ever since Robin's twin brother, Reuben, had split up from his wife some thirteen months earlier. Robin had stopped coming home straight from work. He stopped being there for dinner, and then bath time, and eventually bedtime. There was no more snuggling, no more canoodling. Some days he hadn't gone into work at all and gone fishing, which wouldn't have been so bad had he not forgotten to mention it to Joy. This had caused no end of confusion when she had reported him missing to the police, only for him to turn up three days later covered in mud and smelling like a toilet. He didn't bring any fish home, of course, but then they weren't *really* fishing. Instead, they'd be sat on the bank of some god forsaken old quarry, and then they'd drink. Joy doubted very much whether they even bothered to take rods with them anymore.

At first, she had tried her best to be sympathetic. Reuben was, after all, his twin. The two men were close, despite, much like her own boys, their personalities being as different as wine and butter.

Robin was happy-go-lucky, laid back and rarely managed to match his socks, whereas Reuben was fiercely ambitious, uptight, and a self-confessed perfectionist. He had excelled at college, set up his own IT firm while still at university and which he ran like a well-oiled machine. Robin, meanwhile, was the operations manager of McCrumb's, a local biscuit factory, a job he had fallen into quite by accident. He had the brains to give Reuben a run for his money, but his get up and go had long ago got up and gone, and so, having started on the production line as a 17-year-old in need of money for a boys week in Kavos, they quickly spotted potential and fast-tracked him into a low paid management position so that the old man in charge could retire and live off the profits. While he'd not had a significant pay rise in over twenty years, it balanced out by the fact that Joy hadn't had to spend a penny on biscuits since they got married.

Yet now, Robin had grown ignorant to the fact that he and Reuben weren't teenagers anymore. While his brother was a successful businessman with as much time off as he wanted, Robin's job was conditional on him actually turning up, and from what Joy had gathered from the phone conversations he chose to conduct on the other side of the bathroom door, the company's patience was wearing almost as thin as hers.

A noise outside made her jump, and she hot-footed it back to the window, followed by Pelé. Checking the street again, her heart sunk into her guts as the passing car carried on along and pulled into a drive several doors down.

'Bastard'

Plonking her backside down on the sofa, she searched the side table for a biscuit, and scowled when she found them all gone and her cup empty. She hadn't even noticed herself eat them, which only left her craving more.

She reached for the remote and began to cycle through the TV channels when the front door finally opened, and Pelé made a bolt for the hall.

It still wasn't him.

Elliot and Owen dragged themselves in, soaking wet and covered in mud with their bloody knees brushing against the wallpaper and their grimy wheels scraping against her clean floor.

She flashed them a smile. They were, after all, a whole ten minutes early. "Get showered and bed, you've school tomorrow," she said as they trudged past her. Elliot dumped his bike outside the backdoor as Owen reached over and gave her a grubby kiss before sliding his skateboard under the stairs. As he wafted past her, Joy was sure she could detect the faintest hint of perfume underneath the smell of wet mud, or it could have simply been that he didn't smell like an ash tray like his brother.

Joy briefly considered challenging Elliot, but thought better of it. He would only deny it anyway. Parenting, her mother had told her, was an uphill battle. Parenting twin boys, according to Joy, was like being attacked from every direction while juggling onions on a unicycle with a puncture. Add in a neurodivergent 6-year-old and the malevolent proclivity of an older sister and we're talking space lasers and asteroids. But today, Joy just didn't have any fight in her. She never did anymore. Besides, this was her army, she had grown them and raised them and outside of wishing Elliot and Owen would shower more often, she wouldn't have them any other way.

So instead, she simply ruffled their heads as they both headed wearily upstairs, leaving mucky fingerprints all over the banister that she resolved to wipe off later. She wouldn't.

Eventually the hum of the shower subsided and was replaced with the sound of clean feet climbing the pull-down ladder to the loft room, followed by a muffled "Nice one" and "cheers" as they found a cup of tea and hot buttered toast on their bedside table.

Barely ten minutes passed until the chatter and brother baiting died down, and silence once again filled the house.

Robin still wasn't home.

By that point, Joy hadn't the will to watch anything on the telly, so instead, she sat and stared blankly at her phone, scrolling through posts from friends and old school pals, each one an inadvertent kick in the teeth. Photos of couples enjoying meals out or birthday drinks, first dates and at least one engagement announcement. Joy hadn't posted in months, not since Zachary's birthday in January. Robin hadn't been on that photo either.

She opened her messenger and clicked on his name. *"Last active 7 hrs ago,"* it said next to his profile picture. She slat the phone back down on the table.

Both her head and heart were still restless. She got up, checking the street again. It was dark, with only the rhythmic blinking of a broken streetlight further up on the other side, throwing its intermittent glow on the wet tarmac below like a half-arsed lighthouse calling home all the stragglers once last orders had passed. But that was nearly an hour ago now, and the street was all but empty, save for the cats. At least four who congregated most nights on Joy's wall at the corner and who were presumably waiting for the last of the bedroom lights to dim before staging a heist on the wheelie bins and screeching loudly over the spoils.

Joy sat back down. Then stood up, then walked to the sink and back to the window, and then sat down. This was normal now, almost routine. Over the last few month's she had worn a noticeable path in the carpet running up to the window. Yet, she knew her looking wouldn't change anything. It wouldn't miraculously teleport her errant husband to their front door. She hated herself a little bit more every time she looked out in hope, and each trip to the curtains would only increase her blood pressure and tighten that little rubber band in her head, the one that was keeping all the anger in. And so, it simmered, pricking away at her eyes until they watered, readying itself to boil over should he finally arrived at the door.

But he didn't.

Robin had become as predictable as he had feckless, yet she continued to pace, and against everything in her head telling her not to, and to just give in and go to bed, she'd still hope. And she'd still keep going back to the damn window.

Chapter 4

It was still dark outside when Joy woke the following morning to the sound of Zachary rummaging fervently through kitchen cupboards, with Pelé nipping at his feet, ready to share whatever bounty his partner in crime could liberate from the biscuit tin.

Joy had become quite accustomed to sleeping upright on the sofa. It was old, worn in all the right places and situated right next to the radiator. The only problem was that she would wake with a crick in her neck, which was today joined by a pain in her side where she had been sat on the remote. She jumped up and ran to the kitchen, first plucking the little boy from the countertop and carrying him with her at her hip as she made a beeline back to the window.

Robin's car was still missing from the drive, and after checking the beds upstairs to see if he'd perhaps gotten a taxi home, she was largely unsurprised to see that he was still AWOL too.

Rolling her eyes, Joy sighed as she lowered Zachary back to the floor from where he bolted back towards the kitchen, as Joy glanced over the empty unslept in bed.

She had less than an hour before she had to leave for work.

She settled Zachary down with a bowl full of choco-puffs, giving him a little more than normal in a bid to buy her time to get dressed, and headed back upstairs.

By the time she reappeared in the kitchen, Zachary was in front of the TV, remote in hand scrawling through YouTube, usually a complete no-no before school, but today she didn't have the energy to chase him for the remote or the resolve to deal with the meltdown that would come from unplugging the TV, so she left him where he was and sat herself down in the kitchen with a strong coffee and waited some more.

At 5.40am, she finally heard the key turn in the door, five minutes before she had to leave the house. It would give him enough time to profuse his deepest apologies but not enough time for her to start an argument, and barely enough time for her to tell him where he could shove his sorry

She had spent the last half an hour telling herself not to implode, to play it cool, and to act like she didn't even notice that he wasn't here. But no sooner had he got one foot through the door, she smelt the familiar scent of stale beer and spilt whiskey and that little elastic band that had been slowly winding itself up in her head finally snapped.

"Manage to remember where you live, did you"? she seethed as he appeared in the hall, trying to crack a smile.

Joy glared at him. He looked terrible. He had always reminded her of an 80s Harrison Ford. His wonky smile, high cheekbones and smouldering hazel eyes were all still present and correct, but self-neglect and a love of take-away had left him less Indiana and more raiders of the lost fridge. But this morning, he looked especially awful. His dark sandy hair unkept and straggly, he looked tired and gaunt, his skin the yellowish colour of a past it's best supermarket chicken under the glare of the hallway light. He smelt like one too, and he walked with the gait of someone who was trying desperately not to throw up.

"Don't be like that, babe," he said, his voice faint and frog-like, "You know I've....."

"I know you weren't here when you promised you would," she interrupted. Keeping her voice low as not to startle Zachary. It was amazing how quickly she had learnt how to hold entire arguments without so much as raising her voice or dropping her smile.

"I said I might be a bit late," he said, shuffling past her to the sink.

"This is *not* a bit late," she hissed, "and you knew it was parents evening. They start their GCSEs in a couple of months, it was important."

Robin scratched at his head. "But parent evening's next week."

Sucking her breath in fast through grit teeth, she slapped her hand against the table. "No, Rob, I told you yesterday. And the day before, it's written right there on the fridge, and you said you'd be home. I needed you here with Zach."

"You could have called Mischa," he said, turning his back and picking up the kettle.

Joy let out a long groaning sigh, "Mischa has a life. Zach *isn't* her responsibility. She's not his fucking father. You are."

Robin filled the kettle, sat it back on its dock and flicked the switch before turning around to face her. His eyes still didn't make contact. "Look, I'm sorry, you know what Ben's going through."

"Do you know what I'm going through, Rob?" She bit her lip. She was trying desperately not to cry. "Do you care?"

Pulling a mug from the cupboard, he dropped in two tea bags from the canister on the shelf above. "What do you want me to say? I'm sor . . . "

Joy cut him off before he could even try. She was sick of broken promises, she was sick of pacing to the window, and she was sick of sorry. "You're never here, Robin. Even the boys don't expect you to turn up anymore, even Zach. His consultant says he needs routine, certainty, consistency. The only thing that we have any fucking certainty over is that you consistently let us down."

"I'm doing my best, Joy," he said. His voice was hollow, his mouth crinkled. Joy wasn't sure whether he looked like he was about to cry or vomit.

"Then I'd hate to see your worst," she spat, crossing her arms in front of her.

"I just need more time with Ben," he replied, staring at his feet as he shuffled an errant leaf across the floor that had been dragged in on Elliot's bike the night before and which Joy had been successfully ignoring. "He just needs more time."

"I don't have time, Rob. It's been over a year," she said, rising to her feet and grabbing her cardigan and bag from the back of the chair. She marched into the living room and kissed Zachary before pushing past her husband in the kitchen. Opening the front door, she turned back. Robin hadn't moved. The kettle had boiled, but he was still staring downwards, shuffling his feet. "Is it really that Ben needs more time, or that you *want* more time. That you're not willing to let go of whatever this freedom is that you think you have, because if a year isn't enough, how long will be, two years, three. Five? Do we just have to wait around until Ben's ready to find someone else because you know he will, and then he'll drop you, right? And you expect us just to be sitting here waiting for you?"

Robins face wilted, his eyes glassy as he lifted his head to look at her. He shrugged.

"Look," she said stomping back down the hallway, "I didn't want to do this, Robin, but you don't get to have it all your way, it's not fair on the kids, so choose. Ben, or us?"

"Joy, no, that's not fair?" he stammered, reaching forward and making a grab for her arm.

She snatched her hand away. "Life isn't fair, Robin. If you want to be part of this family, you need to prove it because if you can't, then you clearly don't."

Robin opened his mouth to speak, but no words came. So instead, he stood staring at her like a flailing goldfish tipped out of its tank.

Joy turned and marched out the door, slamming it hard behind her.

She managed to hold herself together during the two-mile drive to the hospital, but as she pulled into the small staff car park right at the far end of the building, she couldn't keep it in anymore, and pulling hastily into the first space she saw, she killed the engine and collapsed across the wheel no sooner had her foot hit the brake pedal.

She let the tears fall. The anger had subsided, and now she was just annoyed with herself for having allowed it to bubble over at all. She hadn't intended to issue an ultimatum, she had thought it often, but it had come out much by accident.

But, she *did* feel relief, a release almost, as if the words themselves had pulled a plug in her head as they had left her mouth and the pressure level had dropped. If nothing more, he might finally realise precisely what he stands to lose if, for a minute, he thought that she was serious.

Through the blur of tears, she could see the little clock on the dash blinking 5:55am while to the east, the early traces of light began to creep along the tarmac ahead of her. She set about wiping her eyes with her cardigan sleeve as she checked the little pull-down mirror in the visor. Her olive eyes were puffy, her slim nose, bright red and her cheeks damp. She looked tired and angry, and her bottom lip was red raw from biting down on it during the drive.

At least the walk to the building would help explain away her red cheeks, and she would excuse away the tiredness on account of Zachary. She always did. Everything else would be blamed on seasonal allergies that she didn't actually have but which had become a convenient excuse. She had even begun to carry an empty packet of antihistamines in her workbag, nothing more than a prop to counteract all the offers from well-meaning colleagues.

Taking a deep breath, she straightened her loose bun, tucked the tufts behind her ears, and climbed out of the car into the crisp morning air.

Striding confidently towards the main entrance, she resolved to call Robin once he'd had time to sober up, and she, time to calm down, and as the wide automatic doors of the main entrance opened, she plastered a smile across her face, swallowed her pain and greeted the security guard with the cheeriest hello she could manage.

Chapter 5

By late morning, the Cardiology ward where Joy was a nurse had largely fallen quiet. Doctors had completed their rounds and retreated to their various day clinics. Patients had been bathed and turned, meds had been deployed, as had tea and biscuits, and Joy found herself with five minutes to think. She didn't want to think. The more she thought about it, the more she thought she had been a twat, and so took the first opportunity to make a bee line for the empty nurses' station and made a grab for the phone before it had the audacity to start ringing.

Tapping her fingers on the top of the counter, Joy wedged the handset under her ear and keyed Robin's work number into the keypad, taking a deep breath as the line clicked and the phone on the other end began to ring in her ear, loud enough, thankfully, to drown out the sound of her own heart beat that was bouncing around in her head.

There was no answer, instead, the ringing stopped abruptly, and a loud beep preceded Robin's cheerful voice. A recorded message.

Joy clicked the receiver down and pressed redial. If he was sat at his desk, he would know it was her. The ward number would come up on his desk phone. She began to wonder if he had made it in at all or if he had pulled yet another sick day.

As the call tone echoed into her ear, she was about to give up and try the landline at home when the ringing stopped, and a voice filled her ear. But it wasn't Robin. It was a woman's voice, giggly, out of breath almost, and incredibly youthful.

"Hello, Mr Lane's office," she chirped.

"Um," Joy's words caught on her tongue. No one other than Robin had ever answered his phone before. His secretary, Steph, had her own line, but she was well into her fifties and sounded blunt and quite bitter. Only Robin answered his direct line.

"Yes, hello, is someone there" came the voice again. It sounded American, northwest if she had to guess.

Joy felt something twang inside of her as she pictured a young creaseless mouth slathered in red lipstick with straight teeth and a tongue that parked itself between them in a way that made grown men readjust their trousers. She gave herself a mental slap and cleared her throat. "Hi, yes, is, um, is Mr Lane there?" she asked, squirming. Even saying the words didn't feel right. "It's, um. It's Joy. It's Mrs Lane," she splurted, adding far more emphasis onto the Mrs than was needed.

"One moment," replied the woman.

Spinning on the chair, Joy turned her back on the ward as down the phone she heard muffled voices, followed by the scrape of chair legs across wooden boards and finally, the phone receiver being picked back up.

"Joy. Is that you? This isn't a good time," said Robin, sounding stern and far more awake than he had when she'd left him.

"Who was that?" she asked.

"We're just in a meeting, Joy, can I call you back?"

Joy bit her lip. "No wait, I didn't want, I don't want to keep you, I'm not trying to ....." her voice trailed off.

"Joy? What is it?"

She didn't answer him. She had spent the entire morning practising what she wanted to say. '*I'm sorry. I was a complete dick. I love you*'. It wasn't all that hard, less than ten words, yet now her entire throat had closed over, and no sound could escape.

"Joy, I really have to go" his voice had dropped to little more than a whisper. "I'll be home early ok, we can talk. I think we need to talk. I'll see you then."

Before she could say anything else, the line shut off and the dialling tone once again filled her ears.

"I'm sorry, I was a dick. I love you," she said quietly into the handset. She let it drop from under her chin, to where it clattered loudly to the desk below. She let her breath out hard, puffing her cheeks as she sat the phone back in its cradle on the desk. She had made a pig's ear of it. She was supposed to have been upbeat, assertive and assuring, instead, she had sounded like a blubbering fool. And to top it all off, a new feeling began to rise in Joy's belly. One she was completely unfamiliar with. And for the first time in their marriage, her heart ran cold as she began to wonder whether Rob had really been spending all that time with Reuben after all.

Chapter 6

Yawning loudly, Joy glared at the little black screen above the elevator door. Reaching forward, she jabbed heavily at the button for the third time. She had watched it drop slowly from seven to six, and then down to five before it had stopped at four, the floor above, at which point it had stopped completely. She had considered running up the stairs to see if she could hurry up whatever the delay was but was sure that no sooner would she burst out of the stairwell that the lift doors would close, and she'd have to start all over again.

She could, of course, just take the stairs to the ground floor, the three flights were far easier on the knees going down than they were going up, but she was tired. She had been on her feet for nine hours, and the lack of sleep the night before was starting to affect her balance.

She was about to lean forward for the button again when the screen finally changed, and the bright blue number four vanished and was replaced with a flashing arrow, pointing downwards.

"At last," she muttered to herself as she adjusted her cardigan and slung her workbag onto her shoulder. But as the lift doors opened, her relief soon turned to dismay.

"Joy, Hi, how are you" chirped a familiar voice.

'Should have taken the stairs,' she thought as she quickly arranged her face into a smile that didn't quite reach her eyes, and holding her breath as she was accosted by the unmistakable scent of nineties Armani and chewing gum.

Dr Callum Goodbody MBChB, MSc, FRCP, CCT stood smiling next to the elevator console. At six foot three, he towered above Joys five foot five, but he was built spindly, with jagged angles, sharp features and jet black hair that betrayed what were essentially warm eyes and a kind smile.

Stepping into the elevator, Joy softened her face and returned his greeting.

Joy and Dr Goodbody had started at the hospital at around the same time; she as a trainee nurse, and he as a very nervous junior doctor fresh out of medical school. Twenty years later and he was still there, having risen to the lofty heights of consultant and clinical director of the emergency department and the longest standing doctor in residence. To Joy, he was also something of an ex.

Over the course of several months in the summer of 2003, they had enjoyed a number of very nice dates. They had gone to nice restaurants and enjoyed nice food. They had watched nice films, visited nice museums and had enjoyed perfectly nice sex. The problem was, while it was all very *nice*, that was all it ever really was. And while many a single mother would have been perfectly happy with the stability and comfort of nice, she wanted more. Her entire life back then was spent either with her head in a book or a dirty nappy, and on the rare occasions that she came up for air, she wanted it to be billowing through her hair and shaking leaves out from the trees, whereas Dr Goodbody had, unfortunately, been little more than a fart in a bathtub.

When along came Robin Lane with his bow and arrow and his wonky smile, it had been like dancing into a hurricane.

"How's life on cardiology?" he asked as the lift doors closed.

"Busy," she said, not dropping her smile.

"And the family?"

"A disaster."

"Very good," he said, nudging her at the waist. "And what about that course, the one I told you about last year? You'd make an excellent practitioner Joy; you know more than most of the doctors around here."

"I think it's a little late for that now," she replied, her eyes dropping to the floor as she felt his fall on her.

"You don't sound very convinced."

"I just don't have the time for study right now. Maybe before Zachary . . . "

"And how is young Zachary?" he asked, noting her discomfort with the conversation.

Joy bit her lip as she pondered what to say. Should she tell him that he never sleeps or that when he does, he prefers to be in the dog's bed than his own? Should she tell him that that he doesn't talk, that he has no friends outside of ~~Pele~~Pelé, and that they nearly got thrown out of the Sea Life Centre on his birthday because he got so excited about the fish in the petting pool that he accidentally punched a starfish.

Or should she tell him about the amazing bear hugs that he gives or the faces he pulls when he's happy. She could tell him about his love of grids, and birds, and that he loves to paint rocks, or about the way he twirls her hair around his finger when he's tired, or the fact that at six, he was far smarter than she would ever be.

Joy lifted her head and readjusted her smile. "He's absolutely perfect," she replied.

Callum smiled back, but his face had changed, his eyes had narrowed, and he looked concerned.

It suddenly dawned on Joy that she was crying. No sobs or whimpers, just crystal clear tears falling gracefully down over her cheeks.

"Are you OK?" he asked, fishing into his pockets and bringing them back out empty-handed. I didn't mean to"

"It's OK," she assured him, fishing into her own pocket and pulling out the tissue that she had squirrelled away that morning. "Allergies," she said, dabbing at her eyes and nodding towards the lift doors as they opened out onto the main entrance with its always opening doors and many hanging baskets.

The doctor nodded for her to go ahead, and so Joy hurried out of the tightness of the elevator, through the short lobby and out of the automatic doors, all too aware that Dr Goodbody was still right behind her as she stepped out into the afternoon sun and making herself look busy by fishing around in her bag for her sunglasses. She managed to push them onto her face just in time to hear his voice beside her.

"Are you sure you're ok, Joy? You do look shattered," he said. There was genuine worry in his voice.

Joy ignored the opportunity to feign insult and grinned emptily from behind the safety of her shaded barrier. "Absolutely fine, Callum, it's just the change over from lates to earlies. That first day is always a killer."

Dr Goodbody nodded. "Well, if you ever fancy a change of pace, you could consider transferring to emergency. We're always looking for an experienced hand."

"Oh no, I'll be fine tomorrow." she said, "Business as usual, but thanks anyway".

Dr Goodbody tipped his head and set off across the carpark. Pulling his keys from his pocket, he clicked the fob and the lights flashed on a brand new Audi Q7 parked in the bay reserved in his name.

Joy sighed, blew her nose on her tissue and turned in the direction of the staff carpark.

She did sometimes wonder if it would have been worth it, foregoing the hurricane in favour of a nice breeze and a brand new Audi as opposed to her battered blue Astra that was older than the twins, and which upon finding it exactly where she had left it that morning, had a parking ticket tucked under the wiper after she had forgotten to display her permit. She promptly removed it and slung it into the rear footwell with the others.

By the time she had made it across town to the school, she was almost half an hour late. Traffic had been a nightmare, and an accident on the ring road had sent her up several side streets that she didn't know the way out of and had thus spent most of the journey driving round them in circles whilst swearing profusely.

Hurrying in through the door, she mumbled her apologies as Zachary appeared on the other side of the entrance hall with Mrs Mortimer, his one-on-one support teacher. Mrs Mortimer was Joy's hero. She was slight, short and had the soft slow voice of a Sesame Street character.

"I'm so sorry sweetheart," whispered Joy, dropping slowly to her knees as Zachary approached. Grabbing him by the shoulders, she pulled him close, running her hands over his thick dark hair. He allowed her a moment before wriggling free and making a dart for the big wall to wall window and proceeding to blow mouth bubbles against it, pushing his gob up against the glass and filling it with air until it he couldn't hold it any longer, then collapsing into a fit of giggles as the escaping air farted against the glass.

Joy reached out and prized him from the window.

"Is everything ok, Mrs Lane?" asked Mrs Mortimer.

"Yes, sure, there was an accident on the way .... "

"No, no, that's no problem" she reached forward and placed her hand on Joy's forearm. Her face, usually warm and full of all the cheer of spring, looked flushed, her eyes staring straight into Joys.

Joy froze, losing her grasp on her son, who shot straight back to the window. Mrs Mortimer had been Zachary's support teacher since nursery. She was a constant in their life for nearly three years, and despite Joy's pleas to call her by her first name, Mrs Mortimer had completely ignored her and continued to address her formally. While she would be incredibly hands-on with Zachary, physical contact with Joy was completely new territory.

"Has . . . has he done something wrong?" she asked, her teeth immediately lurching for the comfort of her bottom lip. Zachary was nothing if not a handful. He danced to his own beat and what he lacked in communication, he made up for in energy, the kind that often bordered on chaos and which was ignorant to both danger or damage. Joy often thought that there was little he could do anymore that she wasn't prepared for, yet he continued to surprise them.

Mrs Mortimer's face softened. "Oh, not at all, no, he's been a darling, no, um," she paused.

Mrs Mortimer never so much as skipped a heartbeat, and her sudden hesitation caused Joy to shift uneasily on the spot.

"No, Mrs Lane, but when your husband dropped Zachary in this morning, he was very, um.."

She paused again, and Joy felt her heart race.

"He was a little distracted."

"Distracted?" asked Joy.

"Bordering on unhinged," she said, her top lip curling into a grimace that did more to explain her concern than any word ever could.

Joy's heart stopped completely. "What did he say?"

"Nothing really. It was mostly incoherent babble. He was late for work, but he looked awful and was shaking."

"He's had a rough year. I told you about his brother."

"The one with the wife?"

"Ex-wife, yes," spluttered Joy, "I'm hoping it will come to a head soon."

"Yes, he did say that," she replied, her tone brightening somewhat.

"Did he?" squeaked Joy, trying to hide her surprise that her husband, who had barely had a whole conversation with her in weeks, had somehow opened up to his son's teacher.

"Well, not in so many words. He wasn't making much sense. He was apologising for being late, and he said something about the end being in sight and changes that needed to be made, but it was all very cryptic."

Joy felt her heart kickstart again with a wallop. The blood rushed back to her face, and she felt the little weight that had wedged itself into her ribcage lift from her chest, until she realised that she couldn't see Zachary.

Scanning the small reception, she soon spotted him lying underneath one of the wide benches next to the door picking at a spot of wood that was missing its paint. Leaning down, she scooped him up and gripped his hand.

"Fingers crossed that we've turned a corner then. I feel for his brother, I really do, but I worry about the effect it's having on Zach," she said.

Mrs Mortimer smiled, "Zachary's fine, Mrs Lane, so long as you are."

Joy returned her smile and nodded that she understood. She'd be lying if she said it didn't bother her that Rob could swan around as he liked, and it would have little to no effect on Zachary, yet her getting annoyed or frustrated at him for it could have such a profound effect that it sent his entire day into a tailspin. It was ironic really that the consultants and the school talked so much about consistency and routine that Robin's disappearance from their home life had been so prolific that it had become part of their normal.

Joy thanked Mrs Mortimer for her concern, and keeping her grasp on the boy, bundled him out through the doors into the sunshine.

Chapter 7

Wanna go for a sleepover, buddy?" called Joy, checking the road ahead of her as she spun the car out onto the dual carriageway into town before checking in the rear view mirror for any sign of reaction. There wasn't one. He was turned with his face pressed against the window, watching the cars pass on the other side of the road. He loved watching them. He counted them. Anywhere they went was measured not in miles or kilometres but in cars passed, or lampposts, or grids. Anything he could take a physical measure of. Thanks to his little jotter that he kept under his pillow, Joy knew categorically that there were 72 lampposts between home and school, 145 drain grids, cars were a little more problematic, yet each day he noted the new number enthusiastically.

"Hey, Spuderoo?" she called, checking back again. This time Zach turned his head from where he had been staring out of the window and faced forward. "Fancy a sleepover? We'll go see Misha, okay?"

Joy waited for noise.

Zach made quite a few noises, none were words, but Joy had most of them figured out by now. Some were obvious. A squeal when scared, a cry when upset, or a self-explanatory giggle. He would gurgle and hum, and sing dum-de-dum, when he was playing. But some were less transparent, like now. Not quite a grunt and yet not really a hum. It came from somewhere deep inside, below his throat. If you listened carefully enough, you could hear it rattle his ribcage and echo up his windpipe. It was the noise he made when he was happy, and Joy liked to think that it came straight from his heart. They called it his grum.

Smiling, she changed lane, indicated and took the next exit towards home. Misha lived barely two streets away from them in a house laid out almost the same as their own, built at the same time by the same people for the same council, although hers was privately rented and had no garden, just a yard with a big bin and a broken patio set. Joy missed her terribly, but study had been all but impossible at home, and so Joy's mother had agreed to pick up half of the rent so long as Mischa picked up the right grades. Something Joy paid dearly for.

On the upside, Zachary had the same back bedroom that he occupied at home, decorated and furnished identically in green and blue. It was the only place that Joy ever felt safe leaving him, although she wasn't sure whether it was the familiarity of the decor or simply the presence of Misha that soothed him so. He missed her too.

Pulling up outside the tiny semi, the curtains were drawn in the middle of the afternoon, and the gate was still open where the postie had made little effort to engage the latch when they left. She checked her watch. It was definitely Tuesday. Mischa didn't work Tuesdays. She had a part-time job at the service station, situated on the southbound carriageway of the M6 where she made coffee and bagels for the passing masses five evenings a week while studying law at the local university. So, while it was entirely possible that she might have forgotten to open the curtains that morning before leaving for Uni, she should have been home over an hour ago.

Rechecking her watch, she didn't have time to drive around to the little car park behind the houses and see if Mischa's car was there. Instead, she would just have to knock and hope, suddenly regretting her eagerness to tell Zachary their plans.

Leaving him strapped into his seat, she slipped out of the car and up the path, knocking loudly at the door before ducking down, opening the letterbox as wide as it would go, and hollering into the opening.

"Misch, it's only mum!"

No sound came back.

She knocked again and waited.

Barely a minute passed before she bent back towards the letter box, but before she could poke it open, a shuffling sound came from behind the thick wooden slab. Joy sprang upright as she heard the key turn in the lock, her mouth gaping open as her daughter finally poked her head around the door.

"Jeez, Misch, you look like shit," she said.

"Thanks," she replied, yawning. Pulling the elastic from her scruffily tied hair, she scraped up the highlighted waves that had dropped around her face, and retied it. "I was in bed."

"Are you sick? You look sick," asked Joy.

"I'm not sick, mum," she replied.

"Is it school? Are you working too hard?"

"It's a revision week, mum," said Mischa, rubbing her red eyes and letting the door swing open "So I picked up a few extra shifts. A double Saturday, and then a six-start straight off the back of a late"

Joy's face softened, dropping her voice. She leaned in closer. "Do you need money? You know if you're struggling, you can always ask us, Misch, you work too hard."

"No, mum, we were short-staffed, I offered"

"Are you working tonight?"

Mischa shook her head. She was about to speak but paused, grinning and waving as she glanced over her mother's shoulder to the car parked at the end of the pathway, and Zachary waving graciously from the back seat. "Mum, is something wrong?" she asked.

"Um, no, not really, at least I don't think so."

"Mum?" snapped Mischa.

Joy gave her daughter a half-smile, "Dad wants to talk. I thought you could take Zach overnight, so we could talk properly, I've already spoken to the other two, they're going to Jay's."

"Talk?" she replied, raising an eyebrow.

"We've barely spoken in weeks, But I think he's finally ready. He said he's going to finish early, and I just want to be able to talk to him without the constant interruption," Joy's eyes dropped to the floor. "But I understand if you're too tired, it's a lot to ask."

"You said things were better," said Mischa, folding her oversized My Little Pony dressing gown across her chest and holding it closed with her arms. "You said he'd stopped all that shit."

"He has, I mean he did, mostly," she said, shifting awkwardly.

Mischa rubbed her face, stifling another yawn. "You think I don't talk to those lump head brothers of mine," she replied, glaring at her mother. "I'm not blind, mum, but yes, I'll happily have Zach if it means you two finally sort yourselves out."

Joy's mouth snapped shut.

Mischa squeezed past Joy and charged towards the car, flinging the door open before plucking Zachary effortlessly from his car seat. The little boy smiled wildly, his big gap-toothed grin stretching from ear to ear as he wrapped his arms around her neck, grumming loudly.

"Give me a ring if you haven't got enough of his night pills," said Joy as Mischa carried Zachary down the path and into the house.

"I've a full box you gave me at Christmas, mum."

"And Jammies?"

"A drawer full."

"What about snacks? Do you need me to run the shop for some bits?"

"He can have my secret stash," she said, winking at Zachary and sending him into a grum frenzy.

"Well here, take this," said Joy, sliding her hand into her uniform pocket and pulling out a balled-up twenty. "Get some pizza for both of you."

Mischa rolled her eyes. "I can stretch to take out mum."

"I know, I know, but my treat, as a thank you," said Joy, dropping the crumpled note into her dressing gown pocket and wrapping her arms around them both. She kissed them each on the forehead. "I'll call you later, and dad'll pick him up for school in the morning," she said, squeezing them tightly before skipping up the path, jumping into the driving seat and setting off around the corner to home.

Chapter 8

The door hadn't even slammed shut behind her before Joy popped the buttons on her uniform, letting it drop and pool around her feet as she charged ahead into the kitchen, where she kicked it off and onto the floor in front of the washing machine.

She opened the back door and filled Pelé's bowl as he did circles on the kitchen floor around her, unable to decide whether he first wanted to eat or piss. She picked him up and turfed him outside, just in case he decided to do both at once, before flicking the button on the kettle.

She paused, then flicked it back off again.

Reaching into the fridge instead, she rooted around at the back, eventually pulling out an unopened bottle of Pinot.

Unscrewing the cap, she lifted the bottle to her lips and took a long hard chug, wincing as the cold acrid wave hit the back of her throat and flooded her mouth with the taste of budget wine. She felt her eyes water as the flavour settled, by which point she could stomach a second, and which tasted much better once her tastebuds had been numbed by the first.

She hardly ever drank, not that she didn't *want* to; give her a long weekend, and a free bar and Joy would knock back anything that was handed to her. She was mostly terrified of the hangover. She had once known a young nurse who, following a birthday night out, had mixed up a cannula with a catheter and scared the shit, or in her case piss, out of a ninety-two-year-old lady who had only come in for an angiogram. Joy had vowed never to touch a drop unless she had a good two days off to recover. Besides, Zachary would almost always wake before 6am and be full of beans, and early starts were hard enough without the brain fog and raging nausea.

But this wasn't a night out or a boozy lunch. No, this was medicinal, something to stop the shaking in her voice and to slow the beat of her heart that was threatening to burst straight out of her windpipe.

She felt giddy, manic almost. She had a million things she wanted to say but couldn't keep them all in her head long enough that they made a single logical thought. She took another swig from the bottle before realising that she was still stood in the kitchen in her underwear, and Robin could be home any minute.

She slammed the bottle down on the countertop and stormed upstairs. Flinging open her wardrobe door, she scanned the sea of colourful fabric until she spotted what she was looking for. The dress she had worn the last time they had gone to the races for their anniversary, a light pink floaty number with delicate green flowers and a ruffle trim just above the knee. Robin had told her how pretty she looked in it, how the green brought out her eyes and how he had spent the entire day telling her how he couldn't wait to take it off. Pulling the dress from the rail, she held it up in the light, ignoring the creases from it being hung in an overpacked closet; if things went well, she hopefully wouldn't even be wearing it long enough for them to drop out. She lowered the zip, slipped it from the hanger and stepped into it. But as she reached behind her to pull the zip back up she stopped.

'*Shit*', she thought. The zip would only go up by about three inches, after which it wouldn't budge.

She glanced over to the mirror on the far wardrobe and turned around, grimacing as she saw the bulge of flesh bursting out over the top of the soft pastel material. Sure, it had been a while since she'd worn it, a couple of years maybe, but she couldn't have put on *that* much weight.

Deflated, she lowered the dress back down over her hips, kicked it to the corner of the room and grabbed another. This one was longer and had a bit more give, but alas, she couldn't even get it up over her thighs and it quickly joined the other on the floor, as did the next, and the one after.

Too short, too frumpy, too much like her mother, too tight, too baggy, too dressy, too young. Admitting defeat, she grabbed her trusted old stretch jeans and her favourite baggy vest, with it's cheerful embroidered sunflowers on the hem and a mayo stain down its front. It would have to do.

She grabbed a can of hairspray from where she'd left it on the window ledge and headed to the bathroom, she slid the elastic from her hair, letting it fall softly over her shoulders and was about to start fixing her curls, but something didn't seem right.

She glanced around the little room. It wasn't even big enough for all of its fittings, the sink overlapped the bath at one end, and a space saver toilet in the corner left barely enough room to fully open the door. There was very little in there to start with, yet it seemed tidier than usual. No damp towels on the floor or pants that had been thrown at, and missed, the wash basket by the door. It wouldn't be unheard of that one of the boys stopped home for lunch, but they weren't known for being neat and tidy. Besides, something was missing. She just couldn't place it.

She stepped back out into the hall and into the bedroom. There was an emptiness that she hadn't noticed before, yet nothing was missing. Everything was where it should be. But the room still felt hollow somehow.

Putting it down to anxiety, she shook the thought from her head and was about to retreat back to the bathroom, but the niggle wouldn't go away, and it was growing. Placing the hairspray can down on the bedside table, she glanced back towards the stairs before crossing the room towards Robin's wardrobe.

Stood in front of its tall, mirrored door, she felt silly. Surely, she was imagining things. But if she just had a look, a quick peek, then she could prove to herself that she was being irrational and that nothing was amiss. It was, after all, just a wardrobe and one that she had opened five times a day for the last decade. It wasn't like it was some secret door she had just discovered or a mystical trunk that would normally be under lock and key, but which she had stumbled upon unshackled. It was a closet, full of very ordinary and largely very dull clothing. She was being ridiculous.

Reaching forward, she grabbed the little chrome handle and flung the door open.

Staring at the open closet, Joy stumbled backwards until the back of her thighs met with the bed, and she slumped down onto its soft surface, not taking her eyes off the contents of the cupboard.

"Fuck," she said softly under her breath, followed by "Bastard," albeit significantly louder.

Chapter 9

Reaching back, Joy didn't so much as blink as she fumbled around on the bedclothes behind her. She only finally glanced away as her hand slid over the cold hard screen of her phone and she picked it up, unlocked it with her thumb, and hit speed dial. She didn't even bother to lift it to her ear. She knew what was coming.

After a moment, a muffled voice came from the earpiece, loud enough to confirm what she already knew, "the person you are calling is unavailable., please try ...."

"He's not unavailable. He's a twat," she screamed at the screen as she jammed her thumb down on the end call button.

Scrolling down to her contacts, Joy's finger hovered over Micha's number before slatting the phone down on the bed at her side. She sat and stared down at it. Her daughter grinned back at her from the screen, albeit a much younger Mischa, stood between a heavily pregnant Joy and Robin as they posed in front of the Eifel tower. It had been Joys favourite weekend ever, a babymoon they'd call it now, a chance to get away before the chaos of a new arrival. Joy never really understood that. She had twin boys; life was already chaos, but her parents had taken them to Blackpool for the weekend, and so she and Robin had taken advantage of a Eurostar deal and a cheap hotel in a part of the city that wasn't really appropriate for a teenage girl.

'You have to tell her.' She thought, almost pleadingly. The screen below her blurring as her eyes glassed over. But telling her would make it real, wouldn't it? There was no going back once someone else knew. Silly really, it's not like she could keep it a secret, if not today, then tomorrow, or the day after. She felt her cheeks flush and her fists tighten. If only she could speak to him first.

She picked the phone back up and hit call.

"The person you have called is....."

"An absolute bastard," she yelled, gripping the phone in her hand, she drew it back like she was about to pitch it at the wall but stopped herself. Instead, bringing the phone back down, she held it at her lips as she breathed in deeply against the worn leather case.

Eventually, once her breathing had slowed and her hand had stopped shaking, she dropped it back to her lap, found Mischa's number and hit call, lifting the handset to her ear as the line clicked into action and began to ring at the other end.

Mischa answered in a heartbeat. "Really, mum. You've only been gone half an hour. We're fine."

"He's gone, Misch. He's taken everything and gone." She blurted, her eyes returning to the empty closet before her. She felt her anger subside and a sadness wash over her, an emptiness. She could no longer feel her heart beating in her chest or her pulse at her ear. She was a husk, just like the empty hollow of MDF that sat before her. "He's left me," she said, almost silently, her voice cracking as she held back the sobs that were building in her throat, the words themselves, like razors blades on her tongue that cut at her flesh as they left her mouth.

"Stay right there, OK? Don't move, just stay" said Mischa, on the other end.

"Ok," croaked Joy, hanging up the call. She lowered the phone to her knees and let it drop to the floor. She didn't even flinch as it landed on her foot. She didn't think that she could go anywhere even if she wanted to.

Laying back on the bed, the pain flowed freely now, as did the tears. Hunching her knees up to her chest, she let them fall, her piercing wails pouring out into the room and echoing back at her from the percussion of the empty closet. She didn't even budge when she heard the jangle of Pelé's collar coming up the stairs or when he jumped up onto the bed and curled himself up in the crook of her knees.

They were both still in the exact same spot, the bedclothes crumpled and damp beneath her when Joy heard the front door open downstairs.

She didn't know how long she'd been lying there. It could have been minutes, or hours. It was still light out and she could hear children playing nearby. She was grateful for their laughter. She hadn't noticed them until now. Her head had been full of black, which was slowly being pushed out by their joyful spring squeals, euphoric after a long winter confined to playing indoors.

Sitting up on the bed, she wiped her eyes as she heard the front door shut and footsteps mount the stairs, accompanied by the sound of rustling plastic and clinking glass.

She stood up, smoothed down her vest and made her way to the landing, "I'm up here, Misch," she croaked, but as she stepped through the door, it wasn't her daughter's voice that greeted her on the way up the stairs.

"No sweetie, it's me," came the reply.

"Carlee," gasped Joy, lurching towards the stairs just as her friend rounded the threadbare little landing that sat halfway up and from where the staircase turned on itself towards the bedrooms. Joy dropped to her knees, her composure, the strength that she had summoned for her daughter evaporated, and the weight of her heart dragged her straight down to the floor.

Carlee dropped the bag she was carrying onto the landing and lowered herself down to where Joy had crumpled, taking her head in her arms and cradling it, almost as if it wasn't actually attached to the rest of her body. Joy just hung from her grasp, drowning in the familiar scent of rose hand cream and furniture polish.

Neither said a word; they didn't need to. In thirty-five years, they had picked each other up so often that it was a wonder that neither had a permanent hunch or a hernia.

Way back in junior School, Joy hadn't understood why some of the other kids were mean to Carlee or why they'd call her names that she'd never heard before. But ten-year-old Joy was sure that when Carlee's mother back in Jamaica had packed her bags and sent her to live with family in the UK, that the better life she had envisioned for her didn't involve her spending her lunch cowering behind a sanitary bin because Darren Moss from year six, with his greasy hair and permanent thick lip, would wait outside of the girls' toilets with a wad of wet loo roll, or that every day she'd offer to help with putting away the gym equipment, just so that she wouldn't be followed home by the year five girls who wore their skirts too short and their hair too high.

Joy had offered to walk with her and quickly found that Carlee was smart, funny and incredibly lonely. That quickly changed. By high school, the two were inseparable. They coached each other through exams, argued over boys, and then cried over them. They took their first sips of alcohol together and once spent the night in opposite hospital beds when the day before GCSE results were released, too much homebrew   resulted in them both having their stomachs pumped.

They were then grounded together too.

When Joy found herself pregnant at 19, it had been Carlee on the other side of the toilet door, waiting as she peed onto the stick that would change her life forever. And a few months later, it had been Joy who was at Carlee's side went she was dragged to court for breaking the father's nose after he told Joy he wanted nothing to do with it. 'It' was Mischa, and to this day Joy regretted not punching him herself.

For thirty years, they had been two sides of the same stone, hardy and strong, yet weather-beaten and a bit worn. And Carlee knew all too well what Joy was going through, after her first husband just upped and left her for his chiropractor a matter of weeks after their youngest daughter was born. Joy, heavily pregnant with Zachary had moved herself in, she had cooked and cleaned, winded babies and wiped noses, and when everything else was done, she lay next to her friend while she sobbed into a pillow.

Grief without death, Carlee had called it, love without purpose is what it was. Pain caused by a build-up of love in the heart, stuck resolutely with nowhere to go.

So, while Carlee didn't say a word, Joy still heard it, Carlee's voice in her head telling her it was going to be ok, that they would get through it, just as they had each done a thousand times before. But, they had always been right. They had both passed the forty mark still standing, and Carlee was a testament to that. She had mourned her loss, and she had healed, and when she met Mark when he arrived to fix the printer at the Post Office where she worked, her heart was ready to let go of all that pent up love. The poor man didn't stand a chance.

Pulling away from her friend, Joy lifted the bottom of her vest and used it to wipe her eyes before blowing her nose into the softly embroidered hem.

"Where's Misch?" she asked, her voice trailing off into uncontrollable sobs, her nose blowing snot bubbles as she tried to stem the flow with her shoulder.

"She wanted to come," replied Carlee, her mouth dropping at the corners as Joys face crumpled. "She said she'd ring when Zach's asleep. She didn't want to disrupt him."

Joy nodded. Mischa was right. She often was. Zachary had been so excited about staying over, if she had tried to bring him home, it would have only resulted in an almighty meltdown, and Joy didn't think that either of them had the head to deal with that right now. Joy was already panicking over what she would tell him, eventually. She was toying with the idea of saying nothing. Robin had barely been home at all for the last few months, and even when home, he was distracted and unengaged. But Zachary was a super smart kid, and while he had a constant air of not paying attention, he noted everything, and he understood it. Joy wondered that he might have already worked it out before her.

"You go freshen yourself up, and I'll pour us a drink," said Carlee, pulling herself to her feet and holding out her hand, "and then we can sit and call him names and make a start on the voodoo doll."

Joy wasn't entirely convinced that she was joking but nonetheless allowed herself to be hauled upright before backing off into the bathroom as Carlee turned and retreated downstairs.

Gasping as she caught sight of herself in the mirror, Joy grimaced. Her face was puffy and red, her eyes swollen and sore, and the little wedge of flesh between her eyes at the top of her nose was so deeply grooved that it looked like a little mini cleavage, right in the middle of her face. Coldwater helped a little, but after splashing half a sink full over her face, she gave up, dabbed herself dry and headed downstairs.

Carlee was already sat at the table nursing a short glass with a tall straw, her crimson weave was scraped up on the top of her head and she was still in her work clothes, her soft pink shirt unbuttoned at the top two, and her name badge hanging lopsidedly at her left breast. As Joy entered the kitchen, she handed her a glass and refused to speak to her until she had drunk at least half. Joy took a big gulp, followed immediately by a second. It was brandy, cognac perhaps, sweet and warm. It tasted like bonfire night. Pausing, she closed her eyes before draining the rest of the glass, ignoring the burning sensation that had begun to rise from her empty stomach and the tingle in her throat, which was hoarse and raw. She handed the glass back to Carlee, who promptly downed her own before pouring another two as Joy took a seat next to her.

"Are you going to tell me what happened, or do I have to guess?" she asked, sliding one of the glasses across the table.

Joy laughed, surprised almost that she still could, "Go on then," she said.

Carlee smirked, "Ok, Robin left home to fulfil a life-long desire to join NASA and fly to the moon?"

Joy shook her head.

"Has he decided to join a monastic order and run away to live in a temple?"

Joy shook her head again.

"Ooh, I know," she said excitedly, "He's gone to look after gorillas in the wilderness like that Foss woman.

Joy giggled, "Nope."

"Don't tell me he's run away with the circus. Oh, Robin, what a bloody cliché," she said, raising one eyebrow and taking a big gulp from her glass.

Joy leaned in and lowered her voice. "He's only gone and left me for his twatting brother," she said before lifting her drink and quickly downing the remainder of the contents, almost as if she was trying to wash the very words out of her mouth.

Carlee drummed her long blue nails on the side of her glass, her eyes narrowing, her mouth puckered. "Thought as much. You did say, though, you did think that it's only a matter of time before he just doesn't come home at all."

Carlee was one of the few people who knew the extent of Robin's behaviour. She only lived at the bottom of the hill and in the early days, she'd sat in their living room while the boys slept so that Joy could drive around to Reuben's and demand that he come home. She had done shopping for her when Zachary had flat out refused to leave the house and Mischa couldn't babysit, she had lied for her when her mother had called, and Joy just couldn't face her, and she had been the only one who had told her what she didn't want to hear. That maybe, it was time to stop fighting it and just let go.

Joy dropped her eyes and stared at a knot of rough wood on the table, trying to ignore the reddening of her cheeks as she clenched her eyes shut. Somewhere in the back of her throat, she could feel the words forming, bubbling up into her mouth. Words she didn't want to admit to.

She cleared her throat. "I made him choose, Car. I made him choose between me and Ben. And he didn't pick me." She didn't dare look up. She felt her eyes begin to sting and rubbery snot form at the back of her nose. She snuffed it in loudly, clenching her eyes shut, but no matter how tightly she held them, tears began to roll from their corners, dripping down onto her hands before slipping into the empty glass that she was clinging onto for dear life. "I was just so sick of it." she said, "sick of waiting around, sick of apologising to the kids, sick of having to rely on you and Mischa and everyone else." She paused and wiped her nose against her forearm. "I was sick of feeling like a fucking burden to everyone but him."

Dropping her head, she rested her forehead against her knuckles and breathed out hard. She heard the chair scratch across the floor, and footsteps on the bare tiles, before she felt Carlee's hands run over her hair and pull her head to her waist. She held it there tightly as Joy's sniffles turned to sobs and her tears to torrents.

"We never carried your burden," she soothed. "We just held you up enough so that you were strong enough to do it yourself."

Joy pulled away from her friends sodden hip, wiping tears and stringy wet snot from her face with a tea towel that Carlee had passed her from the sink.

But before she could say anything else, a noise at the door made them both jump. They spun around, watching as the figure on the other side of the coloured glass panel pushed the handle down and the door slowly opened.

Joy's heart leapt. She could feel it beating in her ears as the rustling on the other side of the door got louder. Half of her wanted it to be Robin, for him to swan in announcing that he'd made a colossal mistake and that everything would be ok. The other half wanted to kill him. The audacity of him thinking he could just come back and that she'd just welcome him with open arms. She bit her bottom lip so hard she felt blood pool around her teeth as the door swung open.

"Only us, girls," came a voice through the open crack. Sitting back and breathing out like a train releasing steam, Joy felt her heart drop back into her chest cavity with a thump.

"Through here, Margot," called Carlee, rushing to the kitchen cabinet above the kettle and grabbing another two glasses.

"Two glasses?" asked Joy.

Carley nodded towards the door.

Joy could just make out another figure behind Margot, and as they stepped into the light of the hall, Joy breathed another sigh of relief to see Meryl, Margot's younger sister trailing behind carrying another three bags.

"Sorry, we didn't know what you needed," said Margot dumping her bags onto the kitchen floor, followed by Meryl, who dumped her bags onto Margot's feet, making her sister squeal, and everyone else jump.

Joy slinked to her feet and hugged them both. "You didn't have to ...."

Margot cut her off. "We didn't, but we did, so shut up. We bought more booze too, which Mez here thought was a bad idea, but sure, if you don't want it, I'll happily take it back with me," she smiled, handing Carlee a litre bottle of pink gin and a six-pack of tonic.

"I did not say that!" demanded Meryl, who was unloading an inhuman amount of hummus into the fridge while trying to brush Pelé away, who had his whole front end inside one of the bags. "I just don't think that drinking your way through a crisis is the best way to deal with it."

"Mez, it's the only way to deal with it," said Margot, shooting a wink in Joy's direction.

Joy laughed. Despite there being barely more than 12 months between them in age, Margot and Meryl couldn't have been more different. Margot was confident and competitive, a high achieving Solicitor. She took no bullshit and didn't tolerate fools. Always immaculate, she wore her long blonde locks perfectly tousled into soft curls, and Joy couldn't remember a single time that she had ever seen her without make-up. Even in their teens, school trips saw Margot awake a good hour before the rest of the class to apply a flawless face full of foundation and once nearly got suspended from school altogether for smuggling hair straighteners on a camping trip to Wales and nearly burning down the chalet.

Meryl, on the other hand, was the polar opposite. She was timid, softly spoken and much shorter. Joy had often wondered whether this was the actual height Meryl was always intended to be or whether she had been somehow stunted from spending her entire life in Margot's shadow. A primary school teacher, she never wore make-up, had a constant smell of PVA glue about her, and had worn her off blonde hair in a high pony since the day she was born. A mother of six, she was compassionate, caring and always in a rush.

Surprisingly when drunk, she turned into Margot, and likewise, Margot became a little more Meryl. When together, they bickered like toddlers and acted out a constant battle of one-upmanship that Meryl could never win, even if she wanted to. Most of the time, she only engaged because she knew how much it winded Margot up that she didn't care how she was *so* much more successful. For everything Margot had and for everything that she achieved, Meryl lived content in the knowledge that, as far as she was concerned, she was, in fact, happier.

Margot poured four gins from the big bottle and handed them out. Joy slid away into the lounge and slumped down onto the sofa, where the dog quickly joined her, and listened as Carlee brought Margot and Meryl up to speed.

"Where's Lauren?" asked Carlee.

"Couldn't get a sitter. Dan's off fishing somewhere," replied Margot.

"And Bernie?"

"Same," replied Meryl, "Mack's fishing with Dan. But Tabitha and Lynn are calling tomorrow, Tab's working late."

"But we can all do Friday, right?" asked Margot.

"Friday?" asked Carlee.

"Impromptu crisis meeting, everyone's been told," said Margot.

"But mums expecting you to take her to Manchester Saturday, *Marg,*" chirped Meryl, cutting Margot of in her stride.

Joy stifled a laugh. She could almost hear Margot's eye's roll through the kitchen wall. She absolutely hated being called Marg, it was in most instances a case of instant friendship dismissal, or at the very least, she would ignore any and all calls for a good week. Meryl was the only one who would dare to and the only one who would get away with it.

Meryl would also usually answer to absolutely any name that Margot chose to call her out of spite, which wound Margot up even more.

"Urrgh, I'll sort it". She snapped.

"I'll ring Mischa in the morning and check she can have Zach," added Carlee.

"Great," cried Margot, smacking her hands and rubbing them together. "Can't remember the last time we had a girl's night out."

"It's not a girl's night out. It's a crisis meeting, for Joy," shot Meryl.

"And what does every girl in a crisis need? A good night out," replied Margot.

Joy dropped her head into her hands and scratched at her eyebrows. She didn't really want to go out. She didn't particularly want to leave the house ever again. The thought of getting dressed up and walking into a bar brought her out in a cold sweat and a sudden feeling of existential dread. But there would be no getting out of it. It was, evidently, being planned and executed by Margot, who would never take no for an answer, and even if she did, she would just guilt Joy into it by pointing out the effort everyone else had made.

When Margot's own divorce had been finalised, she had circumnavigated the fact that many of them had toddlers by hiring the village hall, complete with clown and a face painter. She had still proceeded to drink her own body weight in tequila and then set fire to her wedding dress in the middle of the dancefloor. If the whole affair wasn't depressing enough, standing in the carpark in the pissing rain with butterfly face paint running down your chin while the fire brigade put the roof out is probably not the best way to lighten the mood. It did, though, and while Margot had been hit with a hefty fine and the cost of repair, they still laughed about it.

Taking a sip of her drink, Joy quickly spat it back out into the glass. It was almost entirely gin from where Margot had barely hovered the can of tonic over the top of the glass. She dropped the drink down on the table and lay her head back against the sofa. Groaning as her puffy eyes rolled closed and the weight lifted from her neck. It wasn't even eight o'clock, yet it felt like she had been awake for a week.

She was just getting comfortable when she heard her phone ring in the kitchen and the opening bars of Mr Brightside cut through the chatter of the three women as they filled each other in on their various gossips. She heard Margot answer it, and after first confirming that Mischa was free to have Zachary on Friday, as if she had a choice, she called for Joy to speak to her daughter.

Wandering back into the kitchen, she took the phone from Margot while simultaneously tipping the undrinkable concoction down the sink whilst no one was looking. She then made a dash for the back door. On her way out, she was stopped by Meryl, who handed her another glass, which she promptly emptied into a fake potted Ficus outside the backdoor, before taking a seat on the patio bench and lifting the phone to her ear.

Chapter 10

Joy stood staring blankly into the mirror as she buttoned up her uniform. Her eyes were red and swollen, her face bloated and drained of colour, her pallor wasn't helped by her hair scraped back into a tight bun. *'Those allergies are going to have to do a lot of heavy lifting today,'* she thought, plucking a tube of concealer from the dresser drawer and slathering a thick trail under each eye.

"You're not thinking about going to work, are you?"

Carlee's voice startled Joy, causing her to jerk and smear black mascara straight up her left eyelid.

"I have to," she replied, "And I need to. I need normality. I need to be ..... occupied."

"You need to rest. You've had an awful shock."

Joy ignored her and turned her attention back to her reflection, pulling a wipe from the pack on the dresser and set about cleaning up the angry black smear. She didn't feel tired. She probably got a better night sleep than she'd had in a long time, thanks to the warmth of the brandy and not pacing the living room until the small hours.

As absolutely awful as she felt, Joy couldn't deny that a weight had been lifted. Even when it isn't the one you want, a conclusion is still just that, and the finality that comes with it was, if nothing more, assuring.

She had awoken around 4am feeling surprisingly spritely for another night curled up on the sofa. Carlee and Meryl had helped themselves to her bed, which wasn't a problem as she'd had no intention of sleeping in it. She had considered taking a leaf out of Margot's book by dragging it out to the garden and setting fire to it, but she wasn't in the position to buy new at this point and instead decided that a good exorcism by washing machine would be good enough to get rid of all traces of him. Perhaps she would treat herself to new bedding, at the very least.

"You barely ate, too," came Meryl's voice from behind. Reaching around Carlee's waist, she handed Joy a cup of steaming black coffee and a croissant.

Joy took the coffee gratefully but waved away the pastry.

"Where's Margot?" asked Carlee.

"She snuck out while I was in the shower," replied Joy.

"Yeah, she has to rush home early to check on the portrait in the attic," scoffed Meryl, taking a big chunk out of the corner of the croissant and plonking herself down on the end of the bed.

Carlee shot Meryl a look while Joy sniggered and set about re-doing her mascara.

"Are you sure you're ok for work?" asked Carlee. "I could call in sick for you, and we could just hang out. Shut the curtains, eat junk, pretend like we're in college again."

Joy smiled at the idea but shook her head. "I'll tell the sister in charge what's happened, but I just need to not be . . . . here."

"We could go out for the day, get out of town, I just think . . . ."

"I'm fine," spat Joy, cutting her off. "Absolutely fine."

She wasn't fine at all. She could feel her hands shaking, and it was taking every little bit of effort she had to hold the mascara wand still. But she just needed to get away from the constant reminder of the empty closet and the missing toothbrush. She needed a distraction, a routine. Much like Zachary, so long as everything else carried on as it should, she would be fine.

Without another word, she took a deep breath, picked up her mobile phone from the dresser, and hurried downstairs in search of where she'd kicked off her shoes the night before.

It felt so long ago already. She had come home so full of butterflies and bravado, a married mother of four with a husband and a future full of family. Fourteen hours later and she was leaving a single mother, a cast-aside, with her dreams shattered and her heart broken clean in half.

She lifted her phone and dialled Mischa's number. It was a little past five-thirty, but Zachary would have been well awake by now, and once Zachary was up, it was officially morning for everyone. Mischa answered before the ring tone even kicked in.

"I didn't think you'd be going in today," she croaked. She sounded groggy.

"Morning, sweetie, how did he sleep?" asked Joy, ignoring Mischa's concern.

"Good. I let him sleep in my bed. Do you want to speak to him?"

Joy felt her eyes begin to swell. "No, no, it's ok, um, I'm running late. Tell him I'll see him when I pick him up"

"Mum?" asked Mischa before pausing. She never finished the question, and Joy didn't respond.

"I Love you, mum." Said Mischa.

"Love you too," replied Joy, her voice fading as she slammed her thumb down on the end call.

Slipping her shoes on, she waltzed into the kitchen, grabbed her bag from the countertop before turning to find Carlee and Meryl, who were stood at the bottom of the stairs.

Slinking towards the door, she gave them both a hug before making her way out into the dark and the first day of life 2.0.

Chapter 11

Pulling up outside the school, Joy let her head lag against the headrest and closed her eyes.

Work hadn't been such a great idea after all.

It had all started off so promising. She had arrived to find that Maryanne Mathews, the usual charge nurse, had switched shifts due to a root canal and had been replaced with Janette Pfeffer, the deputy sister. Janette was, compared to Maryanne, a complete pushover. She knew her stuff alright. In fact, Janette had overachieved in everything she had ever done. She consistently topped the boards in training exercises and evaluations, and despite having only been at the hospital for three years, she had quickly moved up the ranks to deputy sister. A position that Joy had reluctantly turned down at least three times, even though she would have been perfect for the role. She knew the inner workings of the cardiology ward inside out. She was popular, highly skilled and had a bedside manner that would put Nightingale to shame, but when Zachary began to show signs of ASD, she just didn't have the mental beans anymore for the extra responsibility or the flexibility required for the sudden shift changes and longer hours that often came with it. So, instead, she had been given a slight pay rise and a lanyard that said, 'Senior Nurse', which she was deeply possessive over.

Janette, on the other hand, wasn't very good with people. She had few managerial skills, couldn't handle conflict and was largely afraid of all the consultants. While this boded well for Joy's request to be put on non-life essential duties for the day in light of extenuating personal circumstances, when a junior doctor had demanded to know why, instead of feigning lady problems as was Maryanne's default excuse, Janette had crumpled, and told him everything. Which meant that by lunchtime, the whole hospital knew. The icing on the cake had been a large bunch of flowers that arrived at the nurse's station just after lunchtime, and which had promptly been sent down to the mortuary, sans the somewhat patronising greeting card from Dr Goodbody, which she managed to refrain from jamming into his exhaust pipe as she passed his precious Audi on the carpark.

Joy wasn't particularly mad that everyone knew. She wasn't even all that embarrassed. This was, after all, a large hospital, and one thing about medical work is that the hospital itself becomes a way of life. Relationships are born and die under the watchful eye of the canteens styrofoam cups, while arguments simmer over chamber pots, and reconciliations take place in linen stores. Hospitals breathe. They have a life of their own, manifested by those whose lives intertwine within its walls. By all accounts, Joy's drama wasn't even scandal worthy, and outside of the unwanted consultant attention, most people had stopped giving her pity smiles and *'You OK, hun?'* nods by the time her shift ended.

Joy's only real issue was that she hadn't even spoken to Elliot and Owen yet *or* told her parents, and many of those who worked at the hospital lived on the estate and had children at school with her boys. Joy worried that they would find out from someone else before she'd had a chance to lie to them, reassuringly, that everything was going to be fine.

It had occurred to her that Robin may try to call them himself and try to explain, but, considering they called her at any given hour in the event that their bike had a puncture or they couldn't find their underpants, she thought that a call from their dad telling them that their family was now defunct would warrant a text message at the very least. Yet her phone had remained eerily silent, which, if nothing else, meant she had one less distraction to contend with.

The ward had also been thankfully quiet. As a dedicated cardiology unit, they acted as a step down from ICU for patients who'd suffered heart attacks and angina flare-ups, along with referrals attending for routine angiograms and heart scans and stent surgery. Those who worked on the ward called it the last chance saloon, a place where people were told that their hearts could be fixed and their lives improved, just so long as they followed doctor's orders and gave up all the things they loved. This meant that on any given day, Joy was present in some of the most beautiful and some of the most painful moments in people's lives. She watched families, faced with loss, reconnect at the bedside while worried visitors sat panicked when their loved ones were wheeled down to theatre. It was a place where second chances were born, and grudges were forgotten. While Carlee and Meryl had worried that this might have been too much for Joy, it actually bolstered her. It cheered her. She found comfort in others happiness, their relieved smiles infectious, even when her own was all but painted on.

"Shit," exclaimed Joy, spotting from the clock on the dashboard that it was already five past three.

Dashing out of the car and down the path, Zachary was already bouncing up and down by the door with Mrs Mortimer.

Muttering her apologies, Joy grabbed the little boy by the hand and, avoiding all eye contact, and promised that she'd explain all later.

Pushing open the front door, Joy was hit with the smell of citrus cleaner and stew. Mischa was already sitting at the kitchen table, scrolling through her phone while a big pot bubbled away on the stovetop.

Mischa spotted Joy before she'd even had the chance to drop her bag and shut the door, launching herself from the chair and running the entire length of the hallway. She threw her arms around Joy, as Zachary took the opportunity to battle his way out of his mother's grasp and skipped off into the living room in search of the dog.

"What's this?" asked Joy, pointing to a suitcase propped up behind the front door.

"That's mine," she replied. "Thought I'd move back in for a few days, help out with Zach."

Joy nodded, patting Mischa on the shoulder. "Not sure how your brothers will feel about that. They were glad to see the back of you."

"Owen's fine with it. He's already home." She said, pointing up the stairs.

Joy felt her heart turn over and her tummy twist. "You, you told him?" she asked.

Mischa nodded. "He figured it out, came home at break to pick up some books. He saw dad's stuff gone."

"Where's Elliot?" asked Joy

Mischa's smile wilted into a tense crease. "He's gone to find dad. Said he's gonna beat him up. He won't," she said matter of factly. "He'll probably shout at Uncle Reuben's front door for ten minutes, call him a few names and be sent straight home."

Joy bit her lip. "Have you spoken to him?"

"Who, Elliot?"

"No, dad."

"I rang and left a voicemail, said Mischa, shaking her head," he hasn't called back."

"Fucking coward" spat Joy, clenching her eyes tight, before following with "Sorry, love."

"You're not sorry, and you shouldn't be," she replied, pulling herself from Joys embrace and heading back to the kitchen. She picked the lid off the big pot and gave it a stir. The smell of too much garlic wafted down the hallway, hitting Joy smack in the gut and sending her belly into a frenzy. She hadn't eaten since lunch the day before, not unless you count a share size chocolate bar for breakfast and two bags of crisps for lunch. She was running on empty.

Turning to hang her cardigan up on the pegs at the bottom of the stairs, the door swung open behind her, and Elliot appeared on the other side, blurry-eyed and spouting angry mumbles.

"You ok, buddy?" called Joy as he pushed past her and marched heavily up the stairs.

"Fuck you?" He called back.

Joy sighed. She had expected this. Owen was rational, and far too level headed for his age. Elliot was teen angst personified, which, to be honest, wasn't all bad because it made him predictable, and predictability could be pre-empted. Most of the time. This would take a little more than a new dart gun and bag of jellybeans, but she understood that he was hurting, and while Owen would ferret himself away to lick his wounds, Elliot would do it loudly and make sure everyone else had to join in too.

Joy called him again, but he didn't answer. She stood at the bottom of the stairs and waited. There was a bang and then a thump from upstairs, followed by a screech, and then another bang before angry footsteps began to descend the stairs again. Joy braced herself for another angry outburst, but it didn't come. Instead, Elliot sloped past her quietly into the kitchen and slumped onto the bench, followed by Owen, who looked just as confused as she did.

This was new.

"Is it true?" he said, eventually lifting his head and glaring at Joy.

"Yes, your dad left. I don't know . . . . "

He cut her off, slamming his fist down on the table. "No, but is it true, what he said you did."

Taking a deep breath, Joy swallowed hard. "What did he say?". She asked. She could already make a good stab at it.

"That it's your fault. That you made him leave," he screamed.

Joy sat down and placed her hand on his. He pulled it away. She could smell the musty scent of cigarette smoke on his clothes and mints on his breath, plus there was something else, something sweet. Cider probably. She had found three cans crushed behind the shed the weekend before. She had initially assumed they were Robin's but he'd barely been home.

Ignoring her son's reluctance, she snaked her hand across the table, slipped her fingers through his and pulled his hand back towards her, gripping it tightly with both hands. He didn't try to pull it away this time. Joy couldn't remember the last time she'd held his hand, probably not since he was at primary school, it felt like a mans hands now, bigger, and hairier at the wrist, yet still soft with youth. She leaned forward, sneaking a peek under the long thick fringe that hung over his face and shrouded his eyes until his gaze shifted and she felt him looking straight at her. "I didn't make him leave. I asked him to make a choice. I never thought he'd choose that, but he did."

"It's not your fault, mum," said Owen, pulling another chair up next to her and laying his head on her shoulder. She felt her uniform dampen against her arm.

"What else did he say?" she asked, watching as little beads of moisture dropped onto the table below Elliot's downturned nose.

He shook his head, "Nothing," he sniffled, "he was really pissed."

"What's he got to be angry about?" scoffed Mischa.

"No, he was pissed," replied Elliot, finally lifting his head. "Hammered, off his face, he could barely stand up."

Joy felt a pang of something rattle against her chest. She wasn't sure what it was. Guilt perhaps, regret, maybe even satisfaction. If it was, it didn't feel as good as she thought it would. "It's us against the world now, guys," she said, taking the deepest breath she could muster and swallowing down the sobs that had been trying to creep into her throat.

Owen wrapped his arm around her shoulder.

"You have me," she continued, "and I have all of you." Through the living room door, she watched as Zachary sat, completely naked and blissfully unaware, playing boat in the long draw that he had ripped out from under the tv unit, grumming loudly as he pretended his hands were paddles, brushing them against the carpet as he swung side to side. And Joy wondered, for a moment, how she could possibly ever want anything more.

Chapter 12

The week had passed in much of a blur. Maryanne had returned to the ward and instantly tried to talk Joy into taking leave, which she cordially and repeatedly turned down. She had, in her personal opinion, been a perfectly capable nurse as a single mother just out of nursing school. She had been an exceptional nurse as the mother of a hormonal teenage girl and rambunctious twin boys. She had been professional and proficient as the mother of an autistic pre-schooler, forced through hours and hours of meetings and assessments, and she functioned seamlessly through the sleepless nights of a child who barely closed their eyes for more than half an hour at a time.

She had, at least, agreed to stay away from anything that had the potential to go awry. She was taken off theatre duties for the week, anything with needles were a no go, medications were double and triple checked at Joy's request, and within a couple of days, she had found comfort in the simple joys of sticking to the basics. She sat with patients. She listened about their lives as she bathed them and dressed their scars. She had listened to 62-year-old double bypass patient Bert tell her about his wife's bunions and his son's new boyfriend, and Maude, who at 58 was getting married for the fourth time, just as soon as she's had her pacemaker fitted.

She spent the entire week avoiding anyone with any kind of seniority, and Dr Goodbody, who she had spotted lingering by the vending machines on at least three occasions. There were plenty of vending machines in A&E, ones that were restocked daily and which, if you knew the right buttons to press, would dispense double the treats for half the money. Joy already knew that Dr Goodbody had no clue when it came to pressing the right buttons, but nonetheless, there was no good reason why he was buying his snickers from the Cardiology corridor other than to bump into her.

By the time Friday came around, and a rare full weekend off, Joy skipped out of the main entrance and off into the sunlight like a teenager on the last day of term. But once home, she found herself ending the week much how she had started it, staring defeatedly into a closet full of clothes that didn't fit her.

Rifling through the rack, she searched through layers of summery colours in chiffon and lace until she felt her hand land on plain-woven jersey. Yanking at the hanger, she pulled it from the closet and held it up in front of her.

Her face fell into a cold grimace.

It was plain black, worn and thinning at the armpits, its long sleeves devoid of any shape, and the delicate layer of beading at the neckline was sparse and uneven.

It was her old faithful and had probably been worn for every night out since before Zachary was even born. It was comfortable, familiar and dull as dishwater.

"You can't wear that old thing," came Mischa's voice from the doorway. She was carrying Zachary on her hip, who was covered from head to waist in yoghurt.

"Did someone get in the fridge again?" she asked, smiling at the boy, who smiled back at her, nodding and clearly delighted with himself.

"You hose him down," said Mischa handing Zachary to his confused looking mother, "and I'll be back in ten."

Mischa turned and left before Joy could get the words out to ask her where she was going. She was starting to think that it might be a ploy, knowing how much Zachary hated the shower, but just as Joy was plucking the squealing six-year-old from the tub some fifteen minutes later, Mischa came charging up the stairs, gripping a coat-hanger, the contents of which trailed beneath it into a crumpled bag for life.

"Try this," she said, thrusting the bag at Joy.

Joy grabbed the hanger excitedly and pulled it from the bag. Suspended from it was a dress. Fashioned in gun-mental lace at the skirt and a bodice encrusted with sequins and crystals that glinted in the light and spread tiny little rainbows on the wall above the bed. Joy pulled the neckline and peered inside at the label. It was an XXL.

"Jasper Conran, eh," she said, raising her brow, "but this isn't your size. You're a twelve, a medium at most."

"I got it in a charity shop in town last month. I was going to give it to you for your birthday." She said, dipping her chin and staring down at her feet.

"And I would have been over the moon with it," she said, sliding it off the hanger and over her head. It fell effortlessly over her shoulders and hung perfectly, if a little baggy, at her waist. Running her hands down her sides, she smoothed the skirt, slipped into her black heels and stepped over to the mirror. "I *am* over the moon with it." She said, giving a little twirl. The soft lace skirt swooshed as she stopped, tickling her at the knees where it came to a rest.

"Gorgeous," said Mischa, clapping her hands together excitedly.

Joy stared back at herself in the mirror and flashed herself a big smile. She felt it too. Even with the rollers still clinging to her head, she felt glamorous and, dare she say it, sexy.

Within ten minutes, she was stood by the front door, her rollers out and her long hair tousled into soft flowing waves. She felt ten years younger.

"What was that?" asked Joy, spinning around on her heels as she heard the sound of a lens shutter, "Don't you dare post that," she said, trying to grab the phone from her daughter's hand.

"Why not? You look awesome," she replied, fiddling with her phone.

Joy grimaced as she heard the notification ping from her phone telling her that she had been tagged in a photo.

"Because your dad'll see it," she said.

"Exactly," replied Mischa, a smug grin creeping across her lips.

Joy wasn't sure why she felt so uneasy about Robin seeing the photo. She looked great. But she felt disrespectful somehow as if she was rubbing his nose in it, or cheating, which was highly ironic considering. There were, of course, other people who might see it, and the last thing she needed was for an overzealous A&E consultant to track her down in the pub. She was about to take the phone out and untag herself when a beep outside confirmed that Carlee had arrived in their taxi.

She swished into the kitchen, kissing Zachary on the forehead and hugging Mischa tightly. "The boys know they have to be in for ten, okay. And no telly after eleven. And no . . ."

"Mum," scolded Mischa, "Just go, it's fine," she said, ushering her mother out of the front door, where Carlee stood waiting by the car, dressed head to toe in black lace.

Chapter 13

Strutting into the Albion on Carlee's arm, Joy felt all tingly. The faint beat of 90's music that filtered into her ears created an involuntary skip in her step that she found impossible to stop. If she closed her eyes, between the music and the unmistakable aroma of stale beer and cheap perfume, Joy could almost imagine that she'd gone back in time. Even her complete inability to walk in heels and the constant fear that her skirt was tucked into her knickers hadn't diminished over the years.

At the far end of the pub, two tables had been pushed together beneath a thin off white tablecloth that was hiding the penises that were scratched into it's surface, and around which sat her friends, who smiled and waved as Joy and Carlee sauntered across the room, which was far longer than Joy remembered. It was early doors, staff were still busy clearing away dirty plates and pepper pots from the teatime rush while all those who remained in-situ were men, draining the last of their post-work, pre-kebab pints.

A number of them turned to look as the pair passed by, causing Carlee to turn full carry on and give them an animated wink and little wave. Joy did not. Joy kept her eyes on the floor and her focus on not falling over.

By the time they made it to their table right at the back by the dance floor, Joy felt an almost birthday like twinge of butterflies as they launched from her tummy and circled in her chest.

Margot, looking immaculate as ever, was sat at one end of the table. Her hair looked like it hadn't moved at all since she'd last seen her and wearing a dress that, if Joy had tried to carry it off, would look like she was trying to escape from a shroud, and which no doubt cost more than she made in a week. At the opposite end of the table sat Meryl, in an electric blue midi-dress that she had presumably been forced into by Margot and which was at least a size too big. She wore her hair scraped back into pigtails that fell playfully over her shoulders and most of her face, which Joy thought was probably intentional.

Making her way around the table, Joy hugged each of her friends in turn. Lauren and Bernie were sat on either side of Margot.

They had all become friends at nursing school, which had led to them being dubbed Charlie's Angels amongst their year group on account of Lauren being blonde, Joy's auburn and the fact that Bernie was, and largely still is, a dead ringer for Lucy Liu. In their final year, Joy had made the mistake of introducing them to Margot, who corrupted them into nights of debauchery and lock ins at the hotel she was working at while at Law School. On one particular evening, Lauren had found herself dragged around the premises by her feet with her trousers around her ankles after losing a game of down in one, while Bernie spent the night locked in the toilets with the hotel manager when the night porter had failed to spot them shagging in one of the cubicles.

Neither had ever been able to turn down a night out ever again, whether that was because of a deep-rooted friendship or bribery, Joy wasn't sure, but in any event, they had both named Margot as godmother to their kids and still holidayed together every other year.

Bernie worked at the same hospital as Joy in paediatrics, while Lauren had digressed into dentistry and worked at a plush clinic in Cheshire. She was also probably the main reason why Joy still had all of her own teeth after promising them all free dental work as a perk of the job.

Next to Lauren, against the back wall, sat Tabitha and Lynne. Tabitha hadn't grown an inch since the day they left junior school, a petite 5 foot one with a mouth like a foghorn and a different hair colour every week. Today she had unicorn hair of purple and candyfloss blue, which fell in a soft bob around sharp eyes and a thin nose. She sat in complete contrast to Lynne, who, with a tight black ponytail, opal eyes and a puckered mouth, looked like an extra from the Matrix. The pair had married on the day that same-sex marriages were made legal and had recently bought a boutique guest house, the Bed&Bakery, where they offered five-star accommodation while selling cupcakes and baked goods from a hatch in the ginnel. This, unfortunately, meant that they were never seen in the same room together outside of the hotel, making tonight a rare treat for them both.

Thankfully there were no pity smiles or *'you ok, hun?'* nods here, Joy had known them each for at least 20 years, and tonight they were out for blood, Robin's blood.

Having all been briefed on the situation by either Carlee or Margot, it meant that one group had got the Jane Austen version, while the others the Tarantino. Both of which had left them with questions, and which Joy was bombarded with no sooner had she sat herself down.

"So, there's no one else involved then?" asked Lauren pushing a large glass of pinot across the table until it was directly in front of Joy, an offering, if you will amongst lady friends, as a show of trustworthiness in exchange for information.

Joy picked up the glass, tipped it in Laurens's direction, and downed a good half whilst shaking her head. But her eyes betrayed her. They always did. When something was bothering her, Joy wore it across her face like war paint.

Throughout the week, one thing had continued to bug her, one tiny thing that she hadn't mentioned to anyone, not Carlee, not even Mischa. The voice on the phone.

She hadn't spoken to Robin since, she hadn't been able to ask him what was going on, and so it hung over her like a pully that tugged at her heart every time she let the thought creep into her head.

"So, there is someone,?" said Margot.

"No" spat Joy, all too quickly,"

"I knew it," said Tabitha, "he couldn't just leave for no reason."

"Honestly, no," protested Joy, "I don't know, its

Just . . . "

"Who is she?" asked Lauren.

"There's a new girl, in his office . . . ."

"It's always the fucking new girl," said Margot.

"Honestly, I don't know if . . . "

"I bet you Ben's behind this," continued Margot, "can't handle seeing Rob happily tied down now that he's single again."

"Didn't you date Ben?" asked Meryl, "after Joel left."

Margot shot her a pernicious look, "Briefly."

"No, you dated for over a year," said Meryl, smirking.

"Long time ago. Just a bit of fun, really. Glad I called it off to be honest," said Margot, tossing her hair behind her shoulders and taking an overly long swig of her G&T.

"Didn't he dump you for what's her face, the ex-wife?" goaded Meryl. She was enjoying this.

"Thank you, Mez," snapped Margot, pushing her chair out and heading off in the direction of the bar.

Carlee pushed another large glass of wine towards Joy, who was sat laughing as she watched Margot storm away, thankful that attention had been drawn away from her. But her relief was short-lived.

"So, what's this new girl like? is she young? I bet she's young," asked Bernie from the opposite side of the table.

"They always are," added Lauren."

Joy drained the second glass of wine, "It was nothing more than a voice on the phone."

"Answering his phone, that's a bit bloody cocky," said Tabitha.

"Or she might have just been standing closest to it," sighed Joy.

"Or" added Lynne, "he wanted you to hear her, odd that you didn't even know she existed until the day he buggered off," she said, cocking her thumb out to the side.

Joy bit her lip. She'd had the same thought.

"Is there anyone in here that's caught your eye?" asked Tabitha, "you know I make a great wingman," she added with a wink.

"What, no," screeched Joy, "Robin left four days ago, I'm not on the fucking pull."

"Why not, you should be having revenge sex. Revenge sex is the best," said Margot, returning from the bar and dumping another full glass in front of Joy.

"I don't even know what that is, but it sounds painful," she replied.

"It's just when you shag someone to get back at an ex," said Bernie, "We've all been there."

Joy hadn't. "And what, you have to tell them about it? Send them a picture or something?" she laughed.

"No," replied Margot, wafting the notion away. "You just shag them to make yourself feel better, like fuck you Robin, I'm gonna shag this hot guy, just because I can"

"That's not revenge sex, that's just getting laid," said Joy, rolling her eyes, "Revenge would be me shagging some random in his brothers front garden while he's inside watching country file."

"You could do that, too" said Meryl.

"Nah," cackled Joy, "Ben's front garden is huge, they'd never spot us."

She emptied her glass, watching as it was quickly replaced by another, as the conversation bounced between what a shit Robin was and whatever random talking point that Joy employed to try and change the subject. Finally, 9pm rolled around, and the speakers perched on either side of the room burst into life with the muffled cries of a DJ who, after 25 years in the same job, still held his microphone too close to his mouth. His introduction was quickly followed by the opening bars of Ricky Martins Livin La Vida Loca, which was met with much hooting and table drumming from a group of young girls who had settled for the night on the opposite side of the room.

Joy glanced over. It was like watching themselves 20 years ago, young, carefree, dressed in skirts that barely covered their arses with spaghetti strap vests, no bra's and heels the height of beer bottles. They were huddled around a small square table in the corner, each gripping a BOGOF vodka Redbull, while the tablecloth below sat littered with toppled shot glasses, their arms draped over each other's shoulders as they belted the misheard lyrics of a song they could, in all probability, have been conceived to.

Joy was just grateful that the decibel level had raised enough to render any meaningful conversation impossible, and the light dimmed enough to make any drink palatable.

Around them, the room began to fill with bodies, mainly younger female bodies, as the ladies in the room seemed to outnumber the men by at least eight to one. Not unsurprisingly, a pint was a pint, and cost the same in almost every bar for a ten-mile radius, but this was the only pub in town that did cocktails for less than a fiver and shots for a quid, with the added advantage that they didn't play any music released after 2001. Often mistaken for a 90s bar, the truth was that the place simply hadn't been decorated since the Spice Girls hit the charts, and the owners were simply exploiting their laziness as nostalgia. Joy didn't mind. It meant that everything felt familiar, comforting somewhat, from the mahogany wood to the worn green seat covers, it was like visiting your nans, that is if your nan had a disco light and a toilet at the top of four flights of stairs.

As Kylie finished and morphed into the impossibly cheery beat of Bewitched's signature C'est La Vie, Carlee grabbed Tabitha and Bernie and headed in the direction of the dance floor, not wanting to be outdone by the younger crowd when there was a poor attempt at Irish dancing to be done, while Lauren and Lynne scoured the cocktail menu that had magically appeared on the table. Margot had snuck outside for a smoke, despite professing all over social media that she had, at long last, quit with the help of some expensive MLM that she had no doubt been given a freebie of, along with a nice kickback and complimentary tickets to the races.

Handbags were downed, shoes were kicked off, and vast Fishbowls full of lord knows what arrived. It didn't really matter what was in them, Margot had announced that she'd be picking up the tab, so Meryl had ordered two of the biggest, most expensive on the menu, which was promptly drained like a herd of thirsty, glitter-covered, stiletto clad, and alarmingly out of tune wildebeest around a magical purple waterhole. These were followed by pitchers of exotically coloured liquor that would undoubtedly look resplendent against the cold hard white of the toilet bowl in a few hour's time.

Joy sat back and watched her friends on the dance floor.

People were a funny breed, she thought. Anyone who'd attended a spinning class or spent any time on social media could tell you that, but never was their absurdity more obvious than when watching a dance floor past midnight. A sea of random strangers jiggling their various body parts about to a beat, or not as the case may be. It didn't make any evolutionary sense, and it served no purpose other than the fact that dancing felt great, for reasons that no one could ever quite explain. Depending on how many fishbowls you'd consumed, you may accidentally fall into, or onto, the love of your life, but more often than not, such a dalliance would only end up with you waking up in a strange bed with only one shoe, no underwear and a night club stamp on your tits.

Yet, the dancefloor was a literal representation of life. Some found it easy, others not so, while some spent the entire time on their arse. Some people were inherently good it and made it look easy, while others had two left trotters and the gait of a drunk pig. But the dancefloor of life was always full, busy with people just doing their best to keep up with the music any way they knew how, and not fall over their own feet. And, of course, when the music eventually stopped, everyone was still always holding out for just one last song, in the hope that it was their favourite.

Joy wasn't much of a dancer. She was more of the drunk pig variety, in dance and in life. But it didn't matter because she was surrounded by people who didn't care if she stepped on their toes, and who instead of showing off their strictly worthy moves, would happily dance to Whigfield with her because that was the only one that she knew all the moves to, and because it made her happy, for reasons that Joy could ever quite explain.

As the tempo of the music changed to something less injury-inducing, Joy took the opportunity to slip outside and check-in at home. Searching around for her handbag, she began to panic. As a teenager, she would wander off into town carrying nothing more than a lipstick and a £20 note shoved into one bra cup, and her house key in the other. She had lost count of the number of times that she'd had to climb in through the kitchen window as her key had slipped out during a taxi-rank fumble. Yet now, she found she couldn't possibly leave the house without her purse, her phone, a large keychain holding the keys to things she no longer even owned, pictures of her kids, Rennies, a hair grip, two aspirin and plaster. And while her breasts, and in turn her bra, had certainly grown big enough to accommodate most of the above, it wasn't really convenient or particularly comfortable. She had received more than one unintentional piercing in her time from an errant hair grip, and she had nearly found out the hard way that carrying loose pills in your underwear was more conducive to finding yourself spending the night in a jail cell, than in the pub, even if they did turn out to be antacids.

Eventually, she spotted the little grey clutch on the floor at the far end of the table, scooped down to pick it up, and trotted hastily out to the veranda, which in reality was nothing more than where they kept the Biffa bins with a couple of fairy lights thrown up and a broken patio heater shoved in the corner.

"Everything alright?" she squealed down the handset, jamming one finger into her other ear upon hearing Mischa answer.

"Everything's fine," came the blunt reply.

"Zach Ok?" she asked.

"Fast asleep."

"And the boys?"

"Out cold."

"So, what are you doing still up."

There was no answer.

"Misch, you ok?" asked Joy.

"I was asleep, mum. It's 1am." She snapped down the phone.

"Already, well, I best let you go, or we'll miss last orders," she paused. "Love you, chicken," she said, hanging up the call without waiting for a reply.

She reached for the door handle, but before she could pull it open, a lone figure caught her eye, hunched face down over a table that sat wedged into the corner behind the bins. Joy would know that mop of blonde and its accompanying shroud anywhere.

"Margot??" she called, louder than she intended.

The head shot up, almost as if it was attached to wire, like the funny dolls you used to find at old fairgrounds. Her eyes were glassy with blackened pools huddled at the corners leaving dark streaks across her nose that met in the middle.

"Huh?" she replied, looking around her.

"You coming in?" asked Joy.

Slapping her hands down on the table top, Margot winched herself up and steadied herself against the wall. "Bit pissed."

"Shall I call a cab?" asked Joy, fumbling around in her bag for the phone, and laughing as she found it still in her other hand.

"Hell no," cried Margot loud enough to make the group of girls at the far table turn around and investigate the noise. "Just needed a little fresh air, here next to this, um, ... Skip," She grinned, "all good now, though."

Stumbling past Joy, Margot grabbed the door handle and swung it open, filling the little outside space with the dulcet tones of Bill Medley and Jennifer Warnes, which was largely drowned out by the not so dulcet tones of 150 drunk women.

Margot, suddenly completely upright and surprisingly sprightly, cocked her arm in out in Joy's direction. "I do believe they're playing our waltz," she said, nodding her head towards the door, as Joy linked her arm and allowed herself to be dragged towards the dancefloor, where she was instantly transformed from a drunken 42-year-old with bare feet and a lemon wedge in her hair, into a dancer supremo, the very ghost of Swayze.

There was skirt swooshing. There was arm linking, there was hand bobbing and lots of swinging around at the elbows before the grand finale. Joy sidled herself up beside their table and braced herself, taking on a stance that resembled a quarterback awaiting a challenge. Egged on by their friend's whooping, and by the amused encouragement of a large group of couples standing nearby, Margot hitched up her dress above the knee and began to charge, launching herself at Joy with the grace and poise of a crocodile being turfed off the back of a boat, and slamming into Joy's chest at full pelt, sending both of them flying backwards into the table.

What neither of them had anticipated was that over the course of the evening, the tables beneath the cheap off white tablecloth had parted, and had Joy stood a matter of inches to either side, all would have been fine. But she didn't. Instead, as she hit the white sheath, the pair just kept on going until they hit the floor, dragging the entire tablecloth and four hour's worth of empty fishbowls with them.

From beneath several folds of foul-smelling fabric, Joy cackled loudly, as Margot writhed around aimlessly on top of her, trying to get enough footing on the now drink-sodden floor to lift herself off,

But they were both wedged solid in the narrow gap.

Finally, after much fuss coming from the outside of their grubby confinement, Joy felt the two tables begin to move away from her enough that Margot was able to roll off her and several pairs of hands appeared from above, pulling her by the wrists and sliding her out.

Joy lay there in hand on heart hysterics, but as she opened her eyes and looked around, everyone else looked serious and concerned. Carlee was shouting furiously into her phone. Tabitha was rushing back from the bar carrying napkins and a big jug of water, while even the DJ had cut the music and turned on the big lights.

Joy carried on laughing, albeit a little more nervously, as Meryl plopped herself down right in front of her.

"You'll be fine," she said, reaching forward and stroking at her shoulder.

Joy looked at her, puzzled. "I *am* fine," she said, "A bit winded perhaps, took a bump to the head and .... "

It was at that very point that Joy realised that she couldn't feel her left leg. It was there, if she reached down with her hand, she could touch it quite clearly, but she couldn't see it. Meryl was in the way.

"Help me up?" she asked.

"I'm not sure that's a good ..."

"For god's sake Meryl, I'm a nurse," she said, pushing her out of the way.

"Fuck a duck," said Joy, her mouth dropping wide open as she felt vomit start to stir. Sticking out from her shin was the fully embedded foot of a long-stemmed wine glass. "Meryl, pass me my bag." She asked.

"Your bag?" asked Meryl.

"I've a plaster in there," replied Joy, assuredly.

"A plaster?" repeated Meryl, slowly.

"Sure, be fine once I get it out," said Joy, reaching forward towards the glass, as every single person who had huddled around the group lunged forward to stop her.

"You can't just go yanking it out, you daft mare, we don't know how deep it's gone," said Meryl, putting herself back in between Joy and her leg.

"Or if it's hit bone," said Carlee.

"Or an archery," added Tabitha, who was hovering wobblily over her, phone out, and taking pictures from every angle.

"It's an artery," cackled Carlee, smacking the phone from Tabitha's hand, "An ambulance is on its way,"

"I don't need a sodding ambulance, it's just a graze," demanded Joy.

"Ok, get up and walk across the room." Said Meryl, moving out of the way.

Joys face crumpled, she tried to lift her leg, to shift it one way or another, to bend it enough to stand, but it was no use. Even if the pain wasn't becoming unbearable, the angle of the glass stem and the swelling that had already started to form around it made it near impossible to budge.

"I need another drink," she said, sliding back down onto her back, just as blue flashing lights filled up the street outside.

Chapter 14

ny other hospital." Moaned Joy, bracing herself against the gurney as the ambulance sped over yet another speed bump.

"It's the closest," replied Meryl.

"This," said Joy, pointing at the glass foot sticking out of her lower leg, "is not life-threatening. I could go to any other A&E in the fucking country."

"It's an ambulance, Joy, not a Taxi. It's up to them," she said, nodding towards the paramedic who was busy slipping a brace around Joy's calf.

"I knew I recognise you." He said, nestling her leg into a fetching, luminous orange box frame. He pulled the straps tight and lowered her dress hem back down, its pretty lace folds now blood-splattered and curled up at the edges. "I Never forget a face."

Joy grabbed the blanket that had been draped uselessly over her lap and pulled it up over her head, covering her face completely. "Forget you ever saw this one," she said, followed by, "any chance of some decent painkillers."

"Sorry, not on top of all the booze, not until you've seen a doctor. I have gas and air, though."

Joy crossed her arms tightly in front of her. "I'm a senior nurse, isn't that good enough. Pete." She said, pulling the blanket down and twisting her head around so she could read the name on his lanyard.

Pete shook his head.

"Any idea who's on call tonight, then Pete?" she asked before yelping as the ambulance hit a pothole, sending her leg sliding across the trolley. "And if you can't give me drugs, can you at least stop driving like a fucking maniac" she screamed.

A voice upfront apologised and pointed out that they were nearly there.

Pulling up outside the ambulance entrance, the doors opened, and two tired-looking porters folded out the ramp and gripped the feet end of the trolley.

"Bloody hell Joy, is that you?" asked the taller, younger and hairier of the two "Can't you keep away from the place."

"Woah, you do know you're supposed to drink the wine, not jam it into a vein?" added the second balding and much shorter guy, shooting Joy a wink as he clocked eyes on the stem that was still protruding angrily from her bloodied leg.

"I'll remember that next time, Pip," she said, returning his wink as they wheeled her out of the ambulance and into the cool, early morning air. Philip Pit, or Pip as everyone except his wife called him, had been at the hospital almost as long as Joy had. He had started working part-time while doing his engineering degree but never left, even after he graduated with honours. He knew every corridor of that hospital better than he knew his own house, partly due to the fact he spent most of his waking life there and liked to brag that he could walk from one end to the other with his eyes closed.

"Any idea who's in charge tonight, Pip?" she asked.

"Callum finished at two, no idea who's taking over," he replied, wheeling her in through the big double doors.

"Fuck," muttered Joy. Checking Pips watch, it was five past. If it was any other doctor in the hospital, they would have been gone in a cloud of dust by the time the big hand hit twelve. She crossed her fingers and hoped that he had somewhere to rush off to. She couldn't cope with this tonight. When she was upright and mobile sure, but she was a literal sitting duck.

Laying back down, she breathed out hard as she was manoeuvred down a long grey corridor until they reached the assessment unit, where she was promptly parked up in a bay while Pip went in search of someone to book her in.

Several minutes passed. She needed to ring Mischa, but Meryl had her bag and was currently AWOL, having not yet found her way in from the ambulance.

She was in the middle of scouring her reachable environment for a call button when the curtains parted and in swanned Dr Goodbody, grinning from ear to ear.

"Back already, Joy?" he chuckled, stood at the end of the trolley, looking down at her legs.

Joy smiled back, sarcastically.

"I was just about to head home when I saw your name pop up on the admissions board. Thought I'd hang on and give you my undivided attention," he said, snapping on a pair of thin blue nitrile gloves. "It's chaos out there, you could be waiting hours, so I've already logged you as an urgent. Need to get you round to Xray first."

Joy's face dropped. "Can't you just pull it out and stitch it up, Callum. You might be happy to hang around, but I need to get home?"

"Sure, if you want to risk infection or losing the leg."

Just as he said it, the curtains behind him parted like the red sea, and Meryl stood, holding them open, giggling.

"Wait. She's going to lose the leg?" she said, trying not to laugh.

"I'm not going to lose my leg," replied Joy, gawping at Meryl, open-mouthed. She was wearing a disposable chamber pot on her head and a catheter around her neck like a scarf.

Meryl let go of the curtains and shuffled to the little plastic chair next to Joy.

"Let me give you a local now, and that way, we'll be ready to rock and roll once we get the all-clear from imaging," continued Callum, patting Joy on the good ankle before turning and swanning back out through the curtain with a swish.

"Wait, I remember him," said Meryl, loudly.

"No, you don't . . . "

"Wasn't he? . . ."

"Nope," said Joy shooting her a look that begged her to just shut up. Meryl either didn't see it or chose to ignore it.

"Didn't you? . . ."

"No . . ."

"Weren't you two? . . ."

"Never happened," said Joy, her voice raising by a whole octave as she shifted nervously on the trolley.

"I'm sure he . . ."

"Stop it, Mez," squeaked Joy as the curtain parted once more, and Dr Goodbody slid back in carrying a tray full of wadding, antiseptic wipes, numbing spray and a large metal syringe.

"Are you going to stick it in her, Doctor?" said Meryl, giggling.

"I'm sorry," replied Callum.

"You want to stick it in her, don't you? Your big needle there."

"Meryl," hissed Joy under her breath.

"I need to inject the injury site, yes," he replied.

"I bet you love sticking it in, don't you," said Meryl, "nice and deep, right?"

"Meryl," squealed Joy, jabbing her in the upper arm with her elbow, her face reddening rapidly.

Dr Goodbody didn't say a word as he cleaned delicately around the wound.

"I'm just going to inject right here, just where the shaft is sticking out," he said, causing Meryl to explode into a fit of the giggles. If Joy didn't know better, she might have thought that he'd done that on purpose.

Joy gripped tightly onto Meryl's arm, in part to brace against the pain, but mainly to keep her quiet as she watched Dr Goodbody plunge the needle into the torn flesh around the glass. She did briefly consider critiquing his sloppy needle position but quickly thought better of it and buttoned her lip. Under the circumstances, she wasn't one to be handing out criticism.

By the time he'd done three little jabs, the pain had eased enough that she released her grip and unclenched her teeth.

"I'll get someone to take you round to X-ray," he said, dropping the needle into the metal dish, before disappearing back out of the curtain.

"What, the fuck, is wrong with you?" spat Joy as soon as she was sure he was gone.

Meryl, could barely get her words out for giggles "Sorry, the nice ambulance man gave me some gas and air, probably a bad idea after all the cocktails."

"Why would he do that?" she stammered, "You're not hurt."

"Because," she said sarcastically, "he asked if I was, and I might have told him that I was. I might have also told him that you landed on me," she said, descending into a long, loud cackle.

Within 15 minutes, Joy was being wheeled out of X-ray and into an urgent trauma bay in the main emergency building. Meryl, who had been sent on ahead with Joy's belongings on account of her messing with all of the instruments, had curled up on the examination bed in the corner, and promptly passed out, which Joy thought was probably for the best.

"You're not looking too great," said Dr Goodbody, pushing a suture trolley into the tiny cubicle, and which he parked up at the end nearest her feet.

"Booze is wearing off. Adrenaline's wearing off. Feel a bit sick to be honest."

A bit sick was something of an understatement. She felt like she had rocks in her stomach, and someone had rolled her down a hill.

"I'm not surprised. You've taken a bit of a knock," he said, pulling a chair up next to her leg. "But the good news is that the glass is still intact, so there's no messy shrapnel to fish out, and it managed to somehow slip right through between the tib and fib. You're very lucky. Can't say I've seen an injury like it in . . . . how long have I worked here again?"

"Too long," she replied, her head lolling back against the bed. "And that's just tonight. Really, you didn't have to hang around."

"What are friends for," he said, pulling on a fresh pair of gloves.

His use of the word friend threw her. He *was* a friend, no matter what their history was, she had known him as long as some of her best friends, and she probably saw him more often. She had forgotten that, and she suddenly felt irrepressible guilt for giving his flowers to the morgue.

"Can you feel anything?" he asked as he pressed at the flesh around the glass.

"Yes," she said, "Shame, remorse, an overwhelming feeling of dread, my head hurts, my stomach feels like it wants to hit the auto-eject, and the call button is digging into my arse."

"I meant in your leg."

"Oh" she replied, scrunching her face up. "No, nothing at all."

"I need you to stay completely still," he said, rising to his feet and positioned himself over her leg. "The quicker I whip it out, the less you'll feel, and the cleaner it'll be. It might spurt a little, but that can't be helped."

Even without Meryl's incessant innuendo in her ear, Joy struggled desperately to hold in the giggle.

"You ready?" he asked.

Joy nodded. She steadied herself against the pillow behind her as he gripped the foot of the glass. Positioning himself directly over it, he gave it a single swift tug.

The long glass shard released with relative ease. Holding up the stem to the light, he showed Joy the inch of blood coated glass. "Looks like a very clean penetration," he said, turning his attention back to the trolley, which afforded Joy a minute or two to snigger into her elbow and be grateful that Meryl hadn't stirred.

"I never thanked you," she said as she watched him carefully loop each suture and move swiftly onto the next. "For the flowers, I mean, it was very thoughtful."

Dr Goodbody smiled but didn't take his eyes from her leg. "I didn't mean anything by them. I just," he paused and wet his lips, Joy felt a pang of guilt ripple in her stomach. "I know how hard a breakup can be. I just thought they might cheer you up."

"They did," she smiled.

He pulled the suture taught as he cut the final stitch and applied a large dressing over the wound, before winding a loose bandage around the whole leg.

"Thanks, Callum, I really appreciate ....." she started, but he quickly shut her off.

"Would you like to go for dinner, one night, maybe, if you feel up to it?" he spluttered, his hand still resting on her ankle, his gaze avoiding hers.

Joy bit her lip. She didn't know how long he'd been waiting to say it, hours maybe, days perhaps, he had clearly been building up to it.

If nothing more, she was thankful that she could rip this particular band-aid off now and get it over and done with. "It's a bit soon," she said, trying to catch his eye. "The separation was . . . . not a mutual decision. I'm just not really . . . . "

"Just as friends of course," he added hastily, lifting his head and looking right at her. He looked like a kicked puppy. He was smiling, but it was flat and empty, the kind of smile you give to a neighbour whose cat has just shit in your flower bed. It was the same smile he'd worn 20 years ago when after she'd told him she wasn't looking for anything serious, and he had then found out she was engaged to Robin.

"Maybe," she said, as warmly and as convincingly as possible. She'd have said anything at that point not to be faced with that look all over again.

Nodding, he pulled himself to his feet, dropped the broken wine glass into the hazardous waste bin and made his excuses before disappearing out through the curtains without so much as a backwards glance.

Chapter 15

Joy had been awake for hours. Propped into a sitting position on a mountain comprised of every pillow in the house, a couple of old baby blankets and at least one stuffed panda. Beneath the covers, her right was leg free to do what it liked, while her left found itself caked in an odd sarcophagus, fashioned from an old wastepaper bin and designed to keep the duvet, Zachary and Pelé off the carnage that had become of her lower extremity. It was only really succeeding on two of those counts, and she could hear the dog snoring somewhere on the other side of her foot, and could feel the occasional wag of his tufty tail across her heel.

Despite her discomfort, she hadn't yet opened her eyes enough to alert anyone to the fact that she wasn't still sleeping. At some point, Zachary had come in and turned on the TV, then immediately walked out again, leaving it playing reruns of some terrible 90s sitcom, full of deadpan jokes and canned laughter. But the remote was over on the dresser. She couldn't get up and get it herself, yet her desire to not let on that she was awake was far more overwhelming than her need to change the channel.

And so, she just lay there, not thinking, not moving. Not that she really could do very much of the latter even if she wanted to. Everything hurt. She had bumps on top of lumps and bruises within bruises, like rungs within a tree stump. Her poor leg felt as if it had been sawn off at the knee and reattached, and it itched like hell, with each twitch sending little electric shocks right into the centre of the tightly stitched hole in her shin.

To her surprise, all of her aches and pains appeared to be fall-related as opposed to hangover, even though she had drunk more in one night than she had in the previous six months combined.

Yes, her head was throbbing, and she could hear the atoms banging together somewhere in between her ears, but she had a nasty bump on the back of her head and a mild concussion to thank for that, along with the canned laughter and an unhealthy dose of shame.

Beneath her pillow pyramid, she heard the faint buzz of her mobile phone ping from somewhere between its layers for at least the one hundredth time in a little less than an hour. She hadn't looked at it yet, though. She couldn't. Partly through fear of being caught awake, but mainly because she knew that the torrent of messages, notifications, and missed calls would only fill in the blanks from the night before, and she wasn't ready for that. She had already spent most of the morning trying to push what she could remember back out of her brain. Yet, that kicked puppy smile lingered, popping into her thoughts whenever her mind wandered from trying to ignore it.

"Stupid fucking tablecloth," she spat, far louder than she intended.

"So, you're up," called Mischa who was already halfway up the stairs, carrying a strong black coffee and a pile of little tablets in a plastic pot. "I was just coming to wake you."

Joy sighed. The peace was over. "Morning sweetheart," she called back, bracing herself for the inevitable mockery.

Perching herself onto the edge of the bed, Mischa handed Joy the coffee and emptied the pills into her left hand. "Painkillers, Anti-biotics, and anti-emetics. They don't do anti-dickhead pills. Else I imagine they'd have sent you home with a truckload."

Joy tried to squeeze out a sarcastic laugh, but the light jiggle that it produced rippled quickly around her body, sending her abused muscles into a spasm.

"How you feeling?" asked Mischa.

"Stupid," replied Joy, tipping the pills into her mouth and swallowing them down with a large swig of coffee. "And silly, and sore, and sick." she paused and burped. "And really fucking sorry for myself."

"Maryanne rang, said she been trying to get hold of you."

Joy's face creased. "Who told her?"

"You did," laughed Mischa, "you rang her at 5am and left a rambling message about being legless."

Joy grimaced. "And? What did she say?"

"She's put you on a week's annual leave starting Monday."

"I'll be fine by Monday," huffed Joy, "a couple of days rest and I'll be back on my feet."

Mischa rolled her eyes, "She said you haven't taken any leave all year and that you need to rest. She said if you turn up on Monday, she'll stab you in the other leg."

Joy crossed her arms and pushed her lips out into a stubborn pout. She had worked with Maryanne for six years, and while she had a markedly macabre sense of humour, Joy knew when she wasn't joking, and therefore had little choice but to admit defeat. "Where are the boys," she asked, quickly changing the subject.

"Still in bed. It's not even nine yet," she replied. A perfectly innocent statement, yet her eyes dropped to the floor, leaving her fumbling with her thumb.

"What is it?" asked Joy.

"Um ... " she started, still trying to avoid Joy's eye until she realised that she couldn't wiggle out of whatever it was that she was trying to wiggle out of. She sighed loudly and turned her face back to her mother. "Dad turned up while you were out."

Joy didn't respond. Inside her chest, her heart began to thump loudly, and she felt her blood pressure begin to creep up.

"He'd seen on Facebook that you were all out," Mischa continued, "he wanted to see the boys."

Joy took a deep breath. Her heart was pounding, her head throbbed, and her chest ached. "And did he? See them?" she asked.

"Zach was already in bed. Owen wouldn't come downstairs," she paused and cleared her throat, "Elliot came down and told him to fuck off."

Joy nodded slowly, trying her best to repress a smirk. She knew this was coming and had already had a stern conversation with herself. She had promised herself that she wouldn't lie to her kids. She wouldn't try to smear Robin or turn them against him. He was still their dad, she couldn't change that, and so she had given them the freedom to choose themselves. Just like he had. She couldn't deny that she felt a considerable amount of smugness over the fact that they had chosen to shun him, although she also wasn't naive enough to not realise that right now they were hurting and that in time that would probably change. After all, teenage boys didn't have the grudge-holding capabilities of teenage girls, and eventually, they would miss him.

"Why didn't you tell me this last night when I rang?" she asked.

"Because you'd have gotten all paranoid and come home, and I didn't want to ruin your night out."

"Probably would have been for the best that I did," cackled Joy in return, quickly grabbing at her hip to stop her leg from moving as she laughed.

"Mum, there's something else," said Mischa, shuffling down the bed.

Joy stopped laughing and turned her attention away from her leg and back towards her daughter. She didn't like that tone. It was the tone of bad news followed by tears. She'd had enough of that right now, and she didn't need anything else to crop up and ruin her already poor mood, but before she could ask her, there was an almighty knock at the front door, followed by an immediate turning of the handle as it flung open, banging loudly off the hallway wall.

"Yoo-hoo, Joy, are you in."

Joy closed her eyes and took a long deep breath, Mischa was staring up at the ceiling.

"Who told my mother." Joy hissed.

"She rang to see if you wanted to go for lunch," stammered Mischa, launching herself off the bed and towards the bedroom door. "I didn't know that you hadn't even told her that dad left."

"I didn't want to tell her over the phone, did I" whispered Joy, "and now she has to bloody well turn up when I can't even run away."

"Up here, gran", yelled Mischa, mouthing a sorry to her mother as she darted out of the bedroom and retreated back downstairs.

Joy listened as they exchanged pleasantries in the hall. Not that any exchange with her mum was ever all that pleasant.

"How are you Misch, no, none of this is fair on you. You shouldn't have to be mothering your own mother at your age. And there's only so much you can do. She has to learn."

Joy rolled her eyes as her mouth moved along mockingly with her words.

"It's fine, gran. I like helping."

"Where is she, still in bed, at this time, I'll find my own way up sweetheart, and tea, with two sugars, when you get a min."

Joy closed her eyes and bit down hard on both her lips.

"What on earth have we been up to now?" asked her mother, breezing into the bedroom, and completely ignoring Joy, marched straight over to the opposite side of the room before throwing open the curtains.

And there was the hangover.

The instant daylight hit her, Joy retreated back under the covers like the spirit of Nosferatu himself. Everything throbbed, her nose bulged, and her eyes filled with little those stringy floatlets that squirmed and swirled so violently that Joy felt like she was underwater.

Peering out from a gap in her duvet fort, Joy stared up at her mother, who looked formidable, staring back at her from the end of the bed. In reality, Verity Peterson was barely 5ft 2. She had overly long arms, narrow shoulders and a blunt blonde bob that Joy thought would look far better at her age if she wore it with a fringe.

"Right, why did he leave then?" she asked, jabbing her hands into her hips.

I'm fine, thanks mother, just a bit battered and bruised mother, can't walk myself to the toilet, but I'll be ok mother. The kids, they're great, all still alive, mother.

"I don't know." She replied bluntly.

"You must know, he's your husband, was there someone else?"

"I don't know. I don't think so . . . "

"And where is he now?"

"At Bens, probably, I don't actually know."

Verity pulled her glasses off and slid them onto the top of her head, before crossing her arms and tapping her foot loudly off the bed frame. "You don't know much, do you?

"I haven't seen him. He won't answer the phone."

"You know I always had my suspicions. I never trusted him."

"Mother," said Joy, pulling down the covers and readjusting her position so she could glare at her all the better. "You paid for most of our wedding. If you had any reservations over whether someone was good husband material, then you might want to mention that before paying two hundred quid for dodgy fucking vol-au-vents."

"Don't swear at me, young lady."

"I'm not swearing at you. I'm swearing at the vol-au-vents," seethed Joy, "but hey, maybe that was an omen. I don't remember any fairy tales that start with the bride spending four days throwing up into a pot plant on the balcony while the groom gets hospitalised with dysentery. Anyway, what's dad said?" she asked.

"I haven't told him yet", replied Verity, stepping over to the window sill and running her finger through the dust, "He'll be devastated. He saw Robin as the son he never had."

Raising her hands to her face, Joy rubbed at her temples and breathed in as deep as she could. "Firstly, mother, you have a son, his names Gary and he lives in Luton with his boyfriend, and you have literally just said that you didn't think Robin was ...... "

"Well, I've always been a much better judge of character than your father. He was the one who got those vol-au-vents, you know, bought them off some guy down the pub called Blinky because the blasted caterer went bump the week before the wedding."

"What do you want, mother? Why are you here?" asked Joy, although she already knew the answer, she was looking for gossip or dirt. Or both. Something she could use to titillate her friends at the community centre.

Verity dipped her gaze, feigning insult. "I'm here to offer you support, sweetheart."

"Ok, can you have Zach a couple of mornings this week so that Mischa can get to Uni?"

"Oh, sorry, no. I have the upholsterers coming on Monday, bridge on Tuesday, I'm at the chiropodist Wednesday, Thursday is book club, I could have him on Friday for an hour if you're stuck."

Joy rolled her eyes and made no effort to hide it. "Ok then, lend me a grand."

"My god, what on earth for?" asked Verity, lifting her hand and holding it against her chest as if Joy had just asked her to cut off an ear.

"Robin emptied the joint account, the spiteful little shit," replied Joy, dropping her voice so that Mischa wouldn't hear. "I've got a bit tucked away, but I need to cover the bills until I get paid."

"Sorry, no can do, all our spare cash is tied up in your sister's business."

Joy's mouth dropped open so fast that she felt her jaw crack. "Wait, you're the mystery donor. You do know she shoved most of that up her nose."

"Don't be silly, Lucy's renting a little room above a hairdresser, and she's had to buy all her own stock. Look, she did me these, aren't they pretty." She said, holding her fingers up a mere inch from Joy's nose.

Joy pulled her head back enough that her mother's fingertips came into focus. They had been painted unevenly in mould green, with pink flowers that looked more like penises.

"So, you're telling me that when the daughter who flunked out of high school, and then flunked out college and who has never held down a job for more than six months suddenly decided on a whim to set up a nail bar in Essex, with no qualifications or experience, you immediately jump to attention and hand her twenty thousand pounds, no questions asked. But when I ask you for a grand to keep a room over your grandkids head, it's a no," said Joy, brushing Verity's hand away. "We are a year away from owning this house outright, and now I'm going to lose it because Lucy wanted to play at being a grown-up."

"Well, why isn't Robin paying his half? It's his mortgage too."

Joy threw herself back against the cushions and lay her hand across her face. "Because, mother, it was before I met him, and I never put his name on it. The whole thing is in my name, and he's not obliged to pay a penny."

"What about maintenance?"

"I can't even get him to answer the phone, I'll have to make a claim, and that could take months. And even then, the boys are 16 in a couple of months. If they don't get into college, he'll only have to pay for Zach. I don't know what I'm gonna do."

"I'm sorry, sweetheart, I wish I could help, I really do, but . . ."

"Gee, thanks." Spat Jot, "I'll trade your wishes in for some magic beans then, for all the good it'll do me, now if you excuse me, I'm supposed to be resting."

It suddenly dawned on Joy that she had nowhere to go. She wanted to stamp away and slam a door, yet she couldn't so much as turn her back on her. She couldn't even wiggle down the bed into a proper lying position. The best she could do was pull the covers back up over her head and pretend that she wasn't there "Goodbye, mother," she shouted, muffled from beneath the duvet.

Chapter 16

By Wednesday, Joy had never been so bored.
Saturday and Sunday had been quite bearable.
There had been a constant slew of visitors,
beginning with Margot, who had turned up not long
after Verity had left, and who came bearing expensive
brownies, profuse apologies and sporting a black eye and a
chipped incisor.

Tabitha had called around Saturday teatime, brandishing
some la carte take out, a box full of strawberry and gin
cupcakes and a spare commode from the hotel's linen stores,
which, after much blushing, turned out to be the most useful
and thoughtful gift that anyone had ever given her.

Lauren, Bernie and Carlee had been in and out most of
the weekend, taking on all the heavy lifting jobs so that Mischa
could focus on keeping Zachary occupied. Even Owen and
Elliot had pulled their weight, helping with the cleaning and

keeping their bed-stricken mother constantly topped up with strong coffee and biscuits.

But as Monday morning had rolled around, the boys had gone off to school, her friends had returned to work, and Mischa had, after much protestation, sulked off to university.

Joy had spent the morning mastering her way up and down the stairs on her bottom. The four walls of her bedroom and the short hop to the commode had quickly grown tedious, and she longed for the widescreen of the living room and better access to the fridge.

By Wednesday, she could make it from the sofa to the kitchen without the need of the clunky uncomfortable hospital issue crutches, and she could now get up the stairs quick enough to negate the danger of wetting herself halfway up, and thus also sparing Mischa the indignity of emptying the commode when she got home.

Now she was bored.

She was too anxious to sleep and too wound up to read. So, within three days of being left to her own devices, she had scoured every corner of the internet, completed online sudoku, filled in caption competitions and entered several dodgy looking prize draws to win a Mini Cooper. She had successfully avoided calling all of her utilities and the bank to arrange payment breaks, vowing to do it tomorrow once she felt up to it. She never did, though, and as the first reminders came through the door in official-looking brown envelopes. She shoved them into the drawer of the shoe rack at the bottom of the stairs and pretended they didn't exist, while simultaneously thinking about them constantly.

In her head, she redecorated the living room, spending hours selecting the right shade of grey paint to match the wallpaper she'd seen in the copy of Good Housekeeping that Margot had left behind. She even went so far as to build a cart on the B&Q website, only to delete it all immediately when she clocked the total, before spending the rest of the afternoon resentful of her current décor. How she could become hostile towards wallpaper, she wasn't entirely sure, but nonetheless, she had found herself cursing the oversized flowers that leered at her from the living room wall and chipped paint on the kitchen doorframe from where Zachary had repeatedly bashed off it.

Come Friday, she finally left the house, albeit just for a wander to the post-box across the road. But Mischa had promised her that if she could make it to the top of the path and back without crutches, that she'd take her on a run to ASDA before picking Zach up from school. To be perfectly frank, Joy couldn't contain her excitement.

But as she sat at the bottom of the stairs waiting for Mischa to get home, there was an unexpected knock at the door. Steadying herself against the banister, Joy opened the door and peeked out. There was no one there. She looked up the street and then down it. But she saw nothing, not so much as an errant child or an escaped pup. She was about to shut the door again when she spotted what looked like a high bun sticking up from behind the rhododendron at the end of the path.

"Meryl?" she called.

"Oh, Hi," replied the bun, bobbing up from behind the bush.

"What're you doing?"

"I'm hiding."

"Who from?" asked Joy, growing increasingly puzzled.

Meryl's voice paused, and the bun shifted position. Disappearing for a moment before popping back up again on the other side of the bush. "You," she replied. "Are you mad?"

"I'm mad at you for not coming to see me all week."

"I'm really sorry."

"What, for not coming to see me?"

"No. For embarrassing you."

"You didn't embarrass me," said Joy, laughing, "Can't say the same for Callum, though. Maybe it's his shrubbery you should be hiding in."

Meryl stepped out from behind the plant, brushing errant leaves and twigs from her long blush skirt and giving Joy a bashful wave. "I brought you this," she said, handing over a large cappuccino and a double chocolate muffin.

Taking a large gulp of the coffee, Joy spat it straight out again, gagging. It was stone cold. "How long have you been out here?"

"I asked Margot how you were," said Meryl, completely sidestepping the question. Smoothing her skirt down over her behind, she sat down on the front step.

Joy slowly lowered herself down next to her, unwrapping the Muffin, she took a big bite, groaning as the gooey chocolate sponge hit her tastebuds.

"And how is Margot?" she asked, swallowing down the mouthful. "You know, last week in the pub, I saw her outside. She'd been crying, I'm sure." Joy held out the muffin and offered up a bite.

Meryl waved it away. "I didn't know she was still capable."

Joy shot her a look. "She looked really upset, Mez?"

"She's going through a bit of shit with Danni" said Meryl. "You know how Joel remarried. Well, Justine, the new wife, she's a complete earth mother type".

"An anti-Margot."

"Exactly," replied Meryl. "She boils her tampons and everything."

Joy's mouth dropped open in horror.

"She's an anti-everything, and Danni seems to have taken a shine to it".

"She's not boiling her tampons, is she?".

"No, not yet, but she got suspended from Uni."

"Ah," said Joy. "What did she do?"

"She and some other girls set fire to the campus football pitch."

"By accident?"

"No," said Meryl, "They wouldn't let them start a girls league, so they set fire to the goals and then spelt out *"Don't move the goalposts, destroy them"* in sanitary towels across the pitch. But wind carried the fire, and all the pads went up and burnt the message into the ground the night before a big game. She got caught because she left behind her rucksack with her iPad in it and then refused to rat out the other girls, so they suspended her until she gives them names."

Devoid of anything else to say, Joy, burst out laughing. They had got themselves into some scrapes over the years, alright, but this was on a whole new level, and while she wouldn't admit it to Margot, she suddenly felt immensely proud of Dannii.

"Thing is," continued Meryl, "Margot has no problem with her wanting to smash the patriarchy, she just wants her to get in to medical school first. And of course, it's a convenient excuse to blame Justine for putting all these ideas in her head, when in reality, what's she's actually doing is rebelling against Margot and her constant need for perfection."

Joy nodded. And then her face dropped as a thought crept into her head. It was a completely new thought. And she didn't like it. "I have all this to come, don't I?" she said, feeling the familiar prick of moisture in the corner of her eyes.

"Mischa wouldn't do anything like that. She's just like you, but cooler."

"No, I mean Justine," replied Joy, "What if Robin meets someone. What if he already has. The kids will have to spend time with them, get to know them. What if he marries again and moves away and then expects to see them at Christmas? I'm not willing to share my kids with some stranger."

Meryl stared at the floor. "I hate to break it to you, but there's an entire world out there that you're gonna have to share them with at some point." She leaned over and nudged Joy's shoulder with her own. "But you'll always be their only mum. Besides, your kids all idolise you. Danni's always been difficult. She takes after Margot."

"I don't know what I'd have done without Mischa these last couple of weeks. She's been a godsend."

"Then why so sad?" asked Meryl, leaning forward and wiping away a tear, just as it fell onto Joy's cheek.

"She's so young, and she's carrying all my shit around with her. She's working, she's at uni, she's looking after Zach, and she's burning herself out. She's tired, she was sick as a dog last night, and she looks so washed out. She should be the one falling into A&E at 3am, not me. I'm supposed to be looking after her."

"She's an adult, Joy. You're not holding her at gunpoint. Remember there was a time when it was just you and her, and she depended on you, and you worked your fucking ass off to get through nursing school with a baby so that she could grow up and be whatever she wanted to be."

Joy nodded, biting down hard on her lip. She closed her eyes. More tears fell.

"Well, she grew up into you. Not because that's what *you* wanted, but because you gave her something amazing to aspire to."

Joy wiped her eyes and lay her head on Meryl's shoulder. "You're too nice."

Meryl reached up and patted her on the head. "You know who else is nice, your doctor friend. He seems lovely."

Joy lifted her head, turned and stared at Meryl, eyebrows raised. "Do *you* want his number?"

"Would be handy," she replied, grinning. "Six kids all trying their best to kill either themselves or each other at any given moment. I'd save a fortune in hospital parking fees and plasters, not sure Devi would take to him though, perhaps I could build him a granny flat in the garden and only bring him out in emergencies, like a pet doctor."

Joy cackled, squeezing Meryl at the shoulders. She planted a big kiss on her cheek just as Mischa's little silver fiesta pulled up at the end of the path.

Chapter 17

Drumming her fingers loudly on the kitchen table, Joy sat, trying to ignore the buzzing. She had not long walked in from a late finish and had barely stopped to take a breath all day. Checking her phone as she'd left the hospital, she'd seen the eight missed calls. There were another two as she was driving home, a third while she was in the chipper, and one more just as she had pulled up outside. All she wanted to do was eat her fish and chips in peace before having to deal with *him*.

She knew it wasn't important. Zachary was tucked up in bed, and the twins were in their room fighting over a video game. Mischa was curled up on the sofa watching a film, despite asserting some 15 minutes earlier that she was going home.

Joy wasn't going to remind her, though. She had got used to having her around again. When she had first moved out, there had been novelty. No more fighting over the remote control, no more bickering over the bathroom, no more punch ups over who had eaten the last of the sausage rolls or finished the bread, especially when, more often than not, it was Joy. She hadn't taken the time to notice just how much in those two short years her daughter had grown up.

Since Robin left, Joy had come home most days to a cooked meal and a calm house, yet she had never once asked her to do any of it. She had rearranged her work schedule, was taking online classes, and when she was home, she'd tidy up, put a load of washing in and make tea. A far cry from the days when she'd throw the hoover across the room after being asked to pick up her crisp crumbs.

Diving her fork into the hot pile of chips, Joy's mouth watered as the smell of vinegar and ketchup rose up and assaulted her nostrils. She was about to take a bite when the phone, now lying face down on the other side of the table, started buzzing again.

She had spoken to Robin only three times in the two months since he'd walked out. Once to arrange a schedule for when he was having the kids. A second time to discuss maintenance. And a third when he'd failed to pay it. The arrangement was working well, and as far as she knew, he had no other reason to contact her. Yet she had an inkling that he probably wouldn't stop calling until she spoke to him, so for the sake of being able to eat her dinner in peace, she gave in, dropped her fork, and answered.

"What do you want, Rob?" she asked, with as much cordiality as she could rally. Which wasn't all that much on top of a nine-hour shift and an empty stomach.

"Did I catch you at a bad time?"

"What do you want?" she asked again.

"Uh, something's come up. Can we swap this weekend for next Saturday? That's ok, isn't it?"

"Nope."

"What d'ya mean, no?" he replied, his voice rising as his own cordiality slipped.

"We agreed every other Saturday, with no swaps. So, you need to arrange your life around that, not expect the kids to fall into place with whatever it is you want to do. Plus, I'm working Saturday, it's too late to swap."

"You have Mischa."

Joy gritted her teeth and clenched her fist under the table. "Mischa has a life. If you want to see more of them, why don't you pick Zachary up and run him to school when I'm on earlies."

"I'm in the opposite direction now. We've been through this. It's just not practical with traffic."

"Not convenient, you mean."

"So, what are we going to do about Saturday?" he asked.

"*You're* going to have the boys as arranged," she said taking the phone and hooking it under her ear. She picked up a chip and tossed it to Pelé who was sat salivating at her feet.

"And maybe this week, Elliot might hang around longer than half an hour before you have to send out the search party."

"It's not my fault he ran away," he said.

Joy could hear the indignation in his voice. She didn't care. "He didn't run away, Robin. He ran home. There's a distinct difference."

"But Saturday ...."

"Is your day. Anyway, the weekend after is the twin's sixteenth, so no can do."

The line went quiet.

Joy's face hardened. "Did you honestly think I wouldn't know what you were trying to pull?" she said, lowering her voice and reaching back, pushed the living room door closed.

"Oh, so I'm the bad guy now for wanting to see *my* sons on *their* birthday. I've promised to take them tubing. It's all booked."

Joy bit her lip, closed her eyes, sucked her breath in hard through her teeth, and waited for the ripple of anger to pass. "What are you talking about?" she said, clearing her throat. "I'm taking them tubing, and their mates. We're going to make a full day of it, big cake, the works."

"But," he paused, "They haven't said anything to me."

"Because it's a surprise, dickhead."

"So, what am I supposed to do?"

"Same as always, just do what you like."

He didn't reply.

She heard him sigh on the other end of the line, and for a moment, she felt a pang of guilt. He *was* their father. It *was* their birthday. "Look, if you really want to see them, then come and pick them up after, take them out for tea, or on Sunday, have them for the whole day."

Rob grunted on the end of the line, and it went silent again.

"Was there something else?"

Still no answer. She was about to hang up when he spoke.

"Actually, I want to have them for a full weekend. I want them to stay over."

"At Reubens?"

"Yeah,".

"Absolutely fucking not," she said, jumping up from the table. She began to pace the room.

"Why not?"

"They hate it there. Rob, Owen says they don't feel welcome. He said Ben ignores them, and so you spend the whole day down the canal, fishing, and Zach just spends the entire day on the iPad. Do you know how long it took me to prize him from behind the sofa last week before you picked him up."

"There's nothing wrong with Ben's house."

Joy could feel the anger bubbling. "It's not the house, Rob. Reuben is a neat freak, his house is like a show home, and kids are messy and clumsy. Our kids are like a tsunami."

"Ben's not that bad."

Joy was now pacing from one end of the hallway to the other. Her fists clamped shut. "Not that bad. Do you remember last Christmas when Zach knocked over that stupid bloody plant pot by the front door? And he was so scared of getting found out that he ate the fucking soil off the floor and spent three days shitting out grit."

"That was a one-off."

"Ok, what about the BBQ we went the summer before, while we were still waiting for a diagnosis, and Reuben went off at him because he pulled down a curtain. He called him an annoying little turd Robin", she took a breath. "To. His. Face."

"But he understands now. He knows Zach can't help it."

"And what about your mum's birthday when .... "

"Ok, you made your point," he said, cutting her off just as she was getting going. "Look, if *you* won't let me have them over the weekend, then maybe we take it to court and let a judge decide."

Slamming her fist down on her thigh, Joy let out a cackle. "Sure, you do that," she laughed, "and then I'll be able to tell them how you haven't given me any child support in nearly eight weeks. Let's make that official too."

"I told you, I had to fix my car."

"No, I agree. Let's make it all official. And that way, they'll take it straight from your wages, so next time you need your car fixed, you'll have to fucking beg friends to help you out, just like I've had to."

"Joy, you're getting carried away."

"Fuck you, Robin," she yelled, pulling the phone from under her chin and shouting straight at the screen. "See you in court."

She slammed her thumb down on the end call button, slat the phone down on the table, and dropped herself onto the seat. She was shaking. Putting her head into her hands, she breathed. Not a normal, life-sustaining breath, but a long drawn-out anger diffusing whine. She felt like she was choking on rage. It stuck in her throat and stifled the air as she tried to suck it in. She breathed again, fighting back tears until eventually, she felt her heart slow, and her lungs fill.

Lifting her head, she found Mischa stood at the kitchen door.

"Too harsh?" asked Joy.

Mischa shook her head. "I was about to head off, but if you need me to stay, I can . . . "

"No sweetie, you go, get a good night's sleep. You look shattered."

"So do you," replied Mischa, stepping over to the table, and wrapping her arms around Joy's shoulders, gave her a big squeezy hug."

Joy squeezed her back, "I've looked like this for 20years love, I think I'm stuck this way."

Grabbing her bag from by the kettle, Mischa leaned over, kissed her mother on the head and stole a handful of chips. Shoving the whole lot in her mouth as she headed for the front door. But before she got around to yanking it open, Joy called her back.

"Mischa, love, you haven't got any plans for next weekend, have you?"

Mischa stopped, turned and shook her head.

"Well, don't make any," said Joy, "we're going to give your brothers a birthday to remember."

Mischa smiled, still chewing. She nodded and raised her fist in the air.

Once her daughter had disappeared out into the night, Joy watched through the door window as her car lights turned on and pulled away. Turfing a forkful of crispy battered fish into her mouth, Joy unlocked her phone, opened the browser and searched for whatever the hell tubing was.

A little relieved to discover that it was nothing more than sliding down a hill in a giant rubber ring, Joy located an artificial ski slope on the other side of town and eagerly opened the website. Scanning the page, she found the booking form and selected a basic party package for up to ten people. She couldn't remember the last time they'd had a birthday party, probably not since Owen and Elliot were in infants. Zachary wasn't the party type, and Mischa had flat out refused one for her 21st. Much to Joy's annoyance.

She put all her details into the form, added on a cake, a banner, and enough chicken bites, fries and soft drinks to feed an army and pressed submit. There was availability. Giving herself a little victory fist pump, she saved the details and clicked through onto the payment screen, stopping as the total flashed up on the screen.

:: £154 ::

Joy minimised the window and opened her banking app, scrunching her eyes closed as her available balance flashed up on the screen. She cracked one eye open to barely more than a slit and peered at the total. There was just enough left in the account to cover some shopping and the overdue mortgage payment that was expected next week.

She dropped the phone to the table and ran her hands through her hair, scratching at the back of her ears with her thumbs. She couldn't *not* book it now. She had told Robin that she was taking them. If she fell through on that, he would surely sweep in and take them. He would be the hero, and she would have ruined everything.

Glancing down the hallway, her eyes landed on the drawer of the shoe rack and the rapidly growing pile of bill demands and default notifications that were slowly taking over it. Then sitting on top of it, were her battered old work shoes that desperately needed replacing, as did the front passenger tyre on her car, and the handle on the washing machine, and the hinges on the kitchen cupboards which had worn loose through constantly being slammed and yanked and hung off. Everything was falling apart.

Closing her eyes, she felt them swell in their sockets. She couldn't do it. She couldn't screw up their birthday. Not after the year they'd already had. She owed them the best day she could give them.

Picking her phone back up, she flicked back to the booking portal and hastily entered her card details, smiling nervously as the booking confirmation flashed up on the screen.

'Another month won't do any harm', she thought as she closed down her phone and shoved it hastily into her cardigan pocket.

Chapter 18

Happy birthday to you, happy birthday to you," squealed Joy, clapping her hands as Owen descended the ladder from the loft room, followed reluctantly by Elliot, who was demanding that all he wanted for his birthday was a lie in.

Ushering them downstairs, still in their Pyjamas, she pushed them down the hall and into the living room. Two brand new bikes sat in the middle of the floor, one green, one blue, their shiny chrome brake handles adorned with ribbons and bows, their wheels surrounded by brightly wrapped boxes and balloons.

"Awesome," called Owen, hugging Joy tightly before diving headfirst into the presents, several of which had already been opened by an over-zealous Zachary who was now eagerly chasing a bright blue balloon around the kitchen followed frantically by Pelé.

Elliot ran straight to the blue bike, jumped up on the seat, and began to wheel it towards the door. "Can I take it out, mum?" he asked excitedly.

"Not right now, buddy, we're going out," she said, pushing him back into the room before he tried to make a break for it. "So go and get dressed. We're getting breakfast on the way."

The two boys sprinted back upstairs, leaving a wake of wrapping paper and gifts sprawled across the floor. Pants, socks, t-shirts, a new dart gun each, a new drone, a football, a wireless speaker for their bedroom and new trainers. Joy began to pick them up and pile them up on the table just as Mischa appeared through the door.

Stood, staring at the carnage, her face creased. "How did you . . . ? "

"I didn't," said Joy abruptly. "Margot did. Said it was compensation over the whole leg thing. She said if I refused, she'd sue herself on my behalf. I've always said I'd give my right leg just to see a smile on their faces. The left leg was close enough"

In all fairness, Joy hadn't been in a position to say no. She'd had the bikes on layaway at a local sports shop for months, she was just shy of the last £50 instalment when Margot had turned up unexpectedly with a car boot full of goodies and handed her an envelope with the express instructions that it was for the boys bikes. Given the smirk that

Mischa was currently trying to hide, Joy now knew which little bird had been whispering in Margot's ear.

"Ouch!!" Screeched Joy as she was hit smack in the face with a dart. Turning, she spotted Zachary, who had clambered up onto the table and was now sat brandishing the big orange dart gun like the Ghost of John Wayne, that was if John Wayne wore Hulk pyjamas that had choco-puffs down their front. The big grin etched across his face soon faded as Joy snapped the gun from his hands, plucked him off the table and carried him upstairs to get dressed.

Pulling up outside of the Ski Centre, Joy's heart soared on the wave of whoops and cheers that filtered forward from the back seat.

Jay, his younger brother Kyle and Simon Wilson from school were already stood waiting, having been picked up by Mischa while Joy was treating the birthday boys and Zachary to a drive-through breakfast. Behind them stood Meryl and Carlee, who was decked out in a full ski suit and brandishing two large helium balloons adorned with game characters that Joy couldn't name even if she tried. She had given up trying to remember most of them. There were just so many. Minecraft had been easy. She had memorised all the sprites, and all the lingo. She knew her nether from her wither and her enderman from her creeper. But now, there were so many games that she couldn't even remember what half of the games were called, let alone any of the players, so she had given up and just referred to them collectively as computer people, no matter how much the boys tried to school her on it. If she was being honest, she missed the Teletubbies. She knew all of those.

"You do know that there's no actual snow?" asked Joy, grabbing the balloons from Carlee and pointing them all in the direction of the chalet/changing rooms.

"I know," she replied, defensively, "but I got this years ago as a hint to Mark that I wanted to go skiing. Unfortunately, he's got all the perception of a doughnut and never got the message."

Evidently, the ski suit never made it to the slopes now either, not even to the end of the safety briefing. After being mistaken for the instructor on no less than three occasions, Carlee sloped off to the car and returned five minutes later in trackers and a hoody that said, 'honk if you feel dirty', a remnant from the days she did some charity work at a community car wash behind the local church. It hadn't gone down very well then either, yet Carlee had never understood why.

Once they had all been briefed on the dos and don'ts of dry slope etiquette, they were all led around the back of the chalet to the practice slope, suitable, according to the website, for beginners and the under nines. The very prospect was met with a degree of hostility from the five teenagers, and Meryl, who promptly made a break for the big boy slope next door.

Joy had no intention of going anywhere near the big slope, she had spent the last five minutes watching people flying down its surface like rats down a drainpipe, and that alone was enough to trigger a nasty bout of vertigo.

Thankfully Zachary wasn't old enough to join his brothers, which suited Joy just fine. Now, she just needed to convince him to walk up the ramp to the top. But he wasn't having any of it. Zachary didn't like new things, or new places, and while she had spent the best part of the last week showing him videos and photos in the hope that it might acclimatise him to the idea, he simply wouldn't budge.

"Come on, sweetheart, it's not a big climb, and then we get to sit down on this big rubber ring and come back down, just like on the video I showed you, remember," she said, pleading with him.

Zachary crossed his arms defiantly across his chest.

Joy couldn't understand it. She knew all too well that he had to be comfortable and inquisitive about an idea before giving it a try. If he showed no interest or walked away, she knew she had little chance of getting him to join in, but he'd looked so excited watching the videos. Staring wide-eyed at the screen as the big inflatable rings whooshed down the slope, coming to a peaceful stop at the bottom where the dry slope met with an edge of thick coir matting.

"Come on, Zach, you'll love it once you give it a try," said Carlee.

Zach uncrossed his arms and pointed to the ramp where a tall, muscular man was lugging a ring up the slope while his little girl sat effortlessly at its centre.

"You want me to pull you up, Zach? Come on, let's pull you up." Said Joy excitedly as Zachary made a dart for the nearest ring. Joy bent down and picked up the thick rope handle and began to heave him up the Ramp. But Zachary was no toddler. His dad's wide build and his need to eat anything and everything that wasn't a vegetable had left him heavier than the average six-year-old, and even wedged inside a vast rubber ring, he was still unable to sit still. Three times joy had to stop on the way up and catch her breath and really only made it to the top at all after Zachary started to meltdown over the delay.

As they finally reached the top, Joy felt ready to collapse. Positioning Zachary's ring at the precipice, she grabbed one of the spares from a pile at the summit and positioned it next to his. Standing in front of it, she plopped her arse into the hole, grateful if nothing more for the sit-down. Then, smooching them both forward, she pushed off with her feet, dragging Zachary's inflatable nest behind her.

Joy closed her eyes as she felt the floor go from beneath her, until she heard Zachary let out a squeal she'd never heard him make before. She opened her eyes to find him smiling the biggest smile, his eyes wide, his arms up in the air as the wind whipped at his hair and ruffled his t-shirt.

As they reached the bottom, he was in a fit of the funnies so fantastic that he couldn't even climb out of the ring. Neither could Joy, but that had more to do with her arse being wedged into it and her not having taken a full breath since lugging him up the hill.

Heaving herself back to her feet, Joy reached down and grabbed the thick rope handle on Zachary's ring, and gave it a tug. It didn't shift. She'd lost all her puff, and staring up at the slope, it suddenly felt like Everest.

She was about to try again, when Carlee came running across the matting and took the handle from Joy's grip.

"Go sit down before you fall down," she said, rubbing Joy's back as she tried to cough up a lung. "Today's your celebration too."

"What have I got to celebrate," she scoffed.

"Er, for a start, you survived sixteen years of twins."

Joy shot her a smile as she watched Carlee grip the rope and pull Zachary all the way to the top without so much as breaking sweat.

Bending over to catch her breath, Joy spotted Mischa sat on a bench by the entrance, flicking through her phone and sipping tentatively on a take-out tea.

"You not joining in, Misch?" asked Joy, sidling over and taking a seat next to her.

"I'd rather be waxed by a bear," she replied, barely looking up from her phone.

"Joy's smile dropped, "Oh, I thought this would be right up your street."

Mischa shrugged, "Another time, maybe. I'm not really in the mood, plus, if I was up there having fun, who'd be able to take blackmail suitable pictures like this one." She said, holding up her phone.

Joy glared at the screen, and a zoomed-in photo of herself, hurtling down the side of the hill, her face red and her legs flailing in the wind, followed by another of her struggling to unwedge her arse from the rubber ring at the bottom.

"You post them on Facebook, and I'll disinherit you." She said, still struggling to catch a lung full of air. "Fancy getting me one of those?" she asked, pointing the styrofoam cup.

Mischa gave her a cheery thumbs-up before disappearing off around the side of the chalet, still gawping at her phone.

Joy returned to the bottom of the slope, just in time to catch Zachary flying down the ramp on Carlee's knee.

His face ecstatic, his eyes closed, and his mouth open with his cheeks, waffling about as he made no effort to stop them from filling with wind as he whooshed.

Landing at the bottom, Joy didn't even get a chance to give him a high five before he jumped back into the ring, ready for Carlee to drag his chariot back up to the top.

Lifting her hand above her eyes, Joy shielded them from the sun as she stared in the direction of the advanced slope, hoping to catch a glimpse of Owen or Elliot. She was about to set off and get some photos when she heard her voice being called from behind.

Assuming it was the instructor ready to call them in for food, she spun around cheerily, her warm smile soon slipping from her face as she found herself face to face with Robin, stood waving from the gate.

"What are you doing here?" she seethed as he pushed open the gate and strode towards her. It was the first time she'd been face to face with him since the day he'd moved out.

Inside, her tummy tingled, and her heart fluttered. He looked so well. He'd lost weight, shaved off the fuzz and cut his hair. In pale grey joggers and a hoody, he looked relaxed, muscular almost. He looked just like the man that she'd spent 17 years madly in love with.

"I wanted to wish the boys a happy birthday, and I wanted to give you this," he said, thrusting an unsealed A4 envelope towards her.

Joy refused to take it. She knew exactly what it was.

"Come on," he said, grinning, "you said to make it official. So, take it."

Joy felt like she was about to pass out. Her lips went cold, and her mouth moistened. She could feel her heart throbbing in her ears. It was still early, but the warm late May sun was busy chasing the morning clouds across the sky, leaving the air dry and stagnant. She felt like she couldn't breathe. "Why'd you have to do this here?" she hissed. "Why today? You could have given me this any time. Why now?"

"Told you, I wanted to see my sons on their birthday." His grin didn't so much as dip. "Two birds and all that."

"Ok, now just fuck off," she sneered, and snatching the envelope from his grip, she turned to leave. She took a step but could hardly walk. Each pace felt like she was being pulled down by the shoulders. She felt her anger rising; it bubbled up her spine and into her arms. Her fists clenched and her jaw lock. She drew her elbow back. All she wanted to do was hit him. To launch herself at him and just not stop.

In the corner of her eye, she saw Mischa by the gate, a look of horror across her face as she stood gripping onto a tray of cups and a big balloon.

Closing her eyes, Joy took a breath and puffed it out slowly, dropping her hands at her waist. She began to walk calmly away.

She didn't realise that she was still on the matting of the practice slope. She also never noticed the chunky rubber ring that was hurtling towards her. Not until it hit her in the back of the legs and sent her flying into the air, along with the envelope.

Landing with a thump and surrounded by scattered divorce papers and the contents of her pockets, Joy scrambled onto her hands and knees to pick them all up as Mischa dumped the teas on the bench and ran to help her up.

"Get out the way next time, you fat fucking pie," called the man who had been aloft the ring as it slammed into her and who himself was no Levi's model.

Joy felt her eyes prick and her knees sting as Mischa helped her back to the safety of the coir and the soothing warmth of weak tea.

By the time she found the guts to look back, Robin was gone, evidently without bothering to say happy birthday to the boys.

Joy didn't eat any cake. She did her best to join in with happy birthday, but cruel words had eaten a hole into her heart and sucked all of the enjoyment from the day.

Carlee, who had witnessed the entire incident from the summit of the practice slope, tried to lighten the mood until joy showed her and Meryl the contents of the envelope while the kids were playing on the vending machines in the chalet.

"Divorce?" she asked, scanning through the papers.

Joy nodded. "He keeps blaming everything on me. I told him to leave, so he left. I told him to make it official, so he has. None of this is what I wanted."

"Have you told him that?" asked Meryl.

"What's the point. It's not what he wants. Why waste my breath or my time? From now on, I have to focus on me. First thing on the list, lose weight."

Carlee shot her a look, "Don't let some fat prick in a rubber ring get to you."

"I'm no use to those kids if I can't even pull a ring full of air up a little hill. If I have to be a single mum, then I have to be able to do it all on my own."

"Not completely on your own" said Meryl, reaching forward and gripping Joy's hand.

Carlee quickly dropped her hand on top of Meryl's.

"No, not completely." She replied.

Chapter 19

All Joy wanted to do was crawl onto the sofa and cry. Her heart ached, and her knees stung. To top it off, the force of a two-hundred-pound man riding an inflatable ring into her legs had triggered a new pain in her shin wound, and all she wanted to do was to get off her feet and not move until morning. Mischa had offered to take Zachary for the night, and Owen, Elliot and Pelé were going camping in Jay's back garden, leaving Joy to look forward to a microwave meal for one and whatever ice cream was left in the freezer.

But as she pulled the car off the main road and into their street, she froze, hitting the brake and stopping dead in the middle of the road.

About halfway down, just outside of her house, sat a shiny new Audi.

She was about to swing the car around and go back the way she came, but a van trying to pull in behind her forced her down the street, and by then, it was too late. He had seen her. How exactly he had seen her, she wasn't sure, but he came out of her gate waving, a takeaway bag in one hand and a bottle of wine in the other.

"Fuck," she said, rolling the car down the hill until it came to a stop behind his.

"There you are," called Callum, waving her over as she clambered out of the car before walking as slowly as she could in an attempt to hide the limp.

"Sorry," she said, slinking past him and jabbing the key into the door. She pushed it open, stepped inside, dropped her bag and turned around to face him. "It's the twins birthday. We were out, um, celebrating."

"Oh, I didn't realise. Another time then." He said, tipping his head and tapping his finger against his brow.

Joy stared at him. He looked so different away from the hospital. Without the harsh glare of all-around overhead lights, his face looked softer, his eyes lighter, and his dark hair fell soft across his temples. He also smelt delicious, the irresistible smell of coconut oil and MSG wafting up from whatever it was he was carrying.

"What's in the bag?" she asked, just as he turned to leave.

Callum spun back around. "Chicken fried rice, prawn balls, something in black bean sauce and a chow mein. You hungry?" he asked, a grin creeping across his face as he took a step closer to the door.

At her feet, Joy spotted the A4 envelope poking out of her bag, and all of a sudden, revenge sex didn't sound all that ridiculous. Without giving herself time for second thoughts, she snaked her arms up and around his neck before planting a soft wet kiss on his lips. He tasted of cherry drops and aniseed, and his open mouth was warm and inviting.

"Famished," she replied. Pulling her hands from around his shoulders, Joy quickly grabbed him by the lapels, yanked him through the door and straight up the stairs, still clutching the bag of food. He didn't even try to stop her.

Lying wide awake, Joy stared up at the light fitting on the ceiling. It was dark outside now, but definitely still night-time. Outside she could hear the cats screeching near the neighbour's bins and the lull of cars passing on the main road at the top of the street. Above it all, however, was the incessant drawn out, post-coital snore of one Dr Goodbody.

Joy had largely reverted back to her original opinion that revenge sex was a complete nonsense, *and* a very bad idea. She had hoped that it would make her feel something. Young, irresistible, desirable, or, at the very least, sexy. All she actually felt was regret, with a side helping of guilt and a big dollop of disappointment.

It had been, after all these years, still perfectly nice. In the same way, that plain digestives were perfectly nice, or un-iced cake was perfectly nice. They were all still enjoyable, to a degree, yet lacked that magic something. After all, a plain digestive was perfectly fine for dipping in tea, but there was no mistaking that a chocolate hobnob gave a longer, more satisfying dunk.

Truth was that sex with Callum today was damn near identical to what sex with Callum was 20 years ago. He'd had plenty of girlfriends in that time, he'd been engaged twice, and he had at least one child that she knew of. She simply couldn't understand why none of his significant others had ever suggested he touch this, or flick that, lick here or stick his thumb there. How no one had ever told him, a little bit faster, a little bit deeper, and a little bit harder. Maybe they had, and he just didn't want to. If anything, Joy thought he'd gotten slower, and he'd developed an odd kind of motion that one might adopt when vacuuming, a kind of long sweeping forward glide that, while still perfectly nice, completely missed the spot every single time. Maybe it was just her, whose spot he couldn't hit.

She also hadn't bargained on him spending the whole night. She had hoped that a bit of afternoon delight, followed by a Chinese feast and a conversation about the finer workings of the radiology department, might have seen him on his way. But as she had cleared away the dishes, he had pulled her back upstairs, and she had given in in the hope that he'd leave afterwards.

Yet he was still here, snoring and sweating all over her new bedding.

Picking up her phone from the bedside table, she opened the camera, snapped a quick pic, and set up a group chat.

Joy

Help, how do I get him to leave?

Bernie

Who is that?

Meryl

OMG, is that Dr Goodloving?

Joy

Goodbody.

Margot

Doesn't look all that great to me.

Lauren

Lol.

Meryl

You got yourself a pet doctor!

Joy

Fuck off. What do I do? He won't leave.

Carlee

Round two?

Joy

Done.

Tabitha

Just move house, leave him there.

Bernie

Burn it to the ground.

Meryl

Sing at him.

Joy

You lot are not fucking helpful.

Margo

Roll him out of bed, down the stairs and straight out of the front door like a giant chiz wheel.

Margot

*Cheese wheel.

Meryl

**Or jizz wheel.

Carlee

Lol.

Joy

Thanks, I'm going now.

Bernie

I can call you, pretend to be Mischa and fake a problem with Zach. Tell him you have to go out, and just don't go back until he's gone.

Joy

I still don't think he'd leave.

Margot

He has to get up and piss at some point. Tell him the truth, that you're going through some shit, and you used

him to make yourself feel better, but that it was a

complete mistake, you feel terrible and you'll see him at

work on Monday.

Lauren

??

Bernie

???

Tabitha

?

Joy

It's the only thing I can do, isn't it?

Meryl

How was it?

Joy

It lasted less time than it would take for me to tell you about it.

Meryl

Oh!

Carlee

Good luck.

Closing her phone, Joy slid out of bed, back downstairs and set about making the loudest cup of tea she possibly could. Slamming every door at least twice, knocking pots out of the cupboard, and turfing cutlery into the sink from across the room. When all else failed, she picked up the now empty wine bottle that Callum had brought with him and threw it straight at the floor. It smashed loudly against the tiles, its sharp shrill drings echoing off into the dark silence of the living room, and up the stairs.

Less than a minute later, Joy heard the toilet flush and footsteps on the landing above her head.

"Everything ok?" he called.

She didn't answer.

"Joy?" he called again, his footsteps quickly padding down on the thinning stair carpet until he was stood at the kitchen door in tented underpants.

Joy was sat at the table, tea in hand.

"You ok," he asked.

She nodded, "It must have slipped out of my hand," she replied, blowing innocuously into the hot cup.

He turned back to the stairs. "Are you coming up?"

"Wait, Callum," she said, cringing. Her tone was wrong. She had wanted to sound upbeat and enthusiastic, instead, it came out like she was about to tell him that she'd ran over his dog. She didn't even know if he had a dog.

"Oh," said Callum, stepping back into the kitchen, and covering the front of his boxers with his hands, presumably because no one wants to be let down gently while sporting an erection. "Is this the bit where you say it's you, and not me .... again?"

Joy offered him a seat, but he declined. "You shouldn't harbour whatever it is you're harbouring, for me. You shouldn't have come here. You shouldn't have come in; you shouldn't have stayed. We shouldn't have. . . . "

"You're the one who pulled me through the door,"

"Are you telling me that you didn't come here in the hope that I would?" she said, raising an eyebrow as she took a sip of tea.

He shook his head for all but a second before thinking better of it. His shoulders dipped, and his hands dropped to his side. He looked deflated in every conceivable way.

"Look, Callum, I think you're a wonderful man,"

"But?"

"But nothing. You're a good friend and a great colleague, and I let you in knowing full well that I have absolutely no intention of making this a thing." She got up and walked to the front door, pulled the envelope from her bag and thrust it into his hand as she passed him on her way back to the table. "I had an utterly shite day, I felt like a complete twat, and I took advantage of you because of it, just because you were here, and he's not."

Callum peeled back the top of the envelope and peered inside. "I'm sorry," he said, placing it back down on the table in front of her.

"It's not that I don't want you, I don't want anyone. I just want to be alone."

Callum nodded, and without saying a word, retreated back upstairs, reappearing a matter of minutes later fully dressed, car keys in hand.

Leaning across the table, he put his hand on her shoulder. "Maybe in another life, eh?"

Joy smiled without looking at him, puffing out her cheeks, she dropped her head into her hands as she listened to him walk quickly down the hall and out of the door.

Chapter 20

Lunging forward, Joy threw herself at the front door with what little strength she had left. Jamming the handle down, the door sprung open, sending Joy hurtling onto the tiled floor below. Rolling over onto her back, her arms flopped at her sides as she gasped for air, her eyes fixed on the ceiling light at the bottom of the stairs, waiting for everything to come back into focus.

She was shaking, her hands throbbed, her heart raced, and the bile in her stomach lapped at her tonsils. She'd have coughed if she hadn't considered that her heart might be propelled out of her mouth with the slightest wheeze.

After a minute or two, her pulse slowed, her heart retreated back into her ribcage, and the blur began to clear.

"Holy shit," she cried, pulling herself upright, only to find Meryl staring at her from the other side of the front door. "Are you trying to kill me?"

"Looks like you're doing a fine job of that yourself," she grinned. "Did I just see you out jogging?"

"I dunno, was I running?" she asked, holding out her hand.

Reaching forward, Meryl, gripped her hand and yanked her to her feet. "No, you were throwing up in a hedge at the top of the street, but, you know?" she said, nodding towards Joy's feet, "In trainers."

Joy managed a weary smile. "Guilty." She said, retreating to the kitchen. She flicked on the tap and grabbed a pint glass from the draining board.

"How far did you get?"

"To the top of the street. I think the mistake was starting uphill," she said. She didn't really think that. The mistake was leaving the house at all.

"Well, if you want a running buddy next time?" said Meryl, jogging after her down the hallway, "just give me bell."

"I don't think there'll be a next time," said Joy, filling the glass and downing it in one mouthful. Gasping as the crisp cold water sizzled its way down her throat.

"Have you thought about cycling instead? I'm sure the boys'll let you borrow one of their bikes."

Joy's face dropped. She used to quite like cycling. She hadn't really gotten back into after having Zachary, until a few years ago she'd had the good intention to get some practice in prior to their annual trip to the caravan, in the hope of joining the boys on a trip down the coast. She had loved it at first. The freedom to weave in and around obstacles, the wind in her hair and the sunlight on her face. Unfortunately, she got more than enough of that when on the final leg back to the house, the brakes failed. She had flown past the house at a dramatic speed, only stopping when the bike plunged into the brook at the bottom of the estate, landing her squarely up to her waist in mud and wedged between a shopping trolley and the passenger door of an old Ford Cortina.

"I've never liked bikes," she said, hastily dismissing the idea. "Was there a reason you called, or did you simply stop by to mock?"

"Yes. No, I mean, I was on the way here anyway, where is everyone, it's so quiet." Said Meryl, popping her head into the empty living room.

Joy sighed. "It's Rob's first full weekend. He's taken the dog too."

"A whole day and night to yourself." She said, clapping her hands together, "will you be paging the good doctor?"

"No," said Joy bluntly. She didn't think he'd come even if she felt inclined. He had spent the week patently avoiding her. No hanging around the vending machine, no parking where he knew her car would be, no flowers. At one point, she thought that he might have taken annual leave, but he was definitely in the building. They had received a number of referrals from A&E over the week, and he'd signed off on the paperwork. Outside of the little knot of guilt she felt every time she thought about him, it was actually quite nice to know that she could get on with work in the full knowledge that there was no chance of bumping into him.

"You ok?" asked Meryl, "with them at Rob's?"

Joy considered lying, plastering the cheery smile she saves for the boys across her face and telling Meryl that some time to herself was exactly what she needed, a candlelit bath, a night in front of the telly and long lie in. But she didn't have the energy to lie, and she was sure that even if she did, Meryl wouldn't believe her. She shook her head and shrugged.

"Tell you what", said Meryl. "Why don't we go for a drink later? No dancing, obviously. You pick a place, and I'll pick you up at say nine, yeah?"

Joy's mood instantly lifted as the prospect of a night on her own faded. "I would love that," she said, nodding her head enthusiastically.

"Brill, I'll see you at nine then," said Meryl, picking up her bag from the chair and charging towards the door.

"Didn't you want something else?" Joy shouted after her.

"Oh, yeah, um, it can wait til later," she yelled, turning back to Joy and flashing her a smile. "Nothing important."

Joy knew she was lying. The smile was the same fake grin she always used herself, the kind that showed way too much teeth and where the eyes didn't quite make contact. Nonetheless, as Meryl pulled the door behind her, Joy opened the fridge, poured a large glass of Chardonnay from the bottle in the door, and headed for the shower.

"What about that guy?" Said Carlee, nodding towards a man stood at the bar wearing dark jeans, loafers and a pink Hawaiian shirt.

Joy shook her head.

"Or that one over there, don't you think he looks a bit like that guy from that zombie show," added Meryl, pointing towards the pool table at the other end of the room, and a man who, from a distance and with poor lighting, could be mistaken for Andrew Lincoln, or up close and with better lighting would adequately resemble the walking dead.

Joy rolled her eyes and sipped at her wine, "I'm not here to pick up men."

"No harm in testing the water thought, right?" grinned Carlee. "What about ..... "

Slamming her glass down on the table, Joy cut her off before she could point her finger at any other guy in the pub. "What is with you two tonight?" she demanded. "If all you're going to do is try to hook me up, I'm going home," she spat, grabbing her bag from the floor.

"Wait," said Carlee, reaching out and grabbing Joys wrist.

"Ok, talk." She replied, dropping her bag and crossing her arms across her chest.

Carlee looked at Meryl, who looked at Carlee, who looked at Joy. Meryl reached down and pulled her phone out of her bag. "You know how at work, us teachers go for drinks at the end of the month and spend a night talking about how much we want to quit."

Joy nodded.

"Well, last night we went over to a new place because John, the year four head's wife, just had a baby," she said.

"Boy or girl?" asked Carlee.

"Little girl," replied Meryl, "called her Primrose, gorgeous little thing, enough to make anyone broody."

Joy coughed, loudly.

"Anyway," continued Meryl, throwing her hands in the air and clearing her throat. "We ended up going to his local because he didn't want to go far from home in case wifey needed him to help with the baby. And guess who just happened to be sat there in the lounge."

Joy felt her heart leap in her chest. "Robin?"

Meryl nodded.

"Was he........" She stalled. She didn't want to ask. She didn't really need to. There was no other credible reason why they were telling her this. "Was he ...... alone?" she stammered.

Meryl shook her head. "I took a photo. Do you want to see?"

Joy felt her eyes bulge and her nose tingle. She shook her head. "Did he see you?"

"No, he ... um, he looked busy," replied Meryl. She was gripping her phone awkwardly between her hands.

Grabbing a napkin from the Cutlery rack on the table behind, Joy dabbed at her under eyes, and blew her nose, took a deep breath, and held her hand out.

"Are you sure," asked Carlee.

Joy shook her head again. She couldn't speak. Everything she was feeling, the hurt, the hate, the pain and all the bad words that she wanted to scream were currently locked, somewhere behind her voice box. She was scared that if she spoke, if she even tried to, it was all going to come tumbling out.

"I feel awful," said Meryl, "should we not have told you."

Joy bit her lip. She wanted to know but didn't at the same time. She wanted to see but couldn't look. It wasn't like she could take the upper ground anyway. It was only a week ago that she was in their marital bed with another man. She wondered if Rob would be so upset if he knew about that. The difference was, of course, that he was the one who left, and if she was perfectly honest with herself, there was still a glimmer of hope that he'd come back. And only he held that power, to walk back in if he wanted to, she couldn't force him. But the more time that passed, the less likely that was to happen. Even less so if he met someone else. At the same time, it had been almost three months. Maybe it was time to draw a line under their marriage and accept that it was actually over.

Gulping hard, Joy jabbed her still outstretched hand towards Meryl, "It's ok, I want to know, now give me the phone."

Meryl opened her gallery and slipped the phone into Joy's hand.

She sat staring at the picture of her husband. He was wearing the bright blue shirt she'd bought him for their last anniversary, but no tie.

There was a female sitting opposite him. She couldn't really see her, only an upturned nose on its profile and skinny shoulders. The rest of her face was mostly obscured by long fiery hair. She was wearing a figure-hugging dress, not that there was much of a figure to hug. Joy imagined that she'd struggle to get such a dress over one of her legs, let alone over her arse. They weren't touching, but Robin was leaning in towards her, looking down, while she was cross-legged and rolling her hair around a perfectly painted, pointed finger. They were both drinking whiskey on the rocks. Robin rarely drank whiskey outside of Christmas, and almost never neat. She had lost count of the parties over the years that she'd had to near carry him out of because one of his uncles had opened a bottle of scotch, and Robin was too embarrassed to tell them that he was a whiskey wuss, that it knocked him sick and that within two shots, he'd be on his arse and shitting into the nearest receptacle. Joy couldn't help but stifle a grin that his date may have to find that out the hard way.

Joy pushed the phone back across the table.

"Is that the girl from work?" asked Carlee, picking up the phone for another look.

Sitting back in her chair, Joy shrugged. "I only ever heard a voice."

"And you don't recognise her?"

Grabbing the phone back from Carlee, Joy stared again at the picture. She was already struggling to think straight, but she liked to think that she'd remember if he worked with a woman who looked like that. For fifteen years, she had gone to every Christmas party, every employee wedding, christenings, funerals. She had organised bake-offs, cook-offs, raffles and charity relays. Granted, after a time, the faces all start to look the same, and the names begin to muddle, but she was sure she'd have remembered that hair.

"You sure you're ok?" asked Meryl.

Joy shook her head. She felt sick, her head was spinning, and her chest hurt. Every time he dropped the kids off, she put on makeup and fixed her hair. When he called to speak to the boys, she made herself sound busy and un-phased. But seeing him with that woman, her hair, her lack of waist, her confident pose, she couldn't compete with that. She let out a loud puff of air, pushed out her chair and stormed off across the pub and straight out of the front doors.

Sitting on a picnic bench at the edge of the carpark, she hung her head in her hands and wept. Her eyes stung, her nose ran, and her throat ached. Carlee and Meryl had both hastily followed her out, but she had waved them back in with a pleading smile and a promise that she wouldn't go off without telling them.

Pulling the napkin from where she had ferreted it away in her pocket, she wiped her eyes. Pretty fruitless, really, the tears were almost immediately replaced with more as they continued to fall with little effort or consideration for her mascara. She had almost expected this. From the moment she heard the voice on the phone, she had been waiting for it, and if not this then someone else, eventually. She hadn't expected it quite so soon, but who was to say that he hadn't had his head turned before he left, and they were just waiting for an acceptable length of time before daring to be seen out in public. She felt her tummy lurch again.

"Are you ok?" asked a voice from behind her.

Joy turned slowly around, her face streaked with blackened trails of muddied makeup, her mouth contorted, mid cry. Behind her stood a man, tall and athletic with whitening hair and an equally white smile.

His face dropped into a horrified grimace as he caught sight of Joy. "Clearly, you're not. Sorry for interrupting," he said, before turning to walk away.

"Did two women set you up to this," she asked, quickly wiping her face and doing her best to compose herself.

"I was leaving anyway. They just asked me to check if you were still out here. So, are you?"

"Still out here? obviously," she scoffed.

He laughed, handing her another napkin from a holster by the door. "Ok. Are you Ok?"

"No, not at all," she replied, watching as a look of panic crossed his face that he might be expected to do something about it. "It's fine, though. I will be ok. I've just found out my husband has a girlfriend."

"Oh,"

"We're separated, divorcing. It was always going to happen," she said, shrugging.

"Well, take it from someone who's on divorce number three. It does get better," he replied.

"Wow," yelled Joy, "Three divorces. What's wrong with you." She laughed, her giggle suddenly vanishing as she heard how that came out, but before she could apologise, the man shrugged and took a seat on the bench next to her.

"First wife left me for our son's swimming instructor."

"Beautifully Cliché," said Joy.

"The second left me because I was always at work,"

Joy nodded, "Relatable,"

"The third, I think, only married me for money."

"Interesting," she replied, looking at his watch. It wasn't a posh watch, or his shoes. Nice and stylish perhaps, but not expensive. "And do you have, *money?*" she asked.

"Not anymore." He said, holding up his empty hands. "It's all hers now."

"And what do you do, to earn your ex-wife's money." she asked.

"I'm a surgeon," he said confidently, "orthopaedics"

"Local," she asked. She knew a few of the nurses in the Orthopaedics department, and Berni's sister had been in training there recently.

"Good god no," he scoffed, "Private practice in Cheshire. Won't catch me in any of those flea-ridden NHS shacks around here. What do you do?

Joy crossed her arms. "I'm a nurse."

"Ah," he said his smile immediately dropping at the corners. "I didn't really ....."

Joy smiled smugly. Turning to face him, she straightened his tie and patted him on the shoulder. "I think we've just solved the riddle of the three divorces," she cooed as she pulled herself from the bench and headed back inside feeling infinitely better. That was until she spotted Carlee, heading towards the door holding a phone aloft. Joy checked her pockets. Her phone wasn't there. She must have left it on the table.

"Joy, quick, it's Robin. He's rang twice, one after the other." cried Carlee thrusting her phone at her.

Joy snatched it from her grip just as the call rang off. But before she had a chance to press redial, it started to ring again in her hands.

"Rob, what's wrong? Is Zach ok?" She shrieked down the phone. She couldn't hear him. She could hear shouting in the background, smashing, Zachary screaming. "Rob," she shouted again, "what's going on?"

"Mum, mum, come quick, please come and get us."

"Owen," she gasped, "sweetheart, where's your dad."

"Please, mum, just come and get us."

"Where are your brothers Owen? What's wrong?" she screamed. By now, half the pub had turned to see what the noise was.

The line cut dead. Joy's heart stopped.

Chapter 21

Meryl had the car out front before Joy had even put the phone back into her handbag. From behind, she felt Carlee bundling her into the passenger seat before launching herself headfirst into the back seat. The doors slammed, the engine revved, and the car pulled out of the carpark with a screech.

"Where are you going," shouted Joy.

"Yours," replied Meryl, switching the gears up into fourth.

"They're not at mine; they're at Reuben's."

"Shit," said Meryl, checking the mirror, "I don't know where that is."

"Turn left up here, go round the block until you come back on yourself, and then carry on until you hit the main road." cried Carlee from the rear.

"Fuck that," said Meryl, slamming on the brakes in the middle of the dual carriageway and pulling a U-turn over a flower bed and nearly knocking down the NO-UTURNS sign.

Pulling onto the opposite carriageway, she slammed her foot down on the accelerator, changing lanes and out of the way on a speeding lorry that was rapidly coming up their behind.

They hadn't even made it into town, and she had already run through at least one red light, two ambers and an ANPR, before mounting the curb on the biggest roundabout in the county, and travelling around it in the middle of two lanes, in the wrong gear and on only two wheels.

"Easy up Mez," screamed Joy, clinging onto the door handle as the other two wheels slammed back down onto the asphalt. Meryl ignored her, veering across the roundabout and out of the exit, narrowly missing a brand-new Lexus, a transit, and a Porshe.

"You're going to lose your fucking license," squealed Carlee, who was on all fours in the back and clinging on to every available seatbelt.

"Don't worry," said Meryl, casually, "Margot has got me out of so many points. She knows all the loopholes. Worst case scenario, I'll dump it on Tesco and report it stolen. You should bear that in mind, Joy, about Margot, should you decide to murder Rob when we get there. Good representation is so hard to find."

"Noted," replied Joy, before squealing loudly as Meryl took a left without so much as tapping the brake.

Pulling into Reubens drive, Joy let go of the door and slumped back into the seat. A journey that normally took Joy the guts of half an hour, Meryl had managed to get them there in ten minutes by ignoring every traffic light and breaking every rule of the highway code.

Scrambling out of the passenger seat, Joy spotted Owen, sat hunched over by the double garage door.

Reuben's house was, in comparison to her own, like a fort. Set on an acre, it had a long blossom-lined driveway leading up to an imposing double gabled front that was clad in expensive Welsh slate and trimmed in smooth black ash. The grass was cut weekly, the eaves scrubbed once a month, and even the gnomes got rotated depending on the season. It was his home, his office, his board room and his entertainment suite, and he ran it like clockwork, except tonight.

Tonight, every single light in the house was on. Every curtain was open, as was the front door. Inside, Joy could hear the screams of Zachary in full meltdown.

Spotting the car, Owen ran over and grabbed his mother around the waist. "Ben smacked Zachary, mum." he sobbed. She hugged him back tightly before instructing him to get in the car, and to stay there.

Storming across the lawn and through Ben's beloved flower beds, she didn't even announce her arrival. She just marched through the doorway and set about locating her other sons, and her dog.

Inside was carnage. Furniture had been upended and wallpaper torn from the stair wall. The large mirror in the hall was smashed, and crockery littered the kitchen floor along with uneaten food and cutlery, swimming in what smelt suspiciously like lager. At the large central breakfast bar sat Reuben, muddied, missing a big chunk of hair from his crown and nursing a large scratch down the right side of his face, and a black eye to his left.

He didn't acknowledge her, and she ignored him, instead following the loud barking and the cries of her youngest son upstairs and into the back bedroom.

Robin was on all fours reaching under the large four-poster bed, pleading, begging, apologising. Pelé was running around him, nipping at his arms as he tried to reach for Zachary.

Joy got down on her hands and knees next to Rob and peered into the space under the bed. There was Zachary, naked, curled up into a ball, squealing at the top of his lungs. His voice was hoarse, his eyes scrunched shut, his hands bloodstained and shaking.

Joy took a deep breath and began to sing.

Zachary stopped screaming and opened his eyes. As soon as he spotted Joy, he scrambled onto his belly, slithered out from under the bed and clambered up onto her shoulders, grumming loudly.

Climbing back to her feet, Zachary slid down onto her chest. His arms gripped so tightly around her neck that it made her eyes fuzzy and her head light. "Where's Elliot?" she seethed at Robin.

Robin didn't bother to get up. He didn't even look in her direction. His eyes were fixed to the floor. "He left, walked out. . . . . . . He punched Ben."

"Good. It'll save me a job," spat Joy, ignoring his sullen tone and obvious upset. Kissing Zachary, she squeezed him tight as she crossed the room, hurrying back downstairs and outside, followed faithfully by Pelé who jumped straight into the car and onto Owen's knee.

Joy had just reached the car when Robin called her back. He was still trying to speak to Zachary. Still apologising. The little boy tightened his grip and began to squeal.

Joy turned around and faced her husband, looking him square in the eyes. "You want to see them again? Then you take me to court, and you tell the fucking judge exactly what happened tonight."

Slipping back into the car, she didn't take her eyes off him. He was crying, his eyes clenched, his shoulders jerking and juddering. She glared at him as she buckled the seat belt around both her and Zachary and followed him with an icy stare as the car pulled off along the driveway and back onto the main road.

Chapter 22

The journey home was thankfully much calmer than the one there. Not a single red light was breached, nor verge mounted.

Joy sat stone-faced in the front, stroking Zachary's hair and kissing his head. He wasn't grumming, but wasn't crying or squealing, and it worried Joy the most when he made no sound at all. It meant he'd completely shut down She held him tighter.

Owen sat in the back, huddled up to Carlee as he tearfully recounted his version of events.

All had apparently started off well with a Go-Carting trip and supper from the drive-through, games were played, balls were kicked, and tummies were filled. However, when Zachary realised that they were headed back to Reuben's and not home, he became agitated. He had screamed the entire way back, and by the time they had gotten there, he was verging on implosion.

When Robin had tried to give him his medication, he had spat it out and threw the yoghurt up the wall. What followed was described by Owen as a rampage of biblical proportions. Pots were thrown, mirrors were hit, and subsequently smashed while bins were tipped up and emptied. Joy remembered similar meltdowns well from the early days before his diagnosis, back when she was arguing with doctors that there was definitely something different about Zachary. He had twice nearly flooded the house, broken every kitchen cupboard hinge and kicked out every tongue and groove panel in the bathroom. *'He's just a boy,'* they'd say, and *'so much younger than his siblings'. 'He'll grow out of it,'* they promised. He never did, he wouldn't talk, he wouldn't play with school friends, wouldn't join in with games, and it had taken him running out into the road, mid meltdown, and a strongly worded letter from the school before anyone had taken her seriously. They had since then planned his routine meticulously. They knew his triggers and avoided any potential pitfalls that might result in a shutdown. Some things they couldn't avoid and so had to approach with caution. She knew this was one of those situations. She had expected it. Robin should have too. She bit her lip, and maybe it would serve him right. She hated herself for even thinking it.

"So why didn't you call me sooner?"

"Dad kept saying it would be ok if we could just get his meds in," wept Owen from his perch on the back seat. "But he just wouldn't take them. We chased him around for ages, then once we had him sitting, Dad tried, I tried, Elliot tried, and then Reuben tried, but Zachary spit it out in his face, then ......

"Then he slapped him," said Joy, sucking her breath in hard. She could feel her whole body tensing.

"So, Zachary ran at him. He was kicking and scratching and biting and screaming, and then Pelé joined in, he was barking and growling, and that just made Zach worse. It was ..... it was ....." his voice trailed off as the sobs returned.

"And what did your dad do?" she asked, her own voice beginning to crack. Her resolve was starting to slip.

Meryl reached across from the driver's seat and rubbed her hand.

"He apologised to Reuben, threw the dog out back and told Zach off," continued Owen.

Holding her face in her hands, Joy rubbed softly at her temples. "So, then Elliot hit Ben?" she asked, watching her son nodding through the visor mirror.

"Elliot was the only one who was able to prize Zach off Ben" he said, sniffling, "and then Ben called him an animal, so Elliot gave him a right fucking smack. And then he ran off."

"And then you rang me?"

He sniffled and nodded again.

"Turn around Meryl," said Joy, as calmly as she could manage. It wasn't easy. She was screaming inside.

"What, no, what for?"

"Why d'ya think?" she hissed. "I'm going to fucking kill him. *please*, turn the car around."

"You're going nowhere other than home," replied Carlee from behind. "Because that makes you no better. And you are better. So were going to get you home, get these boys in bed, find the other one, and then first thing Monday morning, you're going to call a solicitor, and make this shitshow a formal circus, and if you want, if you think you need to, you make a complaint to the police about Reuben striking Zach."

Joy nodded. Carlee was right. She usually was. As much as she wanted to go back and smack them both stupid. There wasn't much point. It wouldn't really make her feel any better, it wouldn't make the situation better, and most of all, it wouldn't help Zachary, who was now fast sleep in her arms.

As Meryl swung the car into their street, Joy sighed loudly as she spotted Elliot sat on the doorstep, his cheeks a web of white tracks where his tears had washed away mud from his face. By the gate, his bike lay sprawled across the path, its tyres flat and its handlebars loose.

He stood up as they approached the door, his head hung low and his hands lolling limply at his side. He stank of beer and wet grass. Joy didn't say anything to him. She just pulled him to her side, opened the door and hurried everyone into the house.

Chapter 23

Have you discharged bed two?" asked Maryanne.

"You haven't asked me to," replied Joy, rooting around in a box of Maltesers that had been found in one of the nurse's station drawers. They were out of date by over a month and misshapen from heat, but Joy thought they tasted just fine, if not a little soft in the middle.

"I did, twice," replied Maryanne, checking her watch. We've a referral on their way over. Angina. I need that bed ready."

"No," replied Joy, "you said bed five, you asked me to canulate three, and change the bag in seven, you said nothing about two."

"Joy, can you discharge two, please?" asked Maryanne, pressing her hands together in front of her chest.

She had been in an odd mood all day. She had arrived late, something that was most unheard of, and had then vanished for an hour after morning ward rounds. Justin, one of the orderlies, said they had spotted her on the phone in her car. But since she had come back, she had been distracted and a little ditsy.

Joy smiled and made a mock salute before grabbing a wad of discharge letters and heading off in search of bed two.

Inside the little side room, she found Elsie, a surprisingly spritely, 82-year-old slip of a woman who looked like she would snap in two if she were to bend over too quickly, and who up until now had survived a childhood in the Manchester tenements, the blitz, the fall of the industrialised north, two heart attacks, a double bypass and three weeks of hospital sandwiches.

"Have you got someone to pick you up, young lady?" asked Joy snatching up the chart from the end of the bed and flicking through the notes.

"Yes, my boyfriend, he's on his way," smiled Elsie, flashing Joy a toothless grin.

"Ooh, do we finally get to meet the elusive Jack?" chuckled Joy, making the old lady giggle like a schoolgirl and clap her hands excitedly off her knees. Since coming round from her bypass, Elsie had talked about Jack, the 22-year-old love of her life, almost constantly. Yet the only visitors Joy had seen was her older brother, her daughter, three sons, a granddaughter who had popped in most afternoons, and a neighbour called Martin who had come to drop off post. They had at first assumed it was post-surgery delirium, then possible dementia, but Elsie was as sharp as a new safety pin and, despite her failing body, was probably more clued in than Joy was. So, they had come to the conclusion that she had simply made Jack up for shits and giggles.

So, Joy's jaw nearly hit the floor when an exceptionally attractive young man entered the room carrying a bunch of yellow roses and a Jacobs cracker assortment. Elsie was, if nothing else, crackers about crackers. And he was a cracker. Chestnut curls and soft hazel eyes offset a strong jaw and wide chest. Standing at least six feet, he was built like a rugby champion and smelt like cafe creams.

Joy watched, open mouthed, as Jack crossed the room and gave Elsie a lingering kiss on the forehead as she sat perched on the edge of the bed, beaming like a streetlight and giggling like a toddler.

Joy picked her chin off the floor and carried on with the paperwork. After removing her canula, Elsie sauntered off to the ladies' room to freshen up and dress, leaving Joy alone with Jack.

"Are you?" she asked, stopping herself at the thought of how utterly ridiculous, if not a little insulting, she sounded. "You do know she tells everyone you're her boyfriend?"

"We go dancing," he said, "and I take her to the theatre and the cinema, and we once went to the opera, which was interesting. I don't think she enjoyed it, but she's so nice, she'd never say so." Leaning forward in the plasticky coated armchair, his trousers tightened around his legs, and Joy felt her mouth sag, and her knees tingle as she found herself completely unable to take her eyes away from his thighs. "But I'm engaged to her granddaughter, we're getting married next month."

Joy checked the door, "Does Elsie know this?" she asked.

Jack laughed, "Yes, she's giving Lilly away."

Joy thought back to the pretty young woman who had visited Elsie often. Joy had admired her delicate summer dresses and would gladly sell her soul for her sunny blonde waves and high cheekbones.

But Joy's thoughts quickly turned to Robin. They often did. Back in the early days of their relationship, he had been so kind and attentive. He would take Mischa to the pictures while Joy worked and once spent a month ferrying her mother around when she was banned from driving after mounting the kerb and hitting a police car because she hadn't realised that the Mimosa's at the WMC charity brunch were alcoholic. But he had relished in his usefulness and basked in the praise of her friends, and Mischa.

Joy felt her heart sink. She just couldn't understand where that man had gone. Surely he was still in there, somewhere. For at least the thousandth time since Saturday, the covert picture on Meryl's phone flashed into her head, and just like every other time, she shook it out before the tears started. She then realised that she was still staring straight at Jack's crotch.

"You're all very lucky to have each other, Jack", she said, dipping her head just as Elsie swanned back into the room dressed head to toe in pea green and giving Jack a twirl before collecting her bags, and her teeth, from the locker.

Stripping the bed after they left, Joy felt her phone buzzing in her pocket. Lifting it out, she saw Robin's name flash up on the screen.

She shoved it back into her pocket.

It rang again while she was in the middle of an observation round and twice more while dishing out meds.

As she finally sat down on her lunch break, about to tuck into the dinner plate sized Cornish pasty she'd been fantasising about all morning, her phone rang again. How did he always manage to ring while she was eating? She slat the pastry back down on the plate, pulled her phone out of the pocket and answered it.

"What?" she spat.

"Joy?"

"What, Rob?"

"Have you done it?"

"Done what?" she asked.

"The text message, the one you sent this morning, have you done it?"

"Aha," she replied, "You want to know if I've been to the police and reported your brother for violently attacking our son."

The line went quiet, but somewhere in the silence, she detected a faint, almost inaudible "Yeah."

"Not yet, Robin. I've been a bit busy this morning. I was going to call in on my way home."

"How is he?" he asked, his voice meek.

"How do you think he is?" she spat, "He's fucking traumatised, Rob. He's barely eaten, he's barely slept, he didn't come out of his room at all yesterday, and he keeps wetting himself. He's fucking terrified of everything."

"I never ....."

"You never do, Robin, do you?

"Please don't report it, Joy. It'll ruin Ben. He could lose everything."

"And what about what Zach, Robin?" she seethed, lowering her voice and holding her hand over her mouth in a bid to keep her business away from the entire canteen. "Zach has lost everything too. His whole life has been turned upside down. But unlike Ben, he doesn't understand why. Then, instead of trying to engage with him, to build a new routine around *our* new circumstances, he gets a fucking slap when he doesn't automatically fall into line."

"It wasn't .... "

"Yes, it fucking was, Robin."

"And what about me, Joy."

"What about you? This is your mess."

"If you report Ben, Zach won't be allowed to stay over at all."

Joy breathed out hard. "We have a plan," she said.

"Who's we?"

"And if you agree," Joy paused, taking another long lingering breath. "Then I won't report Ben."

The line once more fell silent, before he eventually spoke again. "Ok, what's the plan?"

"From now on, if you have Zach overnight, *and the boys*, you bring *your* stuff and have them a Mischa's. That way, Owen and Elliot can come and go as they please with their mate's. It's somewhere Zach is happy and settled. Mischa will stay with me."

"But that's a bit . . . "

"Take it or leave it Robin, it's our only offer, outside of putting it in front of a judge and trying to explain to him that your brother isn't a danger to our kids. Because I'll tell you now, you do that, and you'll end up with an hour supervised contact, once a month in a fucking community centre."

The line dropped quiet again. "Ok, if Mischa's ok with it."

"It was her idea, Robin. I wanted to go to the police," she spat, hitting the end call button.

Dropping her phone into her pocket, she groaned loudly. Her chest hurt and her jaw ached from clenching. She was fed up of clenching, her neck was constantly tense and she had worn permanent grooves into her palm from her nails digging into them. Finally, lifting the enormous pastry from the plate, she went to take a chunk out of its side, but dropped it back down instead, unable to stomach a single bite.

Chapter 24

How far d'ya make it today?" asked Mischa, holding out a pint pot full of cold water and laughing as Joy collapsed onto the kitchen table in a sweaty heap, gasping for air and clutching her side.

It was twenty-two degrees out. Twenty-two degrees was garden weather. It was not, nor should it ever be, jogging weather. But she had finished work at three and arrived home to an empty house, a pile of dishes and a garden that was in desperate need of mowing. In a toss-up between mowing it herself, washing up, and a run, she had chosen the latter, spurred on after not being able to fasten up the shorts she'd bought the previous summer.

Pulling her phone out from the little pocket in her leggings, Joy opened the fitness app that Mischa had installed.

"Nought point six kilometres," she said, in between long, laboured gasps and clumsy chugs of cold water.

"So, not even out of the street?" laughed Mischa.

Joy ignored her daughter's sniggers. "Nope, got to the drive at the bottom and got a stitch. Can't run with stitch."

"You don't have to run at all, mum. Just eat . . less," she replied.

Joy's face dropped into a scowl that could kill at twenty paces. "I barely eat anything as it is."

Mischa plucked the glass from her mum's hand and filled it from the tap. "You barely eat food. And what you do eat is deep fried. You live on chocolate and crisps and pastry and ice cream, or doughnuts and biscuits. Don't think I don't see the wrappers in the bin."

"I haven't had an ice cream in ages."

Mischa splat the full glass down heavily in front of Joy, sloshing water out of the top and over the table. "Mum, you've got choc-ice down your t-shirt. It's still damp," she said, leaning forward and running her finger over the yellowy-brown smudge on her chest. "No wonder you got a stitch."

Joy was about to argue her case when Mischa handed her an envelope, and it knocked the words clear out of her head.

"A guy called while you were out."

Joy sucked her bottom lip in hard. She'd seen the van over the road as she'd set off for her run. It was probably the only reason she had run as far as she did. She had hoped it was there for another house, someone having some plumbing done, or a window quote. But she had seen it outside before. She had spotted the man with the sharp suit and the envelope, stood by her front door as she arrived home from work the previous week, and had ended up driving in circles around the estate until he'd gone. He didn't look like a plumber.

She had stopped answering the door at all when she was home alone, at least not without taking a peek out of the upstairs window first.

She sat and glared at the envelope. It wasn't addressed to anyone. It just had urgent stamped on the front in big red letters with the words hand-delivered written underneath. She knew exactly what it was. She already had quite a collection of them.

"Anything I can help with?" asked Mischa.

Joy shook her head. From the worry in her daughter's voice, she assumed that Mischa knew exactly what it was too. She picked up the glass and sloped off down the hall to put the letter in the shoe rack with all the others. By this point, there were considerably more letters than shoes. She had promised herself faithfully that she'd deal with them as soon as she could. But the maintenance payments from Robin had been sporadic at best, and the longer she left it, the angrier the letters became. The angrier they became, the more she ignored them. When it was just one or two, it ate away at her. She would think about them at night when she lay in bed, sitting there by the door. She could hear them taunting her. Now the pile had grown so big that she could barely close the drawer; she didn't give them a thought at all until another one arrived.

"You ok," asked Mischa, watching as Joy slumped back into the chair, gripping tightly onto her sides.

"This stitch doesn't want to budge," she said, taking deep breaths and waiting for the pain in her ribs to ebb away.

"You know what you need," said Mischa in her best overly cheerful and obviously fake voice.

"A time machine?" replied Joy, grimacing.

"No. A date," exclaimed Mischa.

Joy burst out laughing, further aggravating the pain in her chest and leaving her doubled over. "And where do you suggest I find one of them." Joy didn't want a date. She wanted a lie-down and a Cornetto.

"I just mean something to work towards, an incentive, you know, to lose weight," she sat down at the table next to Joy, leaning in, "and sometimes, dates come with their own exercise," she said, nudging her mum in the arm.

"Mischa!" squealed Joy, her face instantly taking on a beefy shade of pink. "Dates also come with chocolates and dessert and a whole ton of headache that I really don't need."

Mischa's smile faded, "You know, it's a different world out there to the one you met dad in. There are apps designed purely to help people, um, hook up, just for fun. No dessert necessary."

Picking up her phone, Joy opened her browser and searched hook up, her eyes widening as the results popped up on the screen.

'*A casual sexual encounter outside of any defining relationship*'

"Are you trying to pimp me out?" she shrieked.

"I'm trying to cheer you up," replied Mischa, rolling her eyes.

"I don't need a man to cheer me up, Misch."

"I'm not saying you do," said Mischa, "but you can't deny that they're fun. And I see you knocking around this house when the boys are at mine with dad. I've seen you go to the shop for stuff you don't need, just so you can drive circles past my front door. You need a distraction, and if you don't want anything more, there are ways of going about it."

Joy couldn't deny that her daughter made a compelling argument. "And how would I go about hooking up, if I wanted to? I don't go anywhere, Misch. I'm not going to go and sit in a pub on my own or start dropping my handkerchief in the freezer section of ALDI, in the hope that someone might come to my rescue."

"You don't even have to take your slippers off," replied Mischa, her face instantly lifting into a wide grin. "You can live stream to groups on social media and talk to people who have the same interests. Like lonely hearts meets speed dating, but online, and in real-time."

"You sound like you know a lot about these things," said Joy raising an eyebrow.

Mischa didn't answer, but her grin did droop into more of a guilty smirk, the type she used to have as a little girl when she was caught with her nose in the fridge and trifle down her dress."

"So where would I find these groups," asked Joy before quickly adding, "If I wanted to."

Mischa picked Joy's phone up from the table and opened her Facebook app. Scrolling across the screen, she typed '*Dates near me*' into the search bar before handing the phone back to her mum. "Look, you can go local, national, international, you can search based on interests, hobbies, jobs, kinks."

Joy scrolled through the list of groups. *Naughty Nigel's Funtime Forties.* Joy giggled and clicked on it "It won't let me on," she said.

"You have to request to join," said Mischa, "but once you're in, you can watch other people's live videos, or go through old videos, or" she pointed at a little camera icon at the top of the page. "Do you own."

Joy rubbed at her face in an attempt to stop it reddening further. "I dunno. It seems a bit seedy."

"Not at all," scoffed Mischa, "Everyone's doing it. Look this group has 7,000 members. And you can't share the videos outside of a group, and any nasty comments get an instant block. It's in the rules."

Joy didn't say anything. She was busy scrolling through the list of groups on her phone.

"You have the house to yourself tonight," Mischa continued, "the boys are at mine with dad, and I'm out with friends."

"You didn't say you were out. I was going to get take away," said Joy, making no attempt to mask her disappointment.

"It's a birthday, a girl from work. I've pulled the designated driver straw, so I won't be late. Maybe we can have a take-out then, but" she said, a sly smile spreading across her face, "If you want me to stay out, just text me."

Joy shoved her phone hastily into her pocket and downed the rest of her water. "Another time then," she said, kicking off her trainers and heading for the stairs. "I'm going for a shower."

Chapter 25

Three times Joy had opened her old wreck of a laptop, only to slam it shut again. It had taken her nearly an hour to find it buried in the bottom of the wardrobe, and another hour to shower, curl her hair, and carefully apply enough make-up that she no longer looked like she had been dug up. She had tried on several dresses, all of which now sat on her bedroom floor, having been thrown there in a strop. After a spark of genius, she eventually settled on wearing one of her older, tighter, nurse dresses, pinned up at the hem and unbuttoned at the cleavage.

She had started off sitting on the sofa, but the recline left her looking unnaturally frumpy and created a ring around her waist that looked like she was wearing a bicycle tire under her dress. Instead, she had propped the laptop up on the sofa and angled it carefully so that the camera didn't pick up the mucky handprints on the wall, or the broken door on the TV unit, or the cracked pane on the Hi-fi stand. She had removed the ripped lace tablecloth from under the TV and positioned the chair over the bit of bald carpet where Zachary had spent hours plucking at its tuft. At any other time, the subject of the six-year-old who could give Thanos a run for his money in the destruction stakes would have to be high up the agenda of any first date conversation, but tonight, she wanted the focus to be all on her.

The problem was, she still found herself at a complete loss for words every time she opened the laptop and sat down in front of it. Did she really have so little to say? Had she immersed herself in her family so blindly that that was all she was now, dissipated so finely amongst the fragments of their lives that all she had of her own anymore was a name? She felt sick, her heart was racing, and the stitch from her earlier run was lingering, spreading up her side and into a twinge at her shoulder should she moved too quickly the wrong way.

Against her better judgement, she had given in and poured a large glass of wine, followed by a second, and was now halfway through a third. Yet, it had done nothing for her nerves but leave her lightheaded and forgetful. *'You don't know these people,'* she thought while reminding herself of Mischa's reassurance that the video would not be seen outside of the group. The last thing she needed was for that to turn up on someone's phone in the breakroom.

She had carefully joined several local, relatively small groups, watching the archived videos to get an idea of what to say. They were all just like her, lonely, nervous strangers baring their souls to a blinking camera in an empty room. One man told of how his wife had died several years earlier and how he'd lost his confidence to go out and meet people. Another told of how work keeps him away from home for weeks on end and how he's looking for a casual relationship on the rare occasion he found himself in town. Another video was of a young woman, incredibly pretty and deceptively camera confident, and who was looking for a sugar daddy to pay her rent while she put herself through college. They all seemed like normal people, from all walks of life, who simply knew what it was they wanted.

Joy didn't.

Well, she did, it was just something she couldn't have.

She had been through the group's rules several times.

1. No sharing outside of the group.

2. No porn.

3. No explicit nudity.

4. No solicitation.

5. No nasty or offensive comments.

5. Over 18 only,

6. Have fun, which felt like it had been thrown on as an afterthought.

Draining the last of the wine from the glass, Joy took a deep breath and opened the laptop once again.

The screen sprang to life, opening up on the page where she'd left it. She found her profile, clicked on the little camera icon and sat poker-straight against the backrest, her legs crossed, her chest pushed out.

But nothing happened.

She pressed the icon again.

Still nothing.

'Fucks sake,' she said under her breath. Clicking back to the home screen, she located the live button and clicked it again. This time a little white light flashed up next to her webcam.

She was rolling.

Sitting back in the chair, she adjusted her skirt and faced the camera.

"Hi," she said, in her poshest voice, the one she usually reserved for when answering the ward phone. She flashed her brightest smile, making sure to show that she still had all of her teeth.

"I'm Joy," she said softly, "I'm a forty-two-year-old nurse, and I'm . . . . "

Her head went blank. She was sweating, her heartbeat was throbbing in her ears, and the air caught in her throat. She shouldn't have downed that wine. She shouldn't have squeezed herself into this dress. She could barely breathe.

"I'm . . . " she tried to continue, but the words just wouldn't come.

"I'm . . . . not feeling very well," she said, trying to stand, but as she steadied herself against the chair, the stitch which was now deeply embedded in her left shoulder began to spread. She felt it travel down her arm and across her chest, crushing her from within. She was red hot. Her skin felt like it was on fire. Yanking at her uniform, the old worn press studs gave way and it popped open as she staggered towards the laptop and then back towards the chair. She couldn't breathe, she couldn't talk, her eyes had glazed over, and her feet had gone numb. And the pain, the crushing agony felt like it was squeezing the life out of her. As she felt herself flailing towards the floor, she grasped at the chair, slumping over its soft cushioned seat, gasping, desperate to keep herself upright.

Over on the sofa, the little light next to the webcam continued to blink.

Chapter 26

J oy knew that she was in hospital.

She could hear the rhythmic beeping of the monitor behind the bed, the distant chatter from the nurse's station and the sound of thin-soled shoes treading the old lino outside in the hall. She could feel the crinkle of starched sheets on top of squeaky rubber-coated mattresses, and even through the oxygen mask clinging tightly to her face, she could smell the acrid disinfectant that oozed out of the hospital's walls.

She had no idea what she was doing in a hospital and very little memory of how she had got there. She had a blurry recollection of not being able to reach for her phone as it had rung incessantly. She remembered the cold of the air as she had been carried out to an ambulance and the sound of the sirens as she rocked about on the gurney. But faces were a blur, people were fuzzy, noises were distorted, and time had become immaterial. Eventually, everything had been taken over by white.

Until now.

Now she was awake and, evidently, alive. The pain in her chest, the catch in her breath and the warm touch of another's hand resting delicately over her own confirmed it.

She cracked one eye and immediately clamped it shut again. Her head thudding as her sight was flooded with muted artificial light. She waited a moment and tried again. This time squinting her eyelid just long enough to acclimatise. She needn't have bothered. It was mostly blurred, making anything within sight just a mush of greyish blobs. She creaked the other eye open and waited.

Slowly, the grey and green began to meld into shapes, and soon she could make out the off white of the ceiling tiles and the unmistakable diamond shape of the air-con vents above her.

Joy glanced left, and then right, but before she could determine any kind of distinguishing feature, there was a loud shriek.

"Muum!" squealed Mischa right in her ear, followed by beeping and then the sound of doors opening and footsteps.

Joy slammed her eyes shut again.

"Joy? Joy? Can you hear me, Joy?" came a voice, hurried and concerned.

Joy tried to speak but between the oxygen mask and the searing pain in her gullet, it was pointless. So instead, she nodded, it was slow and clumsy and looked more like she was having some kind of spasm, but the voice understood. Over the top of it, the beeping started again as more footsteps and voices filled the room.

"Mischa," croaked Joy, clawing at the oxygen mask, but her hand was pulled away as her eyelids were prized open and once again flooded with light from a pen torch. Joy winced.

"Mischa," she said again, as her other eye was peeled open.

There was no reply. Just the frantic movement of bodies hurrying around her, until she felt it again, the touch of a hand looping through her own as shaky fingers entwined with hers.

Joy glanced along her arm and towards her hand, and there was her daughter tear-stained and tired. She smiled at Joy, biting down on her bottom lip. Joy smiled back before closing her eyes again and praying for the chaos to stop.

Chapter 27

Four days?" stammered Joy. "It can't be."

"Five if you count today," replied Dr Delia Sommers, who dressed in creased scrubs and a Pokemon bandana, was sat reclined on the small plastic chair next to the bed, sipping on a large black coffee and nibbling on a chicken salad sandwich, the smell of which was driving Joy crazy as her stomach growled angrily from beneath her cotton gown.

One thing Joy had learnt about landing herself on a busman's holiday, was that all professionalism had gone out of the window. But, Joy had worked with Dr Delia, the lead cardiologist for her unit, for over a decade, during which time they had enjoyed nights out, camping trips and holidays. They had baby sat each other's kids, bonded over shoes, bickered over BBQ's *and* she was Zachary's godmother. They were friends, they shared the same dark sense of humour and taste in clothes, yet as she sat in front of her now, she couldn't help but feel like a child called into the headmaster's office.

"What day is today?" she asked. She was sure someone had already told her, but for the life of her, she couldn't remember.

"Thursday," replied Delia.

Joy tried to count the days from Saturday on her fingers, but gave up at Monday. "In a coma, you say?"

"Sedated," she replied, brushing sandwich crumbs from her trousers.

"And surgery?" she asked.

"Twice," spluttered Delia, holding up two fingers just in case Joy couldn't hear her over the mouthful of bread and lettuce.

"Did I die?" asked Joy.

The Doctor paused, then nodded as she swallowed down the last of her lunch. "Your heart stopped on the way to the hospital."

"Stopped?" croaked Joy. None of this was making any sense. She was only 42.

"You have myocardial ischemia caused by atherosclerosis. Your infarction was caused by a thrombus in the left anterior descending artery, but there is narrowing in the smaller arteries too." Delia looked especially relieved not to have to explain what any of that meant.

Joys face hardened. "I had a widow maker?"

"Yes . . . "

"But I'm a cardiology nurse."

"You're not immune to poor choices," replied Delia, and for a moment Joy wasn't sure whether she was still talking about her heart.

"Did they fix it? The blockage?" asked Joy.

"We fitted stents, but the angioplasty didn't hold, so we had to go in and bypass the blockage using the saphenous," replied Delia, emptying the last of her coffee.

"Open heart surgery. I only had a bit of stitch," said Joy, trying to summon a laugh, but the added movement pulled on the dressing, and she ended up yelping instead.

"Your heart's taken a bit of a beating, Joy, and you've had a bad year, you didn't notice the warning signs."

"Yeah, duh, like the Titanic didn't notice the fucking iceberg."

Delia shot her a look, "You were . . . *are*, incredibly lucky."

"Could I have another . . . . attack?" asked Joy, staring blankly at the canula in her hand.

"Not while we're looking after you," replied Delia, reaching out and placing her hand over her wrist.

Joy smiled, and lifted head. "When can I go home?"

"Now that your awake, we'll transfer you down to cardiology."

Joy rolled her eyes and muttered *bollocks* under her breath.

"Where," Delia continued, "we'll be able to keep an eye on you and get you back on your feet, so no promises yet."

Delia stood, and brushed the last of the errant breadcrumbs from her lap, "We've got this," she said, giving joy a rub on the elbow before swishing from the room, Mischa quickly jumped on the chair and pulled it back up to the bedside.

"Are you sure Zach's OK?" asked Joy anxiously.

"He's fine" reassured Mischa. "He's at home with dad being spoilt rotten,"

"Your home?"

"No, home home, and Grandma too, she's, um" Mischa paused, "she's helping."

"Your dad and my mum under the same roof," laughed Joy. She leaned over and whispered, "hide the knives."

"They're fine. You're the main concern," she replied.

She was lying, Joy could tell by the twitch in her nose and the way she bit into the corner of her lip.

"Ah, but you don't remember that holiday we had to Porthmadog just before the boys were born, it was a miracle that any of us got out of that caravan alive."

"Mum, don't go getting ..... "

"I can't help it, Misch, I've never been away from Zach for longer than a night. He needs me." her bottom lip began to twinge, "I'm his mum."

"And you nearly died. What would he have done then?"

Crossing her arms indignantly, she winced and immediately uncrossed them after a lightning bolt shot through her chest and along the length of her new 6-inch scar. She knew Mischa was right.

Joy sighed, "I just don't like the idea of those two in the same house, it's like leaving him alone with two angry bears. How *are* the twins, by the way?"

Mischa laughed. "They are ...." She took a deep breath. "They're missing their mum too."

"When can I see them?" asked Joy.

"Not until they move you from ICU, tomorrow maybe," said Mischa.

"And how are you?" asked Joy, running her eyes up and down Mischa's face. She looked tired and pale, and suddenly so much older. "You look awful."

Mischa nodded, her eyes dwelling a little too long on her hands before she answered. "I'm fine." She replied.

She was still lying. Joy lifted her arm to her daughter's face and ran her finger across her chin. "Come on, what's wrong."

Mischa's face crumpled, her eyes clamped shut, and her nose flared. "You scared the shit out of me, mum. You scared the shit out of everyone. When they carried you out of the house, I thought I was never going to see you again."

All Joy wanted to do was reached across and hug. But she couldn't. She couldn't move. Outside of the enormous wound on her chest, there were wires and tubes and monitors and beepers and cuffs. All she could do was run her hand over her daughter's head and tell her that she was sorry, as Mischa lay her head against the bed and wept.

"Misch?" asked Joy once her sobs had quietened and her shudders had all but returned to the normal lull of her breathing. "Who rang the ambulance?"

"What?" replied Mischa, lifting her head and wiping her eyes.

"I was home alone. You were out with friends. Who rang the ambulance?"

"Um .... " stuttered Mischa, her eyes widening as her gaze searched the room.

"Mischa, who?" asked Joy again.

Before she could answer, the door swung open and through it sailed a long clattering trolley topped with cups and plates, a vast urn and an enormous basket of sandwiches.

"Oh Mrs Lane, you're awake," cried the young girl pushing the trolley, and who was barely visible behind the mountain of snacks piled high next to the teabags.

"Claudia." Smiled Joy recognising the blue hair and pierced nose of the hospital's favourite tea lady. A Polish national, Claudia hadn't worked at the hospital very long but had built up quite the following on the cardiology ward for doubling up on biscuits and accidentally leaving trays of muffins lying around. For a moment, Joy wondered whether she could foist some of the blame in her direction, but truth be told, she had bribed enough baked goods off Claudia's predecessor, Brenda, before she retired that she figured that

Claudia had probably been warned in advance that she couldn't be trusted around flaky pastry.

"You are allowed tea, right?" she asked, smoothing her blue hair back behind her ears, "Two sugars. Right? No biscuits."

"Tea yes, but only one sugar," she replied, giving Mischa a *'look how good I am'* nod.

Mischa nodded back approvingly.

Claudia picked up two mugs, dropped a teabag into each and filled them with piping hot water from the urn. She dropped a splash of milk into both and then slid them down onto the table in front of joy.

"Anything for you, a sandwich? Muffin?" she asked Mischa, who shook her head and smiled politely.

Claudia pulled at the trolley and began to back out of the room, "OK, well, if you change your mind, come and find me. That baby won't grow itself."

Mischa's eyes instantly shot back to Joy, who had gone a funny shade of green and looked like she was trying to swallow an invisible apple, whole. Behind her, the little machine with the jumpy arm and the paper printout began to beep a little bit faster as Joy tried to wedge herself upright in the bed.

"Mum, it's not ......" started Mischa, but stopped herself.

"Baby??" stammered Joy, breathing as deeply as she could without bursting her stitches. She was well aware that if she didn't get her heart rate back down quickly that an alarm would go off, and the room would fill with people. Joy didn't want people. She wanted answers. "How far?" she asked, in between slowly sucking in lung full's of air.

"Four months, ish," replied Mischa, half smiling, half grimacing. She clearly knew what was coming.

"Four fucking months," squealed Joy. The little machine started beeping again. "And you never thought to mention it."

"I've tried. There was never a right time, and the longer I left it, the harder it got." she spluttered. "I literally found out the day that dad left. I had the test in my dressing gown pocket when you dropped Zach off."

Joy thought back to all the times she should have guessed, the tiredness, the sickness, the sitting out at tubing, she should have noticed. At any other time, she would have, but she'd been so wrapped up in herself, she'd missed every single sign. "But you had no problem telling Claudia?" she said.

"You were having an X-ray thingy, they wouldn't let me in with you because of the baby, and I was upset. She was passing. She made me tea. She's very kind," she said, dropping her head back down and laying her forehead against the bed.

"And who's the ....?" Joy stopped herself. "No, you know what, none of that matters."

Mischa's head lifted, and her eyebrows narrowed. "What no lecture? Isn't this the point where you tell me how you wanted so much better for me?"

Joy smiled at Mischa and sighed, "Have you ever, at any point, felt unwanted."

Mischa shook her head.

"If I were to tell you that I hoped for better, for you, then that would mean that what I had was bad. I don't and never have regretted you. You were the best decision I ever made." Wetting her lips, Joy rested her hand on Mischa's forearm. "You've had four fucking months, so I assume you've thought it through, but if it's what you want."

Mischa nodded, her acquiesce betrayed only by a single solitary tear rolling down her cheek and into her mouth. "But you gave up so much."

"And I didn't miss any of it," replied Joy "Because what I had was better, and you don't have to give up, you can still finish uni, you can still go to law school, you can do whatever you want because you are strong and smart."

"Only because you taught me to be," said Mischa, laying her damp cheek across the back of Joy's hand. "And I thought I was going to lose you. I thought I was going to have to do it all on my own."

"Nonsense," scoffed Joy. "I'm not going anywhere, and outside of me, you have dad, your grandparents, Carlee, Lauren, Meryl, Tabs, Bernie, Margot, you know Margot had Danni before law school, right? And look at her now. You have so many people who love you and who are going to love that baby just as much."

Lifting her head and wiping her eyes, Mischa stood and climbed up onto the bed, laying herself down curled up in the crook of her mother's arm.

Joy stared up at the ceiling. She had forgotten all about the mystery ambulance caller, and her mother, and Robin. She was going to be a grandma. For now, little else mattered.

Chapter 28

Joy awoke with the sun on her face and butterflies in her stomach. She was so excited that even the chipboard bran flakes that she'd been condemned to for breakfast hadn't dampened her mood.

Firstly, and most importantly, she was going to see her boys. Secondly, she was going to get her phone back, having been banned from using any electrical device while holed up in ICU. She would, at last, be able to message the girls, check-in with Mrs Mortimer, catch up with the news and find out who won Masterchef.

Mischa had arrived at a little past 6am and was now impatiently pacing the corridor outside, waiting for any sign of Dr Delia Sommers and the porters ready to take Joy down to the ward.

Slowly, a steady stream of people had popped in, fiddled with machinery, wrote down numbers and popped out again. She'd had her nasal tube, her drainage tubes and her pacing wire removed, her catheter was very gratefully uninstalled, and she had managed to hobble to the toilet and back without dropping dead. Eventually, all that was left was the heart monitor. Joy didn't mind that though, had grown so used to its constant bleeping that she hardly heard it anymore, and when she did, it comforted her somewhat, reassured her. She was still ticking.

It was already past 10am when Pip and his overtly cheerful smile appeared around the door frame. "I heard our resident celebrity needs a lift," he said, propping open the doors, as Mischa appeared behind him and jabbed him in the ribs.

"Celebrity?" said Joy, her face scrunching.

"Er, the whole hospital's been worried sick," he said, rubbing his side and checking that Mischa wasn't coming in for another shot. "I'm just glad to see you awake. Dr Sommers said she'll see you down there," he added, kicking off the bed brake and manoeuvring the big clunky frame towards the door.

As they approached the cardiology lounge three floors down.

Stopping outside so that Pip could prop the doors, Joy let out a deep breath, and as they opened, a cheer erupted from the other side, followed by applause and the sound of Kool and the Gang's Celebration being played through a mobile phone. Maryanne, Janette and Louisa, a student nurse, were stood just inside the entrance holding balloons and a big sign that read welcome home. Joy wasn't entirely sure that was the right message but valued the gesture, nonetheless.

Behind the nurse's station to the left, Justin, the healthcare assistant, stood brandishing more balloons and a teddy bear with Joy's name written in pink writing on a heart at its chest, while the length of the corridor, heads popped out of side rooms and bays as her colleagues took a second out of their duties to give her a smile and a wave.

Maryanne dropped her balloons to the floor and rushed to Joy, taking her hand and kissing her firmly on the fingers. "What time do you call this? Your shift started six days ago" she said, wiping away loose tears.

"According to my notes, I was admitted at 9.15pm on the Saturday, so I was actually here nine hours early," she replied, clasping Maryanne's hand. "See, efficiency, I didn't even need to ring in sick."

"Let's get you settled in," laughed Maryanne as Pip circled the trolley and backed it into the bay.

"Do I not get my own room," asked Joy, disappointed to not be wheeled towards one of the little rooms that were dotted along the corridor. They had their own bathroom, a TV and a view over the fields at the rear of the hospital, as opposed to the bays, which mainly overlooked the carpark and the dual carriageway on the other side.

Maryanne shot Mischa a look. "This, technically, *is* your own room," she said, gesturing into the bay.

Joy's mouth dropped open as she craned her neck around to see behind her.

The entire four-bed bay had been emptied out of all but one bedspace. The rest was filled, floor to ceiling with cards and balloons, stunning bouquets, teddy bears and banners and a multitude of brightly wrapped boxes.

"What's all this?" she asked as she was parked up at the empty space by the door. "Is this *all* from hospital staff?"

Maryanne largely ignored her as she fussed around the bed, reconnecting Joy to the various monitors and pratting about with the overhead light and the call button, which she draped over the rail closest to Joy's left hand.

"Right, I'm going to get a brew, and then we'll get the step-down forms done, ok." she smiled.

Before Joy could say that it certainly wasn't Ok, and to demand an explanation, Maryanne had turned on her heels and ran out of the door at a pace that would put Usain Bolt to shame.

Joy turned to Mischa, who was stood at the other end of the bed, her teeth clamped firmly on her bottom lip, her eyes staring guiltily at the floor. "Are we not going to address the elephant in the room," said Joy, pointing earnestly to a five-foot stuffed pachyderm in the corner that had its plushy trunk stuck inside a disposable urinal with the words get well soon written on it in sharpie.

"Surprise," cried Mischa, throwing her arms in the air before dropping them awkwardly back to her side and turning her gaze towards her mum.

"Is someone going to tell me what's going on?" said Joy, her confused grin slowly breaking out into nervous laughter as she continued to glance over the display. There were at least three life-size teddy bears. One was wearing a fedora, another had a harry potter cloak and a wand, while the third was sporting a bright pink mankini and sunglasses. Behind the door, there was a pile of confectionary that almost reached the ceiling. And behind that, there was another, just as tall.

There were remote control vehicles, a train set, several stacks of DVD's and at least one games console. Joy couldn't help but wonder that *if* it had all come from hospital staff, why they hadn't just had a whip-round like they did when Miriam from Oncology broke her hip falling off the bar in Zante for her 60th Birthday.

"Well. Um." Mischa paused and thought for a moment. "Um, when you. Before, when you. Um," spluttered Mischa. She had gone as pink as a shepherd's delight sunset and was fiddling so rigorously with her thumbs that she had started to wear off the nail polish.

"Just spit it out. It can't be that bad," said Joy, who by now was getting tired, achy and the overwhelming eagerness to see her sons was leaving her tetchy.

Mischa grabbed a chair from the back wall and pulled it up next to the bed. "Ok," she said, dipping her head and rubbing the bridge of her nose with outstretched fingers. "How much do you remember of the heart attack, or, what you were doing before it."

Joy blushed, her face dropping into a stone-cold grimace, her eyes scouring the room for the best answer. Of course, *she* remembered what she was doing. But she had hoped that under the circumstances, anyone else who knew might just let it drop and not mention it. "I was making one of those stupid video's you talked me into," she sighed.

Mischa continued to rub at her nose and nodded. "Um, yeah . . . . . You went viral."

"I have a virus?" said Joy, laughing, "Is that it?"

"No, mum," she replied, "on the internet, the video, *your* video, you got quite a few views. Lots of fucking views, actually. Millions. It's called going viral."

"On the internet?"

Mischa nodded.

"Because I had a heart attack?" she asked.

"Because you nearly died, live on Facebook." replied Mischa. She was staring Joy in the face now as if Joy should know what on earth she was trying to explain.

"Live," stammered Joy. Still confused.

"Yes, live, in real-time. By the time the ambulance broke the door down, there were hundreds of people watching," said Mischa, keeping one eye on her mum and the other on that little blasted machine behind her that was, once again, starting to beep that little bit faster. "Then people started sharing the video, they put it on YouTube, who kept trying to take it down, but the more they tried to take it down the more interest it got, and so people kept putting it back up, and then twitter picked it up too, and Instagram and . . . ."

"A video?" asked Joy, frantically trying to remember the moment immediately before. Sure, she remembered the short skirt, the heaving bosom, and the little blinking camera light. But everything else was a sweaty blur.

Mischa nodded. "Then you made the local news, which was picked up by the nationals."

Joy, who up until five minutes ago had been thankful to be alive and well and looking forward to seeing her family, suddenly felt very, very nauseous. "Wait, you said that videos couldn't be shared outside of a group, so how the fuck did it end up on YouTube."

"You didn't broadcast it in a group, though, mum. You must have hit the wrong button. You went live on your own profile, publicly."

Joy's face froze as a little tingle worked its way up her spine and into her brain. "Not, in a group?"

Mischa shook her head, her face was stone cold, but there was a smile in her eyes. If Joy didn't know her better, she thought, that she might be trying not to laugh.

"For all the world to see, *and share*?" asked Joy, her voice a veritable squeak. "Fuck," she said.

"No, mum, you don't understand, this is good. If you'd have gone live in a group where no one knew you, no one would have known where to send the ambulance. But everyone you know got a notification to say that you were live, which meant that an ambulance was there in minutes. *I* was there in minutes. Carlee and Tabs were there in minutes. If you hadn't fucked up, you'd have probably died."

"I'm starting to wish I had," said Joy gulping hard. She didn't have that many Facebook friends. Old friends from school, most of the hospital staff, obviously. Families from the estate, some of Mischa's friends from college, those who she'd met on holidays over the years, her family, Robin's family, random people she'd met on nights out, Zachary's ASD outreach team, her actual friends of course. Joy's blood ran cold as she suddenly realised just how big a net she dumped herself into

"You have your own fan club, mum," said Mischa, the smile still trying to break free, "Your left breast has its own Twitter account."

"Wait, what?" asked Joy, her brain now planning how quickly she could be packed up and ready to move to some hot and sunny climes where there was no internet connection. "I need to see this video."

"I'm not sure that's a good idea," replied Mischa. Glancing over to the little machine behind Joy that was still ramping up its beeps and was in danger of triggering the alarm.

"It can't be any worse than what I'm imagining," said Joy. And, indeed, that alone was bad enough. She could picture herself flailing about. She felt sick, her heart was beginning to pulse in her ears, she was breathing too fast, and her head was fuzzy. She felt like she was about to pass out.

She slowed her breathing, clinging onto the bed frame and counting the monitor beeps as they slowed as the panic attack passed.

"Right," she said, keeping her voice low and her breath slow, "you find me that video right now, else you're going to have to trudge me back up into ICU because I think my heart is going to fucking implode."

Misha paused, it looked like she was about to argue the toss but instead jumped from her chair and ran from the room, reappearing thirty seconds later with one of the wards dilapidated old tablets, and after a moment of flicking through the icons, she thrust it at Joy.

Joys eyes scanned the screen, coming to a rest on the title of the video "Lonely lady has heart attack while stripping (NSFW)"

"I was NOT stripping," tsked Joy, gulping as she started the tablet.

The video began. Joy's living room flashed up on the screen, and a little twinge of familiarity in her belly left her pining for home. After a second, she appeared and sat down, smiling awkwardly at the camera. The angle had been perfect for teasing up her skirt, and she was leaning forward, just enough to enhance her cleavage and cover her waist with her arms, squeezing her tits together in the process. "To be fair, I look great." She said to Mischa.

"Fantastic," she nodded back. "Now, watch," she said, pointing towards the screen.

Joy watched, narrow eyed. At first feeling a little chuffed with herself, delighted with how confident she looked as she started to speak. But her face soon changed, and her mouth fell open in horror as she watched herself stand up. First clawing at her shoulder, she ripped open her uniform as she lurched around in front of the camera, her face contorted in panic.

"I'm naked, Misch," she said, her voice quiet against her hard puffs of breaths and the rapidly quickening beeps that came from behind her.

Mischa didn't answer. She wasn't watching. She had her eyes closed and her mouth sucked in.

Joy tried to close her eyes too, but she couldn't. It was the closest she could imagine to an out of body experience, like watching herself driving towards a wall, and there was nothing she could do about it. Instead, she watched on in dismay as the staggering stopped, and she collapsed in loud gasping breaths over the chair in the middle of the room, her knicker-less undercarriage propped up in the air and pointing in the direction of the camera in all its glory.

Feeling the bile rise up her throat, Joy tried to swallow but couldn't. Her entire body was frozen rigid. Her eyes fixed on the screen as the feed jumped ahead to two paramedics bursting into the living room. Joy recognised him as the EMT who'd taken her from the Albion when she hurt her leg. He ran into the room, crouching at her side, draping a blanket over her lower half and knocking the laptop off its tilt. From the doorway, several others appeared. It was hard to tell who. It was all legs and knees. There was crying, shouting, nothing decipherable. Just noise. Eventually, one of the legs stepped forward and closed the laptop. And the video stopped.

Behind her, the beeping reached fever pitch.

"My fanny," whimpered Joy.

"Muum, you need to calm down."

"Calm down," she gasped, "my vagina is on the fucking internet."

"It's been blurred out in a lot of the videos," replied Mischa.

Joy wasn't really listening. Joy was processing. "Why is my vagina on the internet? Why didn't I drop to the floor? If I'd just dropped to the floor, I'd have been out of shot." she muttered.

"I don't think cinematography was a priority while you were clinging to the chair gasping for breath, mother. Why we're you going commando in the first place is probably a better question."

"I wanted to feel sexy," said Joy,

"And how sexy do you feel now?" asked Mischa.

Joy felt her heart sink as she glanced down at the hospital issue support stockings and the large rectangular dressing plastered across her chest. She didn't answer, and instead turned her attention back to the tablet.

"Wait, what are you doing" asked Mischa.

Joy was scrolling eagerly on the screen, "Reading the comments," she replied.

"Nooo," screamed Mischa, plucking the tablet from Joy's grip. "Never read the comments, ever. People can be cruel. But, if you want to feel better about showing your minge to the world, have a read of some of the cards in here. There's some lovely messages. People have taken you to heart. And the media have gone mad for you. The hospital has had to take on communication staff just to field all the calls."

"The media." Joy squealed, "like TV?"

Mischa nodded. "They've offered the hospital thousands for an exclusive hospital bed interview, with your clothes on, of course."

Joy felt the sweat dripping down the back of her neck.

"Maryanne said no," added Mischa quickly, clearly spotting Joy's distress. "And then there's the go fund me."

"What, is a go-fuck-me?" asked Joy, trying desperately to calm her breathing, but the hits just kept coming, and it was a lot to take in.

"FUND, mother, a Go FUND me. It's like online donations," said Mischa. She was laughing now.

Joy wasn't but watching her daughter giggle did more to calm her heart rate than all the breathing in the world.

"People have donated money *to my vagina*?" stammered Joy, trying to take it all in.

"They've donated to you."

"Why?" Joy couldn't for the life of her understand why people would give money to complete stranger just because she'd had the misfortune to do an accidental full monty while almost dying.

"Because there are still good people in the world?" replied Mischa.

Joy bit her lip. "How much?" she asked.

Mischa played around with the tablet for a moment and then held the screen up in front of Joy's face.

The machine began to beep again.

"Two hundred and ninety-eight grand," screamed Joy, pushing herself back into the plush pillow and running her hands over her face.

"That Miller guy on Channel Four is trying to get you over three hundred before the weekend."

"Three hundred grand for falling over and flashing my fanny." She laughed. She wasn't sure why. She didn't find it funny, it was absurd, preposterous, and she couldn't possibly accept it.

"Will you forget about your fanny," spat Mischa.

"Kind of hard not to when it's there in fucking widescreen." she spat in return, "Can I give it back, if I don't want it?"

"This isn't someone handing over thousands of pounds, mum," she said, shaking her head. "This is everyday people giving a couple of quid each. And one guy in Florida who donated thirty five grand because you remind him of his late wife.

"*Florida?*" gulped Joy.

"All over the world, mum, and they've donated because within an hour of your video being shared, people found out who you were. That you've had a tough time, that you have a family and a vulnerable child who you're devoted to 24 hours a day, that you're a real nurse who's barely had a day off in 20 years, that you're lonely."

"And who's told them all of that?"

"Ah," replied Mischa, her eyes quickly dropping back to her thumbs. "Margot has appointed herself your one-woman PR guru."

Joy burst out laughing so hard that she had to steady herself against the bed frame to stop herself from moving.

"It's all true though, mum. Margot just said it out loud. Plus, there were ex-patients sharing stories about how you single-handed nursed them through their own heart attacks. That Shelly from the food bank told everyone about how you'd come in every week in disguise, and hospital staff sharing pictures of you cradling their new-born babies and joining in charity car washes dressed as Mr Blobby."

Joy nearly choked on her own tongue. She had managed to flash her most intimate parts to the world. She'd almost died and was looking at a long recovery. But that all paled into comparison to that bloody costume.

"People think you deserve support, mum, to recover and not have the stress of being off work," continued Mischa, "and for most, all they can give is money."

Joy's face softened. One thought rang in her head above all else. "I'm not gonna lose the house," she said.

"And you never would have if you had just told me how bad it was."

"There was never a right time," replied Joy, mimicking her daughter's excuses, "I guess we both could have been a little bit more open," she said, patting Mischa in the stomach.

"Why don't you take a look out of there?" said Mischa, nodding towards the wide floor to ceiling window and the currently closed curtains.

Joy eased herself out of bed, wincing as she placed her bare feet onto the cold lino floor. She had watched people do this thousands of times, to take those first few steps after open-heart surgery. Told them how strong they were, how brave they were, how they could do it. If nothing more, this was vastly going to improve her bedside manner.

Shuffling slowly, careful not to strain the stitches in her leg from where they'd taken a vein, she inched towards the curtains, with Mischa trailing behind with the drip stand and monitor trolley.

Pulling one of the long green curtains open, the room flooded with bright afternoon sun, and Joy squinted into the light. But before her eyes had quite adjusted, applause rose from below.

Holding her hand up above her eyes, she was met with a small sea of faces staring up at her from the carpark below. Scanning the rabble, she could pick out familiar faces from the hospital stood amongst strangers, adults, children, pensioners. Some were holding signs with her name on it, others had placards that said get well soon, at least one was holding a homemade banner with Joy's photo on it and a row of hearts, and she could count at least two TV crews.

"They've been there all morning, waiting for you," said Mischa, laying a hand on her mother's shoulder. "The TV vans have been waiting for days and the press have tried to make fake ID's to get in and take pictures of you in ICU. But the night you were brought in, a few of the porters lit candles by the main entrance. Lots of people came, and some stayed, they weren't sure if you were ......" her voice trailed off.

Biting down hard on her lip, Joy felt tears prick at her eyes, and she quickly slammed them shut before any had chance to escape. She made a heart with her hands and held it up to the window as more applause rang up from below.

She was about to give a little wave when she heard a noise from out in the corridor. A high pitch grumming followed by a squeal and a bang.

"Zach," she gasped, opening her eyes and turning around to face the door. He hated hospitals. He hated the lights, and the smell and the noise and the lack of things he was allowed to play with, or touch and feel and take apart. To Zachary, a hospital was a place of *No*. No touching, no messing, no climbing. For Joy, places of *No*, were prime meltdown territory. She was amazed that he'd made it up the stairs.

"Mum." said Mischa, her voice tentative.

"Shhhh," replied Joy, watching the door anxiously until it creaked open, and Zachary's head poked around it, followed by Owen, a reluctant Elliot and her mother. For a second, she watched, waiting to see Robin follow them in. But the doorway behind them remained empty until the bay door swung shut with a whoosh. "Spuderoo!" she cried, pushing her disappointment aside and opening her arms as wide as she could.

"Mum," said Mischa, nudging her impatiently in the arm.

But Joy ignored her, watching with glee as Zachary zigzagged erratically across the room, distracted at first by the flowers and the balloons and the stuffed animals and the beeping machines. Until his head turned, and he spotted Joy. His face lit up like a new bulb as he thrust himself at her legs. Joy bent over, stroking his head. She kissed him on the forehead and held him as close to her as she physically could. She could smell the toast on his breath and scent of toothpaste in his ears from where Verity had managed to get it everywhere other than his mouth. Zachary knew how to use a toothbrush, and was well able to brush his own teeth at 3am when he didn't want to go back to bed, yet when it was actually needed, it clearly wasn't as much fun without having to first chase him around the house, jabbing at him sporadically with a fully loaded soft-bristle dinosaur.

Tears fell softly over Joy face as she felt Owen and Elliot's arms sneak around Zachary and embrace her. Joy no longer cared about tears, or her stitches. She felt like her heart was about to burst.

Behind her, from outside, another round of applause erupted, at which point Joy bolted straight upright and turned to Mischa. "There's no back in this gown, is there?" she asked.

Mischa shook her head, laughing out loud as Joy hobbled sideways and back behind the curtain.

Chapter 29

Joy finally made it home seventeen days after she originally left. She might have been able to shave two days off that if she hadn't insisted on Pip wheeling her around the hospital, giving out bunches of flowers and boxes of chocolate that, even as she left, were still arriving on a daily basis.

She had let Zachary pick whichever toys he wanted, and the rest had been donated to the children's ward, except the five-foot elephant which Joy had grown quite fond of, and which now sat proudly on the spare side of her bed.

As Meryl had manoeuvred the car into the street, Joy's tummy turned, and her toes tingled as neighbours came out of their homes and waved her a welcome home.

She had never been one for public displays. As a child, she had once been named carnival queen after her mother had bribed Derek Cooper, one of the parish officials, after he was found with his trousers down in the back room of the local butcher shop while Verity was out buying pork chops. Dressed in her mother's wedding dress, Joy had spent the entire carnival procession trying desperately not to fall off the back of the rickety old, tinsel covered cart that was being pulled by a lame horse that probably should have been put out of its misery many years earlier, instead of spending its golden years giving pony rides around the school carpark every other Thursday. The procession had gone as well as could be expected, but as she had been helped off the cart, she had slipped and landed headfirst in a huge pile of geriatric horse shit and had had to be hosed down outside of the school before she could accept her crown, sopping wet and stinking of dung.

Thankfully, there were no horses on the estate, and after giving several awkward hugs to neighbours, she had finally made it into the house and to the safety of the sofa.

Letting out a loud aching groan, she vowed not to get up for at least another two weeks, as Zachary clambered up next to her and buried himself in her t-shirt until he was tucked up awkwardly under her left armpit.

But if she had been expecting calm, she had been sorely mistaken. Within five minutes of sitting down, there was a knock at the door. More flowers. And thus followed a slow but steady conveyor belt of people passing in and out. Not that there was any lack of people to answer the door. Meryl had threatened never to leave her alone again, and Carlee had turned up so soon after arriving home that Joy was relatively sure that she was waiting around the corner for her to get there. No sooner was she inside, Joy watched through the kitchen door as she started to unload a large holdall full of Tupperware into the freezer.

"Did you do anything other than cook while I was in hospital?" asked Joy as Carlee rearranged a plethora of neatly labelled tubs into alphabetical and chronological order.

"Had to do something in between dealing with your fan club," she replied, pulling out a pile of letters from the bottom of the bag and handing them to Joy.

"What, people still send letters," scoffed Joy, flicking through the pile, "I can't remember the last time I got mail that didn't come in a brown envelope."

"Well, enjoy, because I've another two bin bags full in the car," said Carlee swanning back out to the kitchen.

Joy gulped. Opening the top envelope, she found a handwritten note on pink paper telling her to stay strong. In the second, another letter, this one from a lady called Elsbeth who had been following Joy's story and who had finally been spurred to speak to her doctor about the chest pains that she thought was indigestion. Turns out that Elspeth was a matter of weeks away from her own coronary crisis but was being booked in for angioplasty as a matter of urgency. Attached was a picture of Elsbeth with two small children and a cheque for ten pounds, which Joy immediately tore up before dropping the pile back onto the table.

"And you should see what's waiting for you in your inbox," said Carlee, swooshing back in and handing Joy a steaming hot cup of tea. "So many dick-pics. At this point, you could probably print them off and paper the entire house with them."

Joy grimaced at the thought of a wall chock full of random penises. Or cock full, as the case may be. "Well, I suppose I shouldn't be surprised. I did unintentionally send a collective nude to the world."

Carlee cackled as she disappeared back into the kitchen, only to reappear seconds later with a sandwich. Egg and lettuce, no mayo, no butter, half of which Zachary immediately ran off with, only to leave it on the floor by the door untouched when he figured out it had salad on it. It took less than a second before Pelé had it away under the side table.

Another knock at the door brought more flowers, followed by a flying visit from Margot who hugged her so tightly that Joy thought she might have cracked a rib, and who promised a proper visit at the weekend as she was stuck in Court with a pig of a Jury and was supposed to have only nipped out for a smoke break. As she was leaving, Tabitha and Lynne took her place, along with Bernie, who was bunking off work. Together they helped Joy out into the garden, where they sat and drank sweet iced tea in the last of the afternoon sun. Joy was amazed to see that the grass had been cut, the shrubs had been trimmed back, and the shed door had been fixed. Either

Robin had been busy while she was gone, or her mother had whipped the boys into doing it over the promise of financial compensation and a Big Mac meal.

As the day wore on, Joy fended off a small stream of well-wishers and nosey neighbours, local shop owners and even the local vicar who Joy hadn't seen face to face since the day she got married.

The only face that hadn't turned up that day was Robin's. She could well understand an urgent desire to be as far away from her mother as possible, but she had at least thought he might have faked concern, even if only in front of the kids.

"Has your dad gone back to Reuben's?" she asked Owen as she spotted him snaffling chocolates from a hamper on the kitchen table.

"Um, yeah. He said he didn't want to get in the way," he replied, trying to hide his cache of caramel creams behind his back.

Joy told him to take the box, and he scampered back upstairs to his brother and the brand-new X-box that had arrived at the hospital attached to a nameless note.

Slowly, the slew of people ebbed away as the night drew in, and with Mischa in the bath and Zachary in bed, for the first time that day, Joy found herself alone.

Nearly.

Unable to face another cup of tea, Joy was just about to hit the sack when the front door swung open, and her mother appeared in the hall, carrying a suitcase in one hand and a large Yucca in the other.

Joy rolled her eyes. "I thought you were going home."

"And leave you to fend all on your own." She replied, rearranging the pictures on the hall shelf and positioning the spikey plant smack in the middle.

"I'm not on my own," said Joy flatly. Making a mental note to 'accidentally' leave the plant out in the sun the minute Verity left the house.

"Mischa needs to rest. She shouldn't be running around after you in her condition," she said, pushing past Joy, through the kitchen and into the living room.

Joy followed her. "She told you then?"

"Not at all, I guessed. Grandmothers know these things."

Joy bit her tongue. She was tired. She wasn't in the mood for point scoring with a woman who was known to weight the dice.

"Doesn't dad need you?" she asked. She knew very well that he didn't. Her father would be sat in his pants, beer in hand, watching the darts and farting the theme tune to Columbo by now, happy as a pig in muck and twice as smelly.

Verity knew as much too, so she didn't answer, presumably choosing not to think about it.

"Mum?" asked Joy.

Verity immediately stopped what she was doing and turned to face her daughter. "No," she replied.

"No, what?" asked Joy.

"No, to what it is you're about to ask me, sweetheart," she said, turning away and returning her attention back to fluffing pillows and smoothing down the curtains.

Joy's brow furrowed. "And what was I going to ask you?"

"No," she said again, bluntly. The tone didn't suit her. "We didn't talk about you. I mean, we did, but only to acknowledge that you weren't going to die. But no, we didn't talk about you and him. We didn't really talk outside of the kids."

Joy nodded. She didn't know what answer she was looking for. That he had told her he still loves her. That he was worried about her. That he missed her. That he was glad that she didn't actually die. The slightest little empathetic reaction that might just hint that there was still a care there. A hope, perhaps.

"Mum," said Joy.

She knew her mother was lying. Verity was a werriter, constantly muttering out loud about anything or anyone that bothered her. Only Yesterday, she had jabbered on for almost half an hour about someone putting the sugar bowl back on the wrong shelf and the decibel level of the washing machine. She loved the sound of her own voice, even more so when she was using it to make someone else feel inferior. Her lack of rambling monologue about the dire state of their marriage was a dead giveaway.

"Yes sweetheart?" replied Verity, her voice returning to its usual upbeat and condescending demeanour.

Joy simply shook her head and smiled. "Night, mum."

Chapter 30

Mum, mum, mum," squealed Mischa, jumping up and down and waving a piece of paper in Joy's face.

Joy had barely stepped through the door.

"Mum, you're not going to believe it," she said, following Joy up the hallway, vying for her attention against Pelé, who was equally excited to see her.

"Believe what, sweetheart?" asked Verity, appearing in the hallway behind them and slamming the door shut.

"Do not tell that woman anything," snapped Joy, slatting her bag down on the countertop and reaching for the kettle.

"They recognised me off the news?" protested Verity, nudging Joy out of the way.

Joy had just come out of a painful and slightly degrading physiotherapy appointment to find Verity giving her life story to the waiting room.

"*Sure* they did mother. I'm surprised you don't wear a fucking badge," she snapped, reaching over her and pulling a cup from the cupboard.

"Muuum?" said Mischa, still trying to grab Joy's attention.

"They asked how you were," said Verity, she looked concerned. She wasn't.

"In which case you tell them I'm fine," seethed Joy. Verity opened her mouth to speak, but Joy continued, "you do not tell them how I once flashed my arse during a school performance of Hamlet. You do not tell them that I once shat myself at Alton Towers and had to drive home wearing a bin bag, and you do not tell them that I am desperate for a man."

Verity's top lip curled back.

"MUUUUM," screamed Mischa.

The two women stopped and turned to face Mischa, who shoved the piece of paper right under Joy's nose.

"Jackie Pressley wants *you* to go on Wake-Up Weekend this Saturday. She's sending train tickets and a chauffeur from the station. *And,*" she squealed, her voice rising with excitement, "We get audience tickets. There's a number look, right here at the bottom, you have to call it and confirm." she said, hopping excitedly from one foot to the other.

Joy snatched the letter from Mischa's grip.

She had thought that the furore might have calmed a little once she was out of hospital. Yet still it continued. Her video was not only still doing the rounds on social media, but she had also been remixed, edited, mashed up and memed, and with every new incarnation, came a new news report, a new flurry of letters and emails and a new splurge of cash into the Go-fund-me. She had now received correspondence from as far away as Australia and Canada. On Instagram, she was inundated by get well messages from z-list celebrities, all vying to exploit the #joy hashtag.

Strangers pointed at her in the shop. One guy had asked for a selfie in Wilko's, only to look disappointed when she snapped a picture of her face. She had even been forced to put in a police complaint when reporters from the local rag had jumped out from behind the bushes at Zachary's school, desperate for a quote. All they got was a quick *fuck off* and a threat to shove their cameras up their ethernet cables. It still made the papers, though.

"Maybe it'll all calm down if I do an official interview," she mused. "Maybe then they'll all realise that I'm just a boring nobody and not some modern-day Godiva."

Joy lifted the letter and scoured the page.

Dear Joy,

It is with much excitement that we have been able to secure an opening in our programming and would like to extend an invitation for you to join myself, Jacquie Pressley, on the Wake-Up Weekend Couch on Saturday 24th July for an informal chat, and, if you are agreeable, a makeover.

Please contact our producer on 0161 713458 to confirm your attendance, at which point we will provide you with first-

*class train tickets to Manchester, a driver to the studio, and up
to ten tickets for the show.*

    We cannot wait to meet you.

    Regards

    Jacquie,

Joy burst out laughing. She laughed long and hard until her jaw ached, and her scarred chest pulled tight.

"I think it sounds fun," said Verity, who Joy could see was clearly already imagining herself sat there with her on the show. Joy would rather have another heart attack.

"They want to give me a make-over," she giggled, holding onto her belly as she tried to suppress her guffaws and dampen her hilarity.

"What's wrong with that?" asked Mischa, her smile lolling to one side. "A free haircut, some free clothes."

"I've seen their 'make-overs', they basically cut off all their hair and shoehorn them into clothes that no-one in their right mind would wear to ASDA."

"So just go for the chat," said Verity, "it says you don't have to do the makeover. You did say you wanted to give some of the donations to the cardio unit. It could bolster the cause."

"If nothing more," added Mischa, "You could at least use it as an opportunity to ask men to stop sending you pictures of their willies."

Joy paused. She had a good point. She'd had to set up a new Facebook account because her original one went crazy. She was waking up each day to hundreds of notifications, dozens of new friends' requests and more nudity than she could ever imagine, no mean feat for someone who had spent 20 years as a nurse. So, she had wilfully given the password to Margot and had gone incognito."

"I'll ring in the morning," said Joy, still eyeballing the letter.

"Already done," came Margot's voice, and Joy turned to find her slinking downstairs holding her mobile phone out with train ticket confirmation showing on the screen. "I've rallied the troops. We are good to go."

"How long has she been here?" whispered Joy to Mischa.

"I knew you'd say no," replied Mischa, high fiving Margot as she reached the bottom step.

Joy's face hardened. "But I can't. It's my weekend with the boys. I can't just up and go off on a jolly around Manchester."

"Nope, it's all sorted," said Margot.

"You spoke to Robin," stammered Joy. She felt a little stab in her heart and a flutter in her belly.

"I messaged him on Facebook, pretending to be you," she grinned.

"What did he say?" asked Joy, trying her best to keep her smile flat.

"He said yes."

"Was that it?"

Margot nodded and handed Joy the phone. There it was just one word. No *how are you feeling?* Or *how are the boys?* Just yes.

"Mrs Peterson will you be joining us on Saturday," asked Margot, noting Joy's sudden silence.

"I most certainly will," replied Verity, despite Joy standing behind her dragging her finger pointedly across her neck.

"Ooh, it's gonna be a proper girl's day out. Watch out, Manchester," said Margot, snapping her phone back from Joy's grip and hot-footing it to the kitchen.

"It's not a girl's day out, and mum, you really you don't have to come," she said, turning to Verity in a vain attempt at damage limitation. It was bad enough she was going. The thought of her sat telling Jacquie Pressley about the time she fell off the stage in her year three nativity and broke the donkey's arm filled her with the kind of dread that could only ever be brought out by her mother. A kind of impending doom that smelled like lavender and toilet duck.

"And miss my chance to meet Dr Nash," she said, laying her hand across her chest. "Not on your nelly.

Joy rolled her eyes. Dr Nash was Jacquie Pressley's faithful medical confidante on her weekday show, The Pressley Gang. A bachelor and all-round luvie of daytime TV, he was still clinging to the underside of fifty, tall, blue-eyed and dark haired with go-faster stripes of dappled grey above each ear. If you were a woman of a certain age, it was guaranteed that you had at least once thought of that face while the old man at home was getting busy downstairs.

Joy shuddered at the thought.

"He won't be there, mother. He only does the weekday shows."

"Not when there's a medical guest," said Mischa, eliciting a dirty glare and side-eye from her Joy.

"They had a guy on the other Saturday who got a chess piece stuck up his bum. Dr Nash was there then," scoffed Verity. "Then there was that woman with eight nipples, Dr Nash was there then too, and for that poor fella who had a big toe that looked like Elvis."

"Yes, mother, you're a big fan, I get it, but don't be getting your hopes up. I'm sure he's surrounded by post-menopausal groupies on a daily basis."

"There's one more thing," said Margot.

The look on her face told Joy that she was not going to like it. Margot, as a solicitor, had the best poker face Joy had ever seen, but right now, there was a giggle in her eyes and mischief on her lips. Like a toddler following a cat. "What?" she asked.

"They want you to bring your uniform," she replied, the chuckle breaking free of her grin as she burst into hysterics.

"Fuck," exclaimed Joy.

Chapter 31

Stood on the platform at Stoke station, Joy sipped tentatively at a coffee that was hotter than the surface of the sun and tasted like it had been brewing for at least a week in a yak's armpit.

She had been awake since four, pacing the bedroom, panicked.

Zachary had been dropped round to Mischa's with Robin the night before, and Owen and Elliot were camping. So, she had sat and watched Mischa sleep, curled up in Zachary's bed and snoring like a warthog. She was really starting to show. There was barely anything to her before, but now her breasts had grown, her hips had begun to widen, and the rounded belly poked out from over the top of her pyjamas bottoms as she slept. Joy couldn't help but wonder how she hadn't noticed it before. The sudden baggy jumpers in the heat of summer and the oversized floaty dresses. She really had just not been paying attention at all.

In the station, the sign above the platform flicked from 5.59 to 6am, and despite the early summer sunrise, it was still dark, owing to the thick black clouds that swirled ominously above them. They had enjoyed glorious sunshine for the best part of a month while Joy had been confined to the house, but the great British summertime had, of course, picked today to unleash two week's worth of rain, and it hammered loudly off the lightweight canopy above the tracks.

At 6.04, their train came into view around the bend. Wearily, bodies shrouded in pakamacs, stood from benches and shuffled to the edge of the platform, clutching hot cups and soggy brollies.

"Cheer up, you lot," called Margot, dressed head to toe in pink chiffon, as if she was headed for the executive box on ladies day. She spotted Meryl, curled up on one of the benches further down the platform, and storming over, whacked her over the head with her handbag before turning around, and as the train came to a stop and the doors whooshed open, she strode confidently through the one labelled first class.

Evidently, it wasn't *really* first-class, not like what you see in the movies where there are swivel chairs with champagne buckets attached and flunkies handing out moist towelettes and hot loo roll. To Joy, it looked nothing more than a normal carriage, eight bays of four seats around a table, with a few extra plug sockets and nicer looking headrests. It was, however, much closer to the bar, and they were advised upon boarding that they had the entire carriage to themselves and would be receiving a continental breakfast upon departure.

"Cold Croissant's in a bag," huffed Meryl, stomping down the carriage and into one of the bays at the end before flopping down and putting her feet up on the seats in front. She immediately pulled them down again as a steward arrived carrying a tray full of real porcelain cups and saucers in one hand and a pot of fresh coffee in the other.

Joy dropped her styrofoam cup of molten hot lava into the bin by the door and took a seat at the window opposite Mischa, who was wearing her Christmas morning face. The one that expected magic, even though she knew deep down that it would only ever end in burnt turkey and a fight over the last of the quality street. The magic today, however, was even shorter-lived, and as soon as refreshments had been poured and the train began to chug past 20mph, motion sickness kicked in, and Mischa had to make a dart for the loo before she sprayed choco puffs up the window.

Joy was trying to focus on what she might say once she got there, but the butterflies in her tummy gobbled up every thought she had. She was trying to come up with a witty one-liner as to why she was looking for sex on the internet without sounding sad and desperate. It wasn't really for her benefit though, she had twice bumped into Callum while at the hospital for a routine check-up. She had smiled and he had completely ignored her. He wouldn't even look at her. She couldn't really blame him though, because she'd done it again, hadn't she? She'd told him that she wasn't looking for anyone, and then got caught out in the worst way possible. She knew how it must have looked, but he wouldn't let her explain. Neither would Robin, not that she owed *him* anything, this was partly his fault.

Joy was about to get her phone out and start scrolling when a sound behind her caught her ear.

"Psss, tsk"

Clambering onto her knees and peering over her seat, she found Margot, pulling a silver straw from her bra and jabbing it into a freshly opened can of Pornstar Martini.

"It's six in the morning," she hissed.

Margot looked up, clamped the straw between her bright pink lips and took a big sip. "Girl's day out invokes holiday rules, though," she grinned, the straw still gripped in her teeth.

"We're going to Manchester, not Magaluf."

"We should do that too," replied Margot, her eyes widening. "Can't remember the last time we went away all together."

"Korfu. Tabitha and Lynnes hen week," said Joy, bluntly.

"That was fucking years ago," replied Margot, taking another big sip.

"Yeah, and I still can't drink rum," said Joy, fake retching. She hadn't been able to stomach the stuff following a night that none of them could remember. But if she closed her eyes and thought of the sea, she could still taste it.

"You *can* drink cocktails, though," said Margot, reaching into a holdall under the seat and pulling out a can. She waggled it under Joy's nose.

"I can, but I'm not sure I should," replied Joy, reaching over the seat and tentatively taking the Margharita from Margot's outstretched hand.

"Hope you've brought enough for all of us," called Meryl who was now kneeling up on her seat to get a better view of what they were whispering about.

Margot picked up the holdall and dumped it down in the middle of the aisle. Joy opened the top flap to find it was full to bursting with little silver cans of ready-mixed cocktails.

"Help yourself ladies," grinned Margot, sitting back and clamping the straw back between her teeth as she drained the rest of her can in one gulp.

One by one, they each filled their handbags with a poison of choice.

Joy took four more cans of Margharita, stashing them away under the uniform that was folded neatly in her travel bag. She had spent the entire day before trying to decide what to wear, she had no problem 'bringing' the uniform, but there wasn't a chance in hell that she was going to wear it. Instead, she had tried on every single item of clothing she owned before deciding on a plain grey pantsuit she'd found in a charity shop for a colleague christening and a silver lace blouse that Mischa had given her for her birthday.

"Are you having one, mother?" called Meryl to Verity, who was hanging half out of the toilet, rubbing Mischa's back.

"No!" cried Joy. "I'm not babysitting my drunk mother."

"Oh, don't be a party pooper," said Meryl. "We'll babysit your drunk mother. What you having, mother?"

"Something sweet," replied Verity,

Margot reached into the bag and pulled out two cans of Pina Colada and threw them to Meryl, who handed them to Verity.

"To Joy" said Meryl, scooching into the seat next to Joy on her return, and holding up her can,

"To Joy" came a chorus from around her. Reluctantly, Joy gave in and cracked open a Margharita, and after tapping it against everyone else's, downed it in three big gulps.

As the train pulled into Piccadilly less than an hour later, the Lane party was full of punch and at peak giggle, apart from Mischa, who was just grateful to be back on firm ground and upright.

Gripping Joy's hand, Margot hauled her wrist towards the main entrance and a small group of men holding official-looking signs.

She made a beeline for the one in the middle, a young olive-skinned male whose shirt was untucked and who looked like he had borrowed the driver's hat from his dad.

"Excuse me, are you looking for Joy" she asked.

"Not today," he said in a thick Mediterranean accent, without so much as turning his head to look at her.

Margot rolled her eyes, "No, the sign dipstick, you're here to pick up Joy?"

The man dropped his eyes to the big board in his hands and giggled. It said Joy in big black letters written in thick marker.

"Sorry, I thought you were one of those types who hang around giving out pamphlets," he replied.

"In this dress?" she spat, yanking Joy along behind her as the driver led them out into a very wet Manchester and off towards the pick-up spaces.

Pulling a set of keys from his pocket, he clicked the key fob, and the lights flashed on the back end of a pure white stretch Hummer that was spread across three spaces, sending the group into a spasm of giggles and squeals the likes of which Joy hadn't heard since the stripper came out at her hen party, or that time on an 18-30's holiday to Rhodes, when the rep fell off the back of the booze cruise.

Opening the side door, the driver held out his hands and gestured for them to enter, after which ensued what can only be described as a scrum, as they each vied to get through the tiny opening first.

"Client first, please ladies," said the driver sternly, and reluctantly the sea of floral lace and tulle parted, and Joy slinked forward and into the car, before taking a seat right at the back on the long leather couch, from where she watched as everyone else resumed their rumble and slowly plopped through the door one at a time.

Once everyone was in and seated, a screen at the front wound slowly down, and the driver, who announced proudly that his name was Marco, invited them to help themselves to refreshments, and the left-hand wall began to open to reveal a fully stocked minibar which resulted in more whoops and giggles.

As the car pulled out from the station, another scuffle broke out as Carlee and Tabitha both reached for the huge bottle of Champagne nestled elegantly into an ice bucket at the centre of the display, both eager to pop the cork, while Meryl handed out crystal cut glasses and strawberries, and for the second time that morning, they raised a toast, this time to nearly dying, but not quite.

Joy lay back against the seat and watched rain land in big splodges on the window that spanned most of the limo's roof.

"Smile," squealed Margot, snapping a picture of Joy reclining against the rich leather, fizz in hand.

"What are you doing?" asked Joy, watching as Margot tapped fervently at the screen.

"Just on my way to Wake Up Weekend, make sure you catch me at 11," grinned Margot as she uploaded the picture.

Joy rolled her eyes. She was beginning to think that Margot was enjoying the attention more than she was letting on. In fact, she was sure of it, watching as Margot cackled as she replied to the comments that popped up thick and fast whilst sharing titbits about their morning. To be fair, she was far better at it than Joy was, who barely interacted with people she knew, let alone complete strangers.

Finally, they arrived at Media City, tumbling out of the Limo in one big ball of hairspray and handbags.

Stepping in through the vast glass façade of the studio, Joy felt a little tingle go up her spine. It could have been relief to get out of the rain, or nerves, or too much Margharita. It might, just maybe, have been a little ripple of excitement.

They had been stood for less than a minute when a young blonde came and ushered Joy through a large glass doorway as her entourage were escorted through another much larger door signposted audience. She didn't even get time to give Mischa a hug or to say goodbye to her friends. However, in hindsight, that was probably for the best as Margot would have undoubtedly pulled some more booze from somewhere, and she wasn't sure she could cope with another toast. She was already feeling a little lightheaded, considering it wasn't yet 9am.

Chapter 32

The young woman, who introduced herself as Cheryl and who had a thick cockney accent and a mild lisp, led Joy through a warren of harshly lit corridors.

Every now and then, a face would pop up on an oversized poster that Joy would recognise, and each time she'd get a flutter in her tummy until eventually, they stopped at a door with a big glittery sign at its middle saying *"Premiere guest."*

Joy's tummy did a full somersault and threatened to leap from her mouth.

Cheryl pulled the handle and pushed open the door as Joy stepped inside. Her tummy untwisted itself, and her heart sunk, just a little.

It looked little more than a hotel room, minus any windows or a bed, which was great because if she lay down, she probably wouldn't get up again.

Against the far wall sat a dressing table with a large mirror and a wonky-looking stool, while in the corner lay a small uncomfortable looking two-seater sofa with a cushion emblazoned with the Wake-up Weekend logo on one side and Jacquie Pressley's face on the other.

Cheryl had just ushered Joy inside when another head popped around the doorframe. She looked almost identical to Cheryl. The same makeup, the same perfectly coiffed and highlighted waves, the same sharp suit skirt and crisp blue blouse.

"Ah, Joy, this is Marie," said Cheryl urging the other girl inside. "She's your runner and will get you anything you need."

"I need the loo," said Joy," pointing at her trousers, "and then coffee."

"Second door on the left," said Cheryl, pointing down the hall.

"On her return, only the one girl remained, and Joy could not for the life of her, tell which one it was.

"Just wait here," she said, it was still Cheryl, "Wardrobe will be down soon."

"Wardrobe," asked Joy, her face creasing, "I thought I'd be wearing .... "

"Oh no," said Cheryl, "Everything is perfectly coordinated before the show. We have to make sure the guests don't clash with the set, or each other. Jacquie has picked out a lovely outfit personally."

"It's not a nurse's uniform, is it?" asked Joy, her top lip curling up.

Cheryl laughed but didn't deny it, which did nothing to ease Joy's worry.

"Where *is* Jacquie," she asked.

"Make-up, she'll pop by before the show, so you just relax, and have fun."

As Cheryl turned to leave, Marie reappeared carrying a large steel cafetiere on a silver tray and slid it expertly onto the dresser.

"There's a buzzer by the door there," she said, her strong Liverpudlian tongue taking some getting used to after Cheryl's southern patter. She was pointing to what looked like a doorbell on the wall next to the light switch. "Press that. You get me," she said, slipping out of the door and out of sight.

Joy sat down on the wonky stool, poured herself a coffee, and realised that she was completely alone for the first time in over a month. It was delightful. There was no one talking at her, no one shouting at her from the other room, no one talking about her under her breath, and no one, not a single person expecting her to do *something*.

Joy didn't like it. She felt uneasy and anxious as if she'd forgotten something.

Pulling her phone from her bag, she unlocked it and dialled Robin's number.

"Everything ok?" she asked cheerily as he answered on the second brrrring.

"Fine," he replied.

"Zachary Ok?" she asked.

"Fine."

"The boys?"

"Fine."

"Oh well, I'll just not bother coming back at all then, shall I," she snarked.

She heard him sigh on the other end of the line, "We're all absolutely fine, Joy. Own and Elliot have gone out again. We've just finished breakfast, and nothing is happening of any importance."

Joy bit her tongue. In the background, she could hear Zachary grumming and squealing as he ran from one end of the room to the other.

"He's got the zoomies Rob. Why's he got the zoomies. Is he upset? Did you give him the right breakfast?"

"He's excited," he replied, "I've promised him a game of Kerplunk."

Joy smiled, "He does love kerplunk, but you have to let him win Robin, or else he'll try to eat all the marbles."

Robin didn't answer.

"Will you be watching?" she asked.

"No. Um, I think it will be a bit confusing for Zach to see you on telly, after all the time it took us to convince him that paw patrol wasn't real."

"Of course," she said, closing her eyes and picturing his little face. "Well, give him a kiss from me anyway."

The line cut dead without an answer.

Holding the phone to her chest, she took a deep breath, opening her eyes to find Jacquie Pressley stood in the doorway.

"Oh, I'm so sorry," she said, dropping the phone onto the sofa next to her and jumping up, her hand held out rigid in front of her.

"Not at all," replied Jacquie, crossing the room and taking Joy in a warm and slightly over-familiar hug. Joy breathed in. She smelt like candyfloss and coconut and looked even more glamorous in real life than she looked on the telly. She wore her hair in tight braids, her signature summer style, tied up on the top of her head in a loose knot with a zigzag at the crown. She wore a mustard skirt with a loose-fitting black chiffon blouse tied at the front, and heels that came halfway up Joy's legs.

"Makeup's ready for you," she said.

"Can they make me look like you?" asked Joy, staring at Jacquie's perfect smokey eyes, outlined in subtle glitter.

"Sure, if you were a five-foot ten black woman," she replied.

Joy grimaced, "Sorry, no. I just meant as glam as you?"

Jacquie laughed and waved her apology away. "We'll be keeping it subtle for the interview, but then for the make-over, you can go as glamorous as you like."

Joy felt her tummy knot again, which must have been visible even from the outside as Jacquie put her arms around her shoulders and gave them a squeeze.

"You're going to be absolutely fine," she soothed, holding onto Joy's shoulders and dipping her knees so that they were eye to eye. "Just be yourself, have fun, and if you can, try to drop an accidental shitbomb during the interview."

"An accidental what, now?" spluttered Joy.

"Like an F-bomb or a C-bomb," said Jacquie, as if Joy should know what either of those were either, "But we can't go around saying cunt on lunchtime television, none of us would ever work again, but we are a show for real people, and real people say shit, or bollocks and the viewers really go for it. But try to stay below twat, anything more than that, and it'll bring in Ofcom, and no one wants that."

Joy nodded, half in agreement and half in confusion.

"Come on then," said Jacquie leading Joy out of the door, "Let's get you camera-ready."

Chapter 33

Stood stage left, and hidden from the audience behind a big glittery MDF panel, Joy felt like she was about to have another heart attack. Her hands were sweaty. Her chest was pounding. She was salivating like a hungry puppy and could barely remember how to say her own name. Glancing back at the hubbub of people running around backstage, she caught sight of herself in a prop mirror. She looked beautiful, probably better than she ever had. They had dressed her in a forest green midi dress with a black lustre belt that looked like it cost more than her car. They had teased her long hair into a jazzy parting and tied it up on the top half, better for the reveal later on, they assured her, but she liked it just fine. It made her look younger, fresher. Staring at her reflection, she looked like Mischa.

From out of nowhere, the show's music began to play on the monitor behind her. She heard the audience applause and a faint whoop from the lower stalls, which Joy convinced herself was Margot.

She listened as Jacquie and her co-presenter; Dr Nash addressed the crowd before taking their seats on a vast white sofa. They sat for a moment and chatted casually about their weeks, Dr Nash had been gardening, and Jacquie had been car shopping after her husband reversed hers into a wall.

And then she said it.

"Without further delay, let's give a warm Wake Up welcome to the nations favourite healthcare worker, the one and only Joy Lane."

There was applause, followed by a loud ringing in her ears. Slowly, the screen began to trundle open, revealing Joy to the room like some booby prize on a bad 90's gameshow. *And here's what you could have won, a 42-year-old divorced mother of four with a heart condition and adult acne.*

Glancing out into the audience, Joy's eyes blurred, dazzled by the overhead spotlighting as it turned to illuminate her. Over the loudspeakers, Chumbawumba's Tubthumping began to play, and Joy began to slowly descend the steps down to the stage, grateful that the wardrobe manager had eventually relented and agreed to let her wear flat sandals instead of heels, lest they inadvertently get a live re-enactment of her now-infamous video, although she suspected Jacquie would have absolutely loved that.

Following the instructions to a tee, Joy stopped halfway down and gave a little wave before making her way to the bottom and across the stage to the sofa, where Jacquie and Dr Nash were back on their feet, waiting with their arms outstretched. She hugged Jacquie before being guided to the centre of the enormous semi-circle sofa, where she sat, trying to see out into the assembled throng, which had erupted into wild applause.

From the corner of her eye, she spotted a blur of bright pink, halfway up the rows of seating and smack bang in the middle of the main section. As her eye adjusted to the lights, she could make out faces, Margot, Carlee, Tabitha and Lynne were on one row, right behind Meryl, Mischa, Lauren, Bernie and her mother, who by all accounts looked like she was half asleep, while still waving maniacally.

Joy flashed them all a smile and an excited lift of the shoulders until the music began to fade, and Jacquie crossed her arms on her lap and turned to face her.

"Joy, at last, thank you for joining us," she said, which elicited another ripple of applause.

Joy waited until it had died down, a grateful moment to untie her tongue and un-muddle her mouth. "Thank you for having me," she smiled.

"Now for anyone who's been living under a rock," continued Jacquie, turning directly to the camera, "Joy shot to stardom last month following a Facebook live video that went crazy viral. Unfortunately, we can't show the video for obvious reasons, this is a family show," she paused, and raised a brow,

"But you actually had a heart attack, while filming live, isn't that right." She said, turning back to Joy.

"Yes, Jacquie," Joy nodded.

"And you had no idea that you were so sick?"

"Well," said Joy, "if I had done, I might have thought about putting some underwear on."

The audience laughed, and Jacquie flashed her a well-done grin.

"And how are you now? You look fantastic, by the way. Doesn't she look fantastic, everyone?" She said, holding her hands out and pointing up and down Joy's outfit. "What's your secret?"

Joy breathed in so hard she thought she might pass out.

The audience cheered.

"Well, Jacquie, they've got me on this healthy diet, and I'm just not allowed to eat shite anymore," she stopped and put her hands over her mouth as the audience laughed, "Oops, sorry."

"Well, it's good to hear that they're looking after you," replied Jacquie with a faint but obvious nod.

"Tell that to my tastebuds," replied Joy.

The audience giggled and Joy's heartbeat began to slow. She was actually starting to enjoy this.

"Now, Joy, I understand that at the time, you were making a dating video, is that right?" asked Jacquie.

Joy glanced around. She felt every single pair of eyes in the room staring at her. It suddenly dawned on her that many of the people sitting in that room, that vast room that was absolutely full of people, would have seen her naked. It was like that dream, the one where you're at work and then you realise that you've got no clothes on. She suddenly felt incredibly exposed. She smiled at Jacquie and then turned to Dr Nash, who was smiling back but not looking at her. He was staring at the camera.

She hadn't been introduced to him beforehand as he was running late, but as she scanned his face, something seemed off. She couldn't put her finger on what it was. He looked just like he did on the TV, tall, tanned, distinguished, well dressed, his eyes looked bluer, and his jaw was less muscular, but something was definitely amiss. She turned back to Jacquie.

"That's right," said Joy confidently, "It was a matchmaking video."

"And how's that going, now?" asked Jacquie.

"Well, I'm getting lots of attention, that's for sure. My inbox is full of well-wishes, and, um, pictures. Men sure do like sending pictures."

"And have any of those piqued your interest." asked Jacquie, leaning forward and raising just one brow, a gesture that Joy was sure was more for the camera than for her.

"I'm not sure," replied Joy, "I mean, they're not really sending me pictures of their faces."

"Oh, so it's," said Jacquie, pointing down to her belt before sitting back against the sofa aghast, her hand clutching her necklace. It was all for the show, of course. Joy had little doubt that Jacquie Pressley had been the recipient of her fair share of dick pics over the years.

Joy nodded, her gaze shifting back to Dr Nash, who was comically adjusting his belt to the delight of the audience. She still couldn't place what was wrong with his face.

"That must be quite difficult to cope with," continued Jacquie.

"Some of them are incredibly hard . . . . " Joy paused and gave a sly smile to the camera ". . . . to look at, yes." The audience erupted into laughter.

"So, tell us a little bit about Joy before the heart attack. What led you to that moment. To making that video?" asked Jacquie. She had adopted a serious face and had crossed her arms across her knees as she leaned forward.

The lights shifted, the cameras turned to face her, and the audience hushed to the point that you could hear mouse fart, but as she was about to speak, a loud retching noise came from the crowd, followed by another, and another. and then eventually, a loud splat.

Joy's eyes knew exactly where to look, and so watched on in horror as her mother unloaded a belly full of curdled Pina Colada and flaky pastry all over her own feet. Twice.

"Oooh, sounds like someone has been in the staff canteen," laughed Jacquie as the retching continued, and Joy watched as three ushers filed up the stairs towards her mum, and the sound of violent regurgitation finally stopped. "I'm so sorry, the pitfalls of live TV," said Jacquie, smiling direct to the camera. "Now, you were saying, Joy" she said, reinstating her sombre pose.

Joy cleared her throat, "Well, it's been a tough year. I separated from my husband," she began.

"And was that a sudden change?" asked Jacquie.

"Yes . . . well . . . . not really," replied Joy, "Our marriage had been in decline for a while, we had a lot going on, a lot of stress for both of us, Jacquie."

"So, there wasn't anyone else involved?" she pressed.

"No . . . ." she paused, dropping her eyes from the camera, "no one else." Swallowing hard, she was sure her uncertainty had given her away. "Anyway, after he left, things began to spiral. Debts were piling up, money was tight and I was feeling down and dejected and altogether utterly, utterly lonely."

"So, you were looking for love?" asked Jacquie.

"Not entirely," she replied, taking a deep breath. Joy glanced up to her friends and then back to Jacquie. "I know you're probably looking for me to say something completely salacious, that I was looking for a lover, or a toy boy or a sugar daddy, but I don't really know what I was looking for."

Jacquie was about to speak, but Joy cut her off.

"To be perfectly frank, Jacquie, I'm a woman of a certain age, I have four kids, a grandchild on the way, I work full time, and I run a home. And that's my life. I live for my kids. Our Zachary, he needs round the clock support, so I have one night a month when the boys are with their dad, and I'm off work where I get to be the adult. I get to be me. One night. I don't have the luxury of dates, I don't have the energy for the run-around, and I don't have the heart for the trade-off."

"Trade-off, you mean like losing your freedom, the commitment?" asked Dr Nash.

Joy's head spun around to face him; her eyes narrowed. She stared around him for a moment, not at him, just around his head. She had finally figured out what was amiss. She softened her face into a warm smile. "No, Dr Nash, I mean love. Love is our biggest trade-off because it's pleasure versus pain."

Dr Nash looked both confused and intrigued, as did Jacquie when she turned back to face her.

Taking a deep breath, Joy continued. "Imagine a life where you didn't care about anyone else," she said, "You did whatever *you* wanted, just to please you. You didn't have to worry when they didn't come home. You didn't have to care what they thought. You didn't miss them when they weren't there."

Joy stopped. She looked around at the audience. "Sounds great, doesn't it," she shrugged. "But in return, no one would worry about you, you would never feel like you mattered, and no one would ever miss you." She shuffled uncomfortably, "The truth is, Jacquie, we accept the *pain* of loving for the absolute rapture of feeling loved. A trade-off. But, it can be one-sided, where one person's having all the pleasure and the other, all the pain. I don't have the patience to wait around and see if a guy turns out to be an arse, or if he has some odd obsession, or if he's just a flat-out player. I'm not *planning* a future. I have a future with my family. I just wanted something for now, for one night, something that would make me feel good without having to trade-off for it, without the prospect of pain. And perhaps, to have someone touch me for some reason other than to wipe boogers on me." Lifting her hand, Joy wiped away the tears that had begun to fall. She hadn't tried to stop them. Everyone in that room had seen her naked. How bad would it be if they were to see that she was human too?

There was no applause. No laughter. The audience sat in silence.

"Wow, that's quite an answer," said Jacquie inhaling deeply.

From the audience came a lone, solitary clap. Followed by another. Joy looked up to see Meryl and Tabitha on their feet, hands together. Mischa stood and joined in, followed by Lauren, Carlee and Bernie, until the applaud spread infectiously across every seat and the entire audience were on their feet.

Joy smiled at Jackie, who stood and gave her a hug, as did Dr Nash, who up close smelt like gumdrops and whiskey.

"Well, now, we have to cut to a commercial break," said Jacquie, "but we'll see more of Joy later after her make-over. Now, we'll be back in three with our Billy, who is out and about in Cheshire showing off his big train, and Micheala who wants to get you all hot and sweaty, and not forgetting our Saturday chef Lucas, who's going to be making a delicious brunch burrito from tofu." she said waving at the camera.

"That was fantastic," she said turning to Joy and taking huge breath while holding her hands out to the side, before leaning in and giving Joy another hug.

"We have less than three minutes so let's get you backstage," called Cheryl, who was charging across the stage with a clipboard.

"Just give me thirty seconds," said Joy, hobbling off the stage and towards the crowd. Her friends were already on their way down, rushing over the steps in twos in a rush to get to the bottom.

"You were amazing," cried Mischa, throwing her arms around her mother's neck.

"Where's your grandmother?" asked Joy.

"Back row, out cold," said Tabatha, pointing back up the stairs.

"And where's Margot?"

"Last seen heading towards the car park with the limo driver," replied Carlee, rolling her eyes.

"I have to go, please keep an eye on her," said Joy, nodding up to the very far end of the seating where Joy could just make out Verity's low-heeled loafers sticking out from the end seat.

They all nodded, squeezing in another group hug before Joy clambered back up onto the stage, from where she was quickly jimmied across the floor and, up the entrance steps and back behind the big glittery panel, making it out of shot, just as the music started up and the commercial break came to an end.

Chapter 34

Walking back into the dressing room, Joy was met with an enormous bouquet of roses sitting on a trestle and a bottle of champagne with two glasses in front of the mirror.

She was dressed in her work uniform, having spent ten minutes outside in the rain taking '*before*' photos under a large cherry tree opposite the studio. Dabbing rain from her face with loo roll, she checked her phone and was about to call Robin, when she was stopped by a knock at the door.

"Sorry," said Dr Nash, popping his head around the opening. "I was passing this way, and make-up asked me to let you know that they're running a bit behind. Someone'll come and get you when they're ready," he said before turning to leave.

"So, how old are you really," shouted Joy, leaning back and resting her backside against the dressing table.

The Dr turned and stepped back into the room. Away from the studio lights, his suit looked more blue than grey, which brought out his eyes even more.

"I'm sorry?" he said, checking the corridor outside and pushing the door to.

"Oh, come on," laughed Joy. "Your skin is far too good, and don't think I don't see that grey hair. It's dyed. It's way too symmetrical, and don't even get me started on those eyebrows."

"What's wrong with my eyebrows?" he asked, smoothing them over with his thumb.

"They're not bushy. They're back combed," she said, laughing.

"I assure you, I'm 49," he said, folding his arms defensively.

"Well, I'm a nurse," said Joy crossing her arms, "And I have friends at the medical registry. I could just make a quick call and clarify that. That is if you're even a real doctor."

"Of course, I'm a real doctor," he replied. His voice suggested indignation, but his eyes said otherwise. His eyes were fixed firmly on the top button of her uniform.

"Then why the grift? Are you trying to con little old ladies out of their pensions?"

"No, don't be .... Whatever you're being," he replied, stepping closer. "Viewer polls highlighted that a lot of our viewers don't respect a younger doctor. They think we lack experience. It was all Jacquie's idea."

"So, how old are you?" She asked again.

Dr Nash coughed, his eye's quickly noting everything in the room but hers. "Thirty-eight."

"Oooh, such lies." Said Joy, breaking out into a giggle. "My mother will be distraught, you know, she really thought she was in with a shot."

"How old's your mum?" he asked.

"Seventy-three," she replied, her giggle growing into out and out laughter.

"Well, if she looks like you," he said, stepping closer still.

Joy stopped laughing.

"Are you going to pop that?" he asked, nodding towards the bottle of bubbly.

"Only if you have one with me, Dr Nash. I was never one for drinking alone," she smiled. Inside she wasn't smiling, she was screaming at herself to stop. She didn't know what she was playing at, flirting. She couldn't flirt, she made terrible jokes, and her come to bed eyes were more 'I need to sleep' eyes.

His eyes, on the other hand, twinkled beneath his back combed eyebrows and his fake dyed hair, which under the heat of the studio had worked loose of the hairspray and fell delicately across his tanned smooth forehead. Maybe it was the morning's alcohol or the adrenaline of the audience's cheer, but she was feeling a little braver than she normally would and was intrigued at just how far he'd take the bait.

He leaned across and picked up the bottle, and gripping it in one hand, he gave the cork a single twist and popped it into his hand before pouring two large glasses.

He was right in front of her now as he handed Joy a glass. "It's Dorian, Dorian Nash," he said.

Joy took the glass and sipped at the rim, giggling as the bubbles rushed down her throat and then back up and out of her nose.

"That's a very neat suture," he said, dropping his hand to her collar bone and running his finger down the length of her scar until it finished at her breastbone.

Joy felt her knees tingle. "There's another one on my thigh," she said, looking up at his eyes, biting her tongue as his mouth twitched on one side.

Dorian lowered his hand and placed it on the outside of her knee, running his hands slowly the whole way up her thigh until it stopped at the bottom of her underwear.

"Oh," he said, smirking" I did think you might be wearing your uniform like you did in that video."

Not taking her eyes from his, Joy reached down and wriggled herself out of her knickers and kicked them across the room. "Why don't you try again?" she said, holding her knee out towards him.

He stepped closer, running his hands once again up the outside of her thighs. Her skin fizzed under his touch, and she widened her legs enough for him to slide between them

He leaned forward and planted a tender kiss on the crook of her neck, followed by one on her ear, sucking in the lobe as he reached down and unbuckled his trousers. Lifting her up onto the dressing table, he pushed himself inside.

Joy let out a loud breathy moan. The touch of soft lips against her skin, the grip of firm hands against her hips, and the pressure, building inside her. He was a wonderful fit.

She pulled him closer. She wanted him, all of him, to be touching her as his mouth wandered clumsily to hers.

She came far quicker than she had wanted to. But her feelings of inadequacy soon faded when he juddered to a finished less than a minute later, breathing hard, indiscernible words into her ear as he did.

Running his hands up her torso, he unbuttoned her dress at the top and ran breathy hen peck kisses across the top of her shoulders and down to her breasts as he pulled himself free.

"So, is this the usual premier guest treatment?" she asked as his hot breath tickled at her soft doughy skin.

He shook his head before pulling down her bra and taking her nipple in his mouth, then releasing it. "What can I say? I have a thing for scars. And nurses."

Joy couldn't help but think that if that was true, he had either chosen his profession well, or abysmally.

"But, no," he continued, making his way across to her other nipple. "There's even a clause in my contract about not fraternising with the guests."

Squirming as he took her other breast in his mouth and held it there, "And what if a guest fraternises with you?" she asked.

Releasing her nipple, he stood upright and stared her blankly in the face. He shrugged, "Well, I don't recall there being anything about that in the contract." A smirk crossed his face as he lifted Joy off the table, carried her over to the uncomfortable sofa, and sat her down gently before lifting her dress and disappearing between her legs.

Chapter 35

S at at the table in her little kitchen, Joy stared at the photos that had just arrived in the morning post.

The first was the before photo, the one they had showed on the show right before her big reveal. It was of Joy in the rain beneath a tree. She looked miserable. Her pained smile and *'hurry the fuck up'* glare screaming at the camera.

The second was the after, and what an after it had been.

She had finally been retrieved from her dressing room and brought up to make-up where Susan, the lead MAU, was sat waiting. Susan was probably the coolest person Joy had ever met, with her long, impossibly red hair styled into a sleek ponytail and her youthful lips coated in thick luscious gloss. She wore leggings and an oversized shirt that she made look effortlessly haute couture. Had Joy not have just enjoyed two and half blissful orgasms, she might have felt a little inadequate, but instead, she felt like a goddess, a shagger of much lusted after celebrities and, after downing half a bottle of plonk while her fancy was being tickled, more than a little tipsy.

Susan had been the icing on the cake. She had made Joy look and feel like a movie star. Her makeup was sharp, her wrinkles flattened, and by the time she had been handed over to Jason and his magic curling irons, she could barely believe that it was really her staring back from the mirror. As Susan touched up her make-up and bronzed her shoulders, she had lifted a concealer stick to Joy's scar, but Joy brushed her away. She didn't want to cover it up. It was part of her now. It was part of her story.

They had given her a choice of three outfits for the big reveal, a glittering ball gown, a sharply tailored two-piece, and a floaty summery number that wouldn't have looked out of place in the promenade cafes of Cannes in August. She had picked the summer dress, it fit like a glove, and the audience had gone wild as she strode confidently down the steps on Dorian's arm, grinning ear to ear for reasons that no one else could possibly know.

They had let her keep all three, as well as a generous donation to the cardio unit and a magnum of champagne to take home, which they had all hammered through on the train home.

Now, barely three days later. It all felt like a dream, one that she often got lost in as she clung to the memory. She didn't hear Mischa come in from shopping or Owen, Elliot and Jay raiding the fridge for snacks. She definitely didn't hear the phone ring.

"Mum, there's a message on the answering machine," said Mischa.

"That's nice, love?" she replied, paying absolutely no attention.

"Mum." snapped Mischa from the hall, jolting Joy from a rather pleasant daydream where Dr Dorian Nash lived up her skirt. "The answering machine."

"Who's" asked Joy.

"Yours . . ."

"My what . . ."

"A message. On the answering machine." Mischa huffed loudly, rolling her eyes.

"Who from?" asked Joy.

Mischa shrugged. "Try listening to it."

Joy heaved herself up and wandered down the hall. The phone by the front door was blinking red. She pressed a button on the top, baffled as to how Mischa hadn't had the forethought to do so first.

"Hi, Joy, Hi. It's Cheryl. We met on Saturday at the studio. We've been trying to contact you, its's quite urgent, can you call the studio, extension 459"

The message ended.

The dopey smile on Joy's face dropped to a scowl as quickly as her head dropped from the clouds.

"Oh, fuck!" she spluttered, lifting her hands to her face and striding back down the hall. "Oh, double fuck!"

"What . . ."

"Oh, fuckity, fuck, fuck."

"Mum?"

"Bollocks . . ."

"MUM!" screamed Mischa.

"They know . . ." cried Joy as she turned to face her daughter.

"Who does?"

"Fuck . . ." Joy was pacing the kitchen, clutching her mobile phone to her chest.

"Mum, who knows? What do they know?"

"They know about Dorian," snapped Joy.

"Who's Dorian?" asked Mischa. Her face was growing more confused by the minute. Give it another few seconds, and she'd be completely cross-eyed.

"The doctor," said Joy, in a tone that suggested this was obvious.

"What. Fucking. Doctor?" snapped Mischa, her confusion rapidly shifting to exasperation.

"Dr Nash, Misch. They know about me and Dr Nash."

"Wait. You . . shagged . . . . Dr Nash?" said Mischa, her mouth dropping open into a wide, astonished grin.

Joy nodded, lifting her hand and raising two fingers, "Twice."

"Is that why you took so long to get changed? Is that why we nearly missed our train?" Mischa was laughing now, holding onto her blossoming belly as she stopped it from wobbling.

"I was drunk, Misch, and he had a Jacuzzi bath in his dressing room," she said, her eyes wide with excitement. And then the grin dropped. "But now they know. Shit, what if there's CCTV. They're going to ask for the money back, and the dresses. Oh god don't let them take the dresses."

"Mum, ring them," said Mischa, laughing so hard that she had to pull up a chair and sit down.

"I can't ring them, not now they know."

"You don't know that they know."

"Fuck." Said Joy, slatting herself down on the chair next to her daughter and slamming her face into her hands.

Mischa sighed, hauled herself back up and ambled back to the phone, rooting through the letter rack until she came across the original invite from the studio. She dialled the number into her phone before tucking it under her ear as Joy sat hyperventilating in the kitchen.

Joy waited. She couldn't hear what was being said, Mischa just kept saying yes, and the voice on the other end just kept talking.

"Ok, I'll let her know," said Mischa, eventually hanging up and hurrying back into the kitchen. "You, mother, are a hit," she said.

"A what?"

"A hit. That was Jacquie's assistant," she said, her face lit up with excitement "they were inundated with calls after the show, and they haven't stopped. People are calling. They want your advice."

"*My* advice?" Joy didn't understand. Given her current situation, Joy didn't think for a second that she was in the position to give anyone advice.

"Jacquie wants you to come back and do a segment, an agony aunt type thing where you take live calls."

"Me, tell people how to solve their problems, HA!" she cackled, "Don't be so silly."

"No, mum, I'm serious, and if it's successful, to make it a regular slot."

"On the telly?" asked Joy.

"Yes, on the Pressley Gang, with Jacquie and Dr Jacuzzi, starting Friday." she paused, "and, they'll pay you for it."

Joy felt her heart leap. But it quickly sank again. "Wait, on a Friday. I can't. What about Zach? It's school holidays" she said, nodding into the living room to where she could see him sat on the floor building a fort out of Lego.

"I can change my rota, and we can just tell him it's work," said Mischa.

"But I'm not supposed to be driving yet," said Joy despondently, pointing at the scar that poked out the top of her t-shirt. "I've only been to the shop and back."

"Mum, you don't understand," she replied, circling the kitchen. "They. Want. You. So, make some demands. Tell them you want a driver and ask them for an early slot so you won't be away so long." She stopped pacing. "That is unless you were planning on hanging around for some Jacuzzi fun?".

"No," snapped Joy. Her eager answer unconvincing when combined with the plum face and the twinge in her tummy, somewhere just below her belly button. "That was a one-off."

Mischa let out an exasperated sigh, "What's the worst that could happen?"

Joy tried her best to suppress the smile that was fighting its way across her face. "What are you waiting for then? Ring them back and tell them yes."

Mischa turned to leave.

"Wait," called Joy, "so they definitely don't know about Dorian."

"No," called Mischa as she marched back up the hall, making retching sounds, "but I do."

Chapter 36

Joy lay draped over the vast king size bed, wearing nothing but a delicate golden bracelet and a smile. A big smile. Huge.

Her heart was still all a flutter as she listened to the rhythmic whir of the air conditioning and the faint sound of clinking glasses somewhere further down the hall. Stretching across the soft Egyptian cotton sheets, she stared out across the river that wound gracefully around the quays, the sun glittered decadently atop the waters crest as seagulls circled, and pleasure cruises passed by in quick succession.

Her second life at Media City had quickly become her escape. She was a different person here. She wasn't Joy, mother of kids, mopper up of shit. Here she was Joy, TV luvvie and sex kitten.

She ate breakfast 'on the go', sipped coffee she couldn't pronounce from enormous paper cups and wore outfit's she could have only ever dreamed of. In the ten weeks since her heart attack, she was down over 20lbs and back in her size fourteen jeans, albeit with a touch of muffin top.

"You were wonderful today," said Dorian, sliding back in under the sheet next to her and pushing himself against her, nuzzling deep into her neck.

She really had been, the segment had been a hit since day one, and the number of calls for help they were getting had almost tripled. They had to be heavily vetted by the producers first, of course, with two then chosen for the live show. One a heartfelt plea, usually for help with a philandering husband or how to spice things up in the bedroom, the second an amusing public interest question that Joy, Jacquie, and Dr Nash would anecdotally discuss, dissect and eventually skirt around an answer.

Joy had slipped seamlessly into the team. She looked like a natural sat between Jacquie and Dorian, laughing about life's little mishaps. Whenever they were side by side, Dorian tucked his pinkie and his ring finger into the waistband of her skirt, rubbing tentatively at the lace band of her underwear. 'Our little indiscretion,' he called it, a way for her to know that he was thinking about it, even when he couldn't do anything about it. What it did, was push Joy's confidence through the roof, along with her libido.

So far, they had talked to a man who couldn't have sex with their new dog in the room because the dog had initially thought he was an attacker and had bit him in the nuts, to a banker who got aroused by socks, the smellier, the better, apparently. And today's gem. An octogenarian who had been gifted something from a niece but who didn't know what to do with it. After a short description from the caller, they had managed to determine that the gift was a vibrator and evidently, had been sent to her in error.

Joy had been on top form, suggesting initially that she could use it as a back massager, a foot scratcher, or if all else failed, it could be used to stir custard, breaking up all those hard to stir lumps. Jacquie had added that she could use it as a bookmark or something to press the fiddley little buttons on the Tv when she couldn't find the remote. It was eventually left to Dr Nash to explain exactly what the contraption was for and to advise that there was no shame in returning it to the sender with a note. Evidently, after finding out what it was, the caller didn't want to do that, and Joy was now left with a mental image that would forever be burned into her memory.

"I have to go," she said, pulling back the cover and searching the floor for her knickers, which she eventually spotted hanging from the floor lamp.

"Stay, a little?" he pleaded, pulling her back down onto the bed and wriggling himself in between her legs.

She had been so determined to say no. She had been decidedly steely that first day, arriving in the studio. She had at first ignored him, she had then derided him, but it was futile, and the first mention of joining him for dinner ended in them eating pot noodles in bed in the hotel next to the studio, something that was now a regular fixture in her diary, along with cardio appts, football practice and the PTA.

She couldn't say no to him. Nor did she want to. It wasn't actually him, though, that she couldn't fight. She couldn't resist that feeling. He made her feel alive, he made her feel young, he made her feel irresistible, and she was addicted to it.

Buttoning up her jeans, Joy checked her hair in the mirror as Dorian appeared from the bathroom. "Why don't you stay the night?" he asked. "We could go out to eat in an actual restaurant, or you could come to mine."

Joy's heart sunk. He asked every week. She explained why not, every week. "I have to be home before Zach goes to bed. He thinks I'm working."

"You are working," he replied.

Joys eyes widened.

"Um . . . . you were working, earlier," he added, hastily correcting himself. "He survived you being in hospital, didn't he? It's only one night."

"Mischa's seven months pregnant, Dor. She's shattered doing nothing, and Zach is a lot of work."

The truth was, she could have asked any of the girls to stay overnight with Mischa, she could have asked her mum. But she didn't want to have to ask anyone else. Mischa was the only person who knew why she wasn't home after each show, and she didn't ask questions. Others would, her mother especially, and Joy wasn't ready to answer any.

"What about Robin?" he asked.

Joy bit her lip and scowled. She didn't know why, but she didn't like him saying his name. "He'll be working."

"Then come over the weekend when he does have him," he said, snaking his arms around her waist and pulling her close.

"But what if someone sees, Dor? I don't want to be seen. People will jump to conclusions."

"And they'd be right, wouldn't they?" he laughed, laying a lingering kiss on her ear, "Anyway, what's so wrong with that?" he said. He looked dejected. Not quite kicked puppy, but she still hated herself.

"Why me?" she asked. "You could find any woman who would be delighted to sit in a restaurant with you."

"I've been burnt in this business, babe" he said, pulling his hands from her waist and slinking over to the large balcony doors. He crossed his arms and stared out at the quays. "There's always someone who wants to use you as a springboard, to make a name for themselves off the back of yours. Ask Jacquie, she's been there too."

"And is that what you think I'm doing?" she asked.

"No, that's the point, you found yourself here unexpectedly, like Dorothy in Oz, you don't have those aspirations, you're happy with just being here," he replied, "And that makes you a breath of fresh air in the middle of a tornado."

Joy smiled, "This, Dorian," she said, pointing around herself, "Is my perfect. I don't want to share this, and I don't want the attention. The local rag has literally only just stopped following me to the shop. Right now, this is all I can give you. Can you accept that?"

"Do I have a choice?" he asked.

"You have a choice to have this, and all of me, for a short time, or not at all." As soon as she said it, she hated herself, another ultimatum. Another me or them. She grimaced, staring at him as he remained focused on the window. Fortunately, the scorn she had been expecting didn't follow. Instead, he turned back to her, pulled her close again, and kissed her, wrapping his arms around her.

"I can accept that," he replied.

And he did. Over the following weeks, Joy reached a level of equilibrium that she had never thought possible. Owen and Elliot we're doing well at college, having got in by a hair's breadth, and Zachary, having gone up a year when the school went back in September, was adapting really well to the new routine. Mrs Mortimer had even commented on how even his meltdowns were becoming less sporadic, he was reading, and writing and taking an interest in what the rest of the class were doing, even though he still didn't want to join in.

Robin had stopped threatening her with court action every time she dropped him off. But then, he had mostly stopped speaking to her at all. There were no pleasantries. No '*how do you do*,' or '*goodbye*'. Just acknowledgement.

And every Friday, she got to forget it all for a morning, and just exist in a bubble of her own creation.

She had even begun to embrace her newfound fame. People would stop her out shopping and ask how she was. They would tell her how well she was looking or ask if Dr Nash was as lovely in person as he seemed on the telly. She always told them that he wasn't. She had even grown used to the ever-present photographer from the local paper; she had befriended him, to a degree. His name was Graham, and he was married with seven kids, two grandkids and an ageing Staffordshire Bull Terrier with rampant colitis. Every now and then, Joy would throw him a bone and let him get that perfect picture, lest he be forever hanging around waiting for her to take out the bins.

To top it off, The Go-Fund-Me had finally reached its end date and released the money, so she had been able to pay off the bailiffs, clear the mortgage and buy a new car, one big enough for ferrying around her soon to be expanding family. She also made good on her promise of donating fifty grand to the cardio unit, if nothing more than to keep them sweet, seeing that they wouldn't let her go back to work yet, and so she was swanning about on the telly instead. They returned the favour by making her a hospital ambassador, which sounded fancy enough, but involved nothing more than mentioning on live TV how amazing they were for not letting her die.

If Joy was in any way an optimistic person, she would have thought that she had finally found her happy ever after, her fairy tale ending. However, Joy wasn't an optimist, for a very good reason.

Chapter 37

Joy woke to the sound of Mischa screaming downstairs. Throwing on her dressing gown, she rushed out of her room and down the stairs, only to find her daughter, sat on the bottom step, laughing maniacally, while gripping the paper.

"Is it the baby," cried Joy, reaching the bottom of the stairs.

"No," squealed Mischa. She could barely get a word out for laughing. "It's you," she snorted, holding out the newspaper.

Joy snatched it from her hand and stormed into the kitchen. Flicking on the kettle, she sat down at the table and slat the paper down in front of her.

It took a moment for her to realise what she was seeing.

"Oh, bollocks," she said, staring at the front page.

It was a full-page image split into two. Both had been taken through a long-range lens and focused on a hotel balcony. In the first one, through the glass, you could make out two naked figures, one straddling the other atop a large bed. A small inset photo zoomed in on the top figure, confirming that it was most definitely female.

The second showed the same woman on the small balcony, wrapped in a sheet sipping champagne. Behind her in the doorway stood a man, naked as the day he was born with his genitals blurred out.

Above the photo's, the headline screamed, "Look who's playing doctors and nurses," in bold type.

"Oh fuck!" said Joy.

"Mum?" asked Mischa.

But Joy wasn't listening. Her head had gone completely numb and had inadvertently shut out all sensory input. She just sat there, open mouthed, staring at the pictures.

"Mum," said Mischa, leaning down and wrapping her arms around her mother's shoulders. "It's not that bad," she soothed.

"How did they get this, Misch? We were ten floors up?" she asked.

Mischa shrugged, "Helicopter, drone, camera pigeon, they have their ways."

"But how do they make it look so seedy. This isn't an affair. We're both adults."

As she scanned the page again, Zachary appeared from upstairs, grumming excitedly and chasing Pelé with one of his brother's dart guns, but on spotting Joy, he quickly shoved it behind his back and dropped it to the floor, instead stopping and scouring the countertops for errant treats. Joy ruffled his hair, picked up the newspaper and launched it into the bin, out of his view. She handed him an apple from the fruit bowl, and he immediately sat down on the floor and began to take chunks out of it.

"Mum," said Mischa, "You were in a hotel room, in the middle of the day with your co-host. To you, it's just sex. To them, and everyone who reads that shit, it looks like scandal."

"It's my fucking life Mischa, it's the only thing I had that was just mine. Now, they made it feel . . . smutty."

"That's showbiz," replied Mischa. Nervously flittering between and smile and a grimace.

Joy's phone began to ring on the table in front of her. She glanced at the screen, and picking it up, rolled her eyes as she answered. "What, mother?"

"Are you sleeping with that lovely doctor off the telly?"

"I'm fine mother, how are you?" she replied sarcastically while simultaneously mouthing *fuck off* into the handset.

"I don't care how you are, sweetheart. I just want to know if it's true," snapped Verity.

Joy put her hand over her face and lay her elbows on the table, rubbing her eyes. "I take it you've seen the paper."

"Hasn't everyone?" asked Verity.

"Well, I can assure you, I was *not* giving him CPR."

"How long have you been carrying on?"

Joy puffed her cheeks out. "we're not ca ...."

"Is it serious?"

"I'm not .... "

"Why didn't you tell me? I'm your mother," she snapped.

Joy sighed, "While I was in hospital, you gave a full expose to the Mail where you told them I had D cup breasts at nine and that you thought I was going to be a lesbian until I came home pregnant. You gave The Mirror photos of me in a bikini at 12. You told The Sun about your disappointment that I was a gym slip mum, which I bloody wasn't, by the way."

"Yes," replied Verity, completely ignoring Joy's scolding, "But this is good news, he's a successful doctor, a handsome TV personality, rich too, I imagine. See, I always told you that you could do so much better than . ."

"Bye, mum," said Joy, shutting down the call and turning her phone off.

She was about to slat that in the bin too when there was a knock at the door.

"If that's the press, get rid of them." She whispered to Mischa, ushering Zachary into the living room and slumping onto the sofa. He quickly crawled up onto her lap, spitting chunks of apple everywhere as he grummed softly.

"Love my Spuderoo," she said, quietly stroking his head. "Don't worry, Mummy's not going anywhere again, I'm literally never leaving the house, ever. It's just me and you kiddo"

"Mother," called Mischa, from the hall.

"Did you tell them to fuck off," she shouted back.

"Well, I will if you like," came Dorian's voice as he appeared around the corner, followed swiftly by Pelé, who was barking loudly whilst snipping at his heels and trying to cock his leg up his trousers.

Joy's mouth dropped open. She wasn't dressed, toys littered the floor where she hadn't tidied up before going to bed and her hair was full of half chewed apple chunks.

"What are you doing here?" she asked, smoothing down her hair and running her fingers under her eyes as Zachary disappeared under her dressing gown.

"I wanted to see if you were OK," he replied, brushing the dog away with his foot. Pelé ran straight back to him, sniffing enthusiastically at his shoes.

"You could have called."

"I wasn't sure you'd answer," he replied.

Joy raised her eyebrows and paused. She probably wouldn't have. "They have me on the front page of the paper, Dor. Shagging. On the front page."

"They have *us* shagging," he said, stepping into the room, still trying to brush the dog from his feet. He didn't sit down.

"Oh, my mistake, I don't recall them zooming in on your tits."

"I've got my cock out," he argued back.

"It's blurred out. You look like a hairy action man," she snapped, "How did they know we were there?"

Dorian shrugged. "It was booked under a false name. Either someone saw us going in, or someone at the hotel tipped them off. Is it really that bad?"

"My boys will see this, Dorian. It will be the top hit when someone searches my name. It's going to be all over the internet. I've already caused them so much fucking shit this year."

"They're teenage boys, Joy," he reassured her. "And they're your kids. I'm sure they're thicker skinned than that."

"And what about school? Zach's teachers. I'm supposed to be his carer. He's supposed to be my priority."

"Fucking hell Joy, would you listen to yourself." He stammered. Joy shifted uneasily. He'd never raised his voice before. "Do you really think you don't deserve a little fucking happiness? That you can't enjoy a bit of fun, and heaven forbid a shag. It doesn't make you a bad mum, Joy. it makes you human."

Joy shot him a look as Mischa made blatantly mock retching noises from the kitchen.

Joy put her finger to her lip as she heard Zachary's grumming getting louder, it was verging on changing into a growl. "Keep your voice down," she hissed.

"Joy . . ." he started, but she stopped him in his tracks.

"It's over Dorian," it was a lot of fun, but I'll call Jacquie later and tell her I'm not coming back."

Dorian's face crinkled, his face lilting to one side. "Why on earth do you think that this would be the end. And I've just spoken to Jacquie. She already thought we were screwing. Everyone on the set does."

Joy's face dropped into a horrified scowl.

"Jacquie think's it's fantastic, she said the chemistry will take the segment to another level," he carried on.

"Oh well," spat Joy, throwing her arms up to her head. "That's ok, so long as the segment doesn't suffer."

Mischa appeared behind Dorian in the doorway, handed them both a coffee, plucked Pelé off Dorians trousers, and Zachary from under Joy's robe. But the little boy quickly scrambled from her arms and ran over to Dorian, tapping him on his knee. He first pointed to the knee and put his hand up for a high five before pointing at the TV and then darting under the table, from where Mischa fished him out and carried him upstairs.

Joy's heart dropped, and her face froze. She had never seen Zachary do that before. He wasn't good with strangers. Occasionally he'd be ok with people if he recognised them. And then it occurred to her that Zachary did recognise him. He had seen them on the TV together, and seeing as he was at school every Friday, and that Mischa flat out refused to watch them together when he wasn't, the only time he could have done that was that first show, when he was with his dad. *Robin had watched.*

"Look Joy, I'm not ...." began Dorian, but was cut off once more by the sound of the front door opening and heels storming down the hallway.

"Well, well", said Margot, barging into the living room, followed swiftly by Meryl and Carlee, who was holding up her phone.

"Are you filming me, asked Joy" pulling her robe tighter.

"No, Tabs, Lauren and Bernie," replied Carlee pushing the phone up against Joy's nose, "they couldn't come."

Joy waved into the camera, and her friends grinning faces waved back.

"We came to see if you were ok, but I guess you're just fine," said Meryl smiling widely and eyeballing Dorian up and down.

Joy smiled awkwardly, "And good morning to you too, Ladies."

"Why didn't you tell us you were sleeping with the hot Doctor?" said Margot, completely ignoring the fact that he was stood less than a foot away.

"I haven't seen you, you swanned off to Portugal with that driver guy, and no-one's seen you since."

"His names Marco," she replied, crossing her arms at her chest.

Joy burst out into an uncontrollable cackle. "Margot and Marco, my god, you two shagging must be a narcissists wet dream."

"I saw you twice last weekend and you never mentioned it," said Carlee.

"I'm not going to blurt it out in the fucking co-op am I." replied Joy, her eyes offering an apologetic smile to Dorian.

"You could have called us." Said Meryl.

Joy readjusted her dressing gown and shuffled forward to the edge of the sofa "This year, I've had my heart ripped out, metaphorically *and* literally, and perhaps I just wanted to *not* be the one everyone was talking about. I would have told you when I was ready."

Joy knew this wasn't strictly true, just like when Robin had left, once other people knew about it, it became real, and real couldn't be taken back. Joy just wasn't ready for real.

Carlee dropped her eyes to the floor while Meryl shuffled her feet and mumbled under her breath.

"You know he's only 38," said Joy, offering up the only other juicy gossip she could think of by way of an apology. "They make him look older for the show."

"Ooh, you got a toy boy too," squealed Margot, clapping her hands. "Is yours an absolute animal in bed too?"

Dorian coughed loudly, "You know I am in the room."

"Then go and find something constructive to do," replied Margot, followed with "Oooh," as she heard her phone ping in her pocket."

"Jacquie Pressley just posted a statement to the gram," she said, "clicking open her notifications."

"What does it say?" asked Joy. She could feel her heart throbbing in her throat.

Margot tapped the screen. "We are aware of reports about an ongoing relationship between two of our show's friends. We would like to remind our viewers that Dr Nash and Joy Lane are both single, consenting adults, and what they choose to do in their own time is not any of our business. But ...." read Margot, raising her index finger. "We wish them all the love in the world on what is no doubt a difficult morning and want to reassure everyone that this will not affect the scheduling of your favourite daytime show."

"See, I told you she's fine," said Dorian smugly, "Which reminds me, have you got the kids tonight?"

Joy shook her head. "It's Robins weekend."

"Only now," he said, stepping forward and wringing his hands together, "You've got no reason not to be seen out with me, and I've got this little thing tonight."

"Wait," said Meryl, checking her phone, "Isn't tonight the . . . ?"

"The TV awards, yes," he replied, cutting her off.

"Is that tonight," asked Joy. Jacquie had been trying to bribe her into it for weeks, but she had been reluctant given her track record on nights out.

"Come with us," he asked, holding his palms together, "If we turned up together, it would really show those hacks thinking they've got one over on us. Plus, you might actually have some fun."

Joy thought about it. She couldn't deny that an evening of glitz and glamour sounded better than a night in front of the TV, eating healthy steamed vegetables while her heavily pregnant daughter gorged her body weight in chocolate ice cream.

"But I've got nothing to wear," she replied.

"Ha-ha," said Margot, clapping frantically, "You've got that gown they gave you for the make-over."

Joy felt her tummy somersault itself into knots. Between her friends egging and Dorian's eyes, there was nothing else she could say but, "Ok then," while nodding anxiously and flashing a nervous smile at Dorian.

Meryl and Carlee squealed, jumping up and down. They launched at Joy, ambushing her on the sofa.

Margot held up her phone and logged into Joy's Facebook, snapped a picture of Joy grinning like a Cheshire cat. She tapped "Cinderella will go to the ball." hastily into the keyboard, before uploading it to the world.

Chapter 38

*O**uch!***" screamed Joy as Carlee yanked tightly on the back of her dress. It had been far too loose with just the zipper, and being made almost entirely of chiffon and sequins, had been far too complex to take in with only a few hours to spare. Carlee had rushed to the rescue, adding eyelets and a ribboned corset tie to the back, which she was now using to try and crack the wiring in Joy's sternum.

"You don't want it falling down and having a nip slip on the red carpet, do you?" said Meryl, who was sat crossed legged on the bed, flicking through a two-year-old copy of vanity fair for 'inspiration'.

At this point, Joy didn't really care all that much if she did flash her nipples. Her hoo-ha had already been featured in every available media, and she had been plastered in the full throes of passion across several tabloid front pages, so what would a little areola matter now.

"I still need to be able to breathe though, and walk, and talk," she groaned, as her friend squeezed the last of her breath from her lungs with one final tug before tying it off with a neat double bow.

"I still think this is a bad idea." She said, jiggling about in an attempt to rearrange her boobs, which, thanks to all the tugging, were now pointing in opposite directions. One up, one down.

"You're going to have great fun," said Mischa, applying another coat of varnish to the false nails she had spent an hour trying to attach.

"I'd have just as much fun with you," said Joy.

"I'm going out. I . . . . have a date," replied Mischa, lifting her chin.

Joy pulled her hand from her grasp. "Who with? You're nearly eight months pregnant."

"I'm sorry, I didn't get the memo where it said I have to live in a box until the baby's born," she snapped, yanking her mother's hand back to her knee.

"Does he know?" she asked.

"I couldn't hide it if I tried. And we're only going to the cinema. It's not like he's taking me out raving. He's from Uni, a post-grad. He's been tutoring me."

"Is that what the kids are calling it now," chuckled Meryl, not even looking up from the magazine.

"Is he the father?" asked Joy.

Mischa scowled, "You promised you wouldn't ask about that. But no, he's not," she said, shoving the varnish brush back into the bottle before heaving herself up off the end of the bed.

"Did you tell dad not to let Zach have any more treats tonight? He ate an entire packet of KitKat's this morning after one of your brothers left them out on the side."

"Yes," said Mischa. Sighing loudly as she tried to leave the room.

"Did he say anything, when you dropped Zach off?"

"Who?" asked Mischa.

"Your Dad."

"About what? The KitKat's?"

Joy glared at her. It would appear that the baby brain was well and truly kicking in early. "About the papers?"

"No, he didn't really say much at all."

"Maybe he hasn't seen them," added Carlee.

"He had," said Mischa, "I saw the newspaper in the wheelie bin on the way out."

"If he can run around with a younger woman, then you can do what you like," said Meryl.

"Has he ever mentioned her, his girlfriend?" asked Joy.

Mischa shook her head, "But I've never asked him. Should I?"

Joy didn't answer.

"Wow," gasped Joy, as she placed herself in front of the hallway mirror. Her hair had been curled into Real Housewife worthy waves, pinned up on one side and coated in at least two cans of hairspray. Meryl had done her make-up as close as she could get it to her make-over look, all sultry smokey eyes and heavy kohl, while the long black dress clung to her perfectly, the bodice keeping all of her lumps and bumps tucked up under its bones, while the trailing sequin skirt gathered at the hip in a swirling rose of black and silver taffeta.

"I do believe that Cinderella is good to go," said Carlee, spritzing Joy's shoulders with shimmer spray while brushing errant cotton threads from her back.

Running her finger over the soft skin beneath her eyes, Joy glanced up at the clock in the mirror, but her sight missed its aim, and she found herself staring straight at a picture that sat above the coat rack. A much younger Joy, and Robin, stood staring down at her from a Christmas party, taken in the late noughties. It was probably the last time she remembered feeling like a princess, although her puffy tulle dress wasn't a patch on the designer threads that currently encased her. Nonetheless, she had kept it perfectly preserved up the loft, unable to part with it. The same could be said for the picture, she had removed her wedding photos from the dresser and the living room walls, replacing them with pictures of the kids and a print she got cheap off eBay. She knew that that picture in the hall was still there, it wasn't that she had forgotten to take it down. She simply didn't want to. It was one of her favourite memories, and she didn't want to have to erase it from her life, just because he had removed himself from it.

A double beep outside jolted her back to her reflection in the mirror.

"Sounds like your carriage has arrived," said Carlee, clapping her hands together and squeezing Joy's arm excitedly.

Chapter 39

Opening the door, Joy held her hand to her chest as the glinting black limo came to a stop at the end of the path. Slipping her feet into the glitter-encrusted heels she'd borrowed from Margot, and which were at least half a size too small, Joy strut down the path, followed hastily by Mischa and Carlee, holding their mobile phones aloft and yelling for her to smile.

Around her, curtains twitched, and nosey faces popped out of front doors before venturing out onto the street in their Saturday sweatpants and slippers, just as the limo door opened and Dorian Nash stepped out, dressed in a sleek black tux and holding a bunch of flowers that contained more heads than the whole of Joy's front garden, waving to the neighbours who hastily lifted phones and tablets, eager to be the first to post the sighting to social media and get in on the heavily trending #doctorsandnurses.

As Joy reached the gate, a small ripple of applause erupted and floated up into the sky, getting louder as she crossed the threshold where she was welcomed into an embrace by Dorian, who was wearing his best TV grin.

Climbing into the Limo, she flashed a wave to her neighbours before glancing back towards her little house, with its wonky curtains and peeling soffits. The amalgamation of her two worlds, completely separate up until now, felt ludicrous, much like a child waking up to find a theme park in their garden, it felt impossible, and yet it was happening.

Another small cheer followed as the door closed, and the car pulled off towards the glittering lights of the big city, and once more, her worlds parted.

Joy's stomach had hit the spin cycle as their car joined the long queue of limo's that lined the street outside the Manchester Central Convention Centre. Its imposing glass façade and elegant sloped roof lit up in shades of pink and blue, with searchlights strategically placed at the front exit, reaching their arms up into the cloudless October sky above.

Dorian, who was old hat at these types of occasions, had given her a crash course in award show etiquette, starting with how to get out of a limo whilst teasing the threat of showing your underwear, but without actually doing so, something that apparently Jacquie was an expert at. Where Joy was concerned, she thought that this was a case of the horse not only having already bolted but it was now several miles up the road and taking hostages.

Next up, smile. And keep smiling, don't stop smiling even if your jaw aches so much it feels like it's about to drop clean off your face. Smile if you win. Smile if you don't win. The only reason to stop smiling was to yawn, and if so, to not catch yourself yawning on camera, else you'll never be invited back again. Yawning was to be reserved for toilet breaks or masked by taking a drink.

Thirdly, don't get pissed. The rule of thumb was to pace yourself. The event was several hours long, and a lot of it was spent waiting around for other people to stop talking. Considering there would be a constant supply of champagne on every table, it would be easy to get carried away, especially with all the drinking that was being done whilst trying not to yawn. Apparently, many of the big names circumvented this by having a bottle of apple juice brought to them, which they kept under the table and topped up during commercial breaks. The younger crowd hadn't quite worked this out yet, and Dorain couldn't remember a single event where at least one reality TV star hadn't had to be carried out for getting smashed and pissing on something. Apparently, once they got inside, there would be wagers available on who it would be this year, although Joy already had an uneasy feeling that she would probably be odds on favourite by the end of the night.

Lastly, if all else fails, smile and nod.

At last, the car pulled up next to the steps, and an usher stepped forward and opened the door.

The camera flashes began before she'd even got one foot out and didn't stop until she had made it up the steps, across the forecourt and onto the pink carpet outside the entrance. They stood for a moment and posed for photos before being ushered inside where they joined a conveyor belt of stars, jumping through hoops in an attempt to get into the hall and find their seats.

All was going swimmingly until Joy set off the handheld metal detector being wielded by a security guard, and had to explain to three burley men, with big guns and big 'guns' that it was the wires keeping her rib cage together that had triggered an evidently over sensitive body scanner. Fortunately, one of the security guards recognised her from the morning papers and waved them through with a smile, despite not taking his eyes off her cleavage. This was one of the pitfalls of lowcut tops and between the breast scars, and Joy had grown somewhat used to it.

Having taken an hour to get through the lobby, they were finally squeezed through the double doors and into the main room, where they were each handed a glass of champagne and directed to table five, To Joys horror, table five was right in front of the stage, and where Jacquie was already waiting for them with her husband Oscar, Michaela, the Saturday workout girl, and several members of the crew. Joy had hoped to sit near the back and run out as soon as it was over.

They were up for two awards this year, best weekend show and best lifestyle show, both of which they had won the previous five years, and which was Jacquie's entire focus for the months leading up to the awards. Joy had no doubt that it was why she had been so determined to get her on the show before the nominations were released.

Taking her seat, Joy accepted a glass of ice-cold bubbles from their server, a young girl with a thick plait and a name badge that said Suky, and then sat and gawped around the room. To call it as such did it no justice. Being a converted train station, it was enormous, and with its resplendent arched ceiling coated in thousands upon thousands of twinkling lights, it was like sitting under a sea of glistening stars.

Joy made it through the first half with little issue. She had managed to stick to only two glasses of fizz and had spurred Dorian's advances for a joint trip to the loos. But by the time they were halfway through the second half, her face felt like it was melting off her face, and her lips had gone numb. She had, at least, found a moment to apologise to Jacquie for finding herself naked in the national press, and Jacquie had simply laughed it off as a PR dream. Joy didn't like to think that her sex life was now being used as a viewer magnet, but they were paying her incredibly well, and she felt loathe to complain that she didn't particularly like seeing her tits in print.

Finally, their big moment had arrived, and as they announced the results of the Best Lifestyle Show award, Jacquie made them all hold hands around the table and close their eyes, knowing full well that they'd be on the big screen.

Unfortunately, Joy was so focused on trying to keep her eyes closed while smiling, and definitely not yawning, that she didn't even hear them announce the results and so still had her eyes closed as Dorian grabbed her by the arm and dragged her towards the stage.

Joy hadn't wanted to go up on stage. She was quite happy where she was. But neither Jacquie nor Dorian would accept no for an answer, and so instead of going full Cinderella and running off into the night as they beckoned her onto the steps, she had taken Dorian's hand and followed them up.

Stood on the stage, she looked out over the sea of faces. She knew most of them, some of them she'd watched since she was a little girl. Joy had expected to feel out of place, like an imposter. After all, this wasn't her show, this wasn't even her real job, but as Jacquie made her speech and the sea of TV faces applauded, Joy felt at ease, welcomed, and immensely proud. She had never won anything before, not on her own or as part of something bigger. If anything, at school, it was pretty much guaranteed that whichever team she was on would lose, so she had stopped even caring about winning.

But, she had to admit, it felt pretty good. She was also grateful that their host decided to hand them the best Weekend Show award while they were up there in a bid to wind things up a bit quicker, which also meant that she only had to go up and down the steps once. They were remarkably high and very thin, and she didn't want to get this far and then ruin it by being wheeled out on a stretcher at the final inning.

Joy's head was still very much up on the stage as their car veered into a wide leafy street and pulled up outside of formidable metal gates. They opened automatically as they approached and closed again behind them, as the limo trundled up a driveway that was longer than Joy's entire street.

Yet, the house was smaller than the grounds suggested, two-story with four bedrooms, it had its own cellar, a loft bar and an underground pool. He had a gym, a hot tub, a full-sized tennis court and a kitchen that was bigger than both hers and the house next door put together. The whole place reeked of fresh-cut flowers and was decorated in anxiety raising wall to wall white.

"Do you even live here?" she asked, her mouth dropping open at the sight of smudge-less windows and countertops full of expensive barely touched gadgets that still glinted in the overhead spots.

But there were no family photos, no coat rack full of muddy shoes, no dishes in the sink and no notices stuck to the enormous double fronted fridge. She pulled the handle, and it swung open to reveal that there was very little inside of it either, bar a neat row of beers stacked onto the bottom shelf. She ran her finger around the worktop. Everything looked brand new, knives were razor-sharp, cutlery wasn't watermarked, and there wasn't a single crumb in the bread bin.

"I do," he replied, "I mean, it is my house, but I'm either at the studio or at the flat in town, which I assure you smells like a gym locker. I'd say the cleaner probably spends more time here than I do."

Pulling his phone out of his pocket, he turned off the mute, and it began to ding incessantly. He quickly turned the mute back on.

"We're still trending," he said excitedly.

"Of course, we are. We won," she replied, pulling two bottles of beer from the fridge.

"No, *we*," he said, slipping a bottle opener from a hidden drawer in the centre island, and handing it to Joy. "As in us, hashtag doctors and nurses. It's number one on insta and Twitter."

"Oh," said Joy, deflated. She already knew this. She had checked her phone in the car and had chosen to ignore it. She did, after all, prefer it when her notifications didn't involve her name, or her breasts. She snapped the top off the two bottles and took a swig.

"It says we make a handsome couple, that we look like a natural match," he continued, taking the other bottle and gripping it under his middle finger.

"That's only because they still think that you're several years older than me. I wonder what they'd think if they realised that you were my young bit of stuff. They'd probably call me a harlot."

"You *are* a harlot, and that's why I love you," he said, glancing up from his phone.

That one word stopped Joy completely in her tracks. She bit her lip and stared blinkingly at him.

"I meant *love* as in figuratively," he said, dropping the bottle and the phone down onto the countertop and turning to face her. "The same way that I love wine and cheese."

"You love me like you love *cheese*," she said slowly, her eyes narrowing.

Sliding towards her and running his hand up her side, he located the top of the zipper and ran it down slowly. "I like to eat cheese, I like to eat you, it's a fair comparison," he said.

Joy made a loud audible groan as, for the first time in several hours, her lungs fully filled with air, and her back cracked as it arched. The dress dropped to the floor, and she stepped out of it, where it stayed almost perfectly upright as if being worn by an invisible child.

Pulling her close, he kissed her neck as she undid his bowtie, and grabbing her hand, he led her out of the kitchen and up the winding staircase into the master bedroom.

Picking her up, Dorian lay her down gently on the bed. It was pitch black, with only the light coming in through the crack in the door and illuminating his face above her. Running his hands up the inside of her thighs, his mouth made its way down her body to meet them, but he had barely made it past her belly button when Joy heard the unmistakable sound of the Killers emanating from her handbag where she had dropped half way up the stairs.

"Ignore it," he said, his voice muffled.

Joy tried but no sooner had it stopped than it started ringing again.

"It's Mischa," she said, pushing his head away. "She knows how big tonight is. She wouldn't ring if it wasn't _really_ important." Joy sat up. "It could be the baby."

Dorian rolled over onto his back as Joy climbed down from the bed, and ran from the room, only to reappear again less than a minute later, panicked.

"What is it?" he asked, sitting upright on the bed.

Slatting her phone back into her bag, she slid her legs back into her underwear. "It would appear my house in on fire," she replied.

Chapter 40

The taxi pulled up just as the fire engine was winding up its hose. The street lit up for miles around with flashing blue lights that flittered off into the sky and which they'd been able to see as the car sped along the main road to the estate.

Joy had the car door open and her bare feet out on the tarmac before they had come to a stop, her loosened off dress trailing behind her, and her shoes gripped tightly in her hand. Dorian, dressed in cargo shorts and a hoody, followed close behind. Mischa was sat on the kerb opposite, holding a mug of tea and a blanket.

"Misch, are you hurt," squealed Joy, dropping to her knees in front of her and cradling her at her shoulder.

"I'm fine," she replied, "I wasn't here. It was already on fire when I got home."

"How? we were all out," asked Joy, glancing back to the house.

"Not all," replied Mischa. She was twiddling her thumbs around in the loose threads of the blanket, her eyes fixed to the floor. "Elliot had a row with dad and stormed out. He came home and skinned up, fell asleep."

"Skinned up?" asked Joy.

"Pot mum, he was getting stoned."

Joy knew exactly what it meant. She had just never imagined one of her boys mixed up with that. "Is he . . ?" she couldn't even bring herself to ask it. Instead, she scanned the street for more bodies huddled under blankets. She felt her heart race as she realised he wasn't there.

"He's OK, mum," said Mischa, sensing her panic. He'd gone outside to watch the stars. They found him asleep in the grass. The dog too. Looks like he'd dropped his joint butt on the sofa before he went out."

"I'll fucking kill the little shit," seethed Joy, holding her hand to her chest and collapsing onto the curb next to Mischa. "Where is he?" she asked.

"Police station."

"What, why?"

"He had a lot of weed on him, and they're trying to do him for possession. Margot's already there," said Mischa.

"Shit," exclaimed Joy, standing up and turning to the steaming pile that *was* her house. "Has anyone checked on next door?"

"He's in hospital," said Mischa.

"Will he be ok?"

Mischa quickly realised Joy's confusion. "Oh, no. He was already in hospital. Hip replacement a couple of days ago, a stroke of luck, really."

Joy bent back down and hugged Mischa tightly, then told her to go home. Giving one last glance to the house, she turned and left, clambering back into the taxi with Dorian hot on her heels.

By the time they made it to the police station, Margot had already managed to get Elliot released based on a first offence and him having less than ten grams of weed. Joy found them sat on a bench in the park opposite the police station. Elliot was bent over double, sobbing into his hands.

Without saying a word, Joy sat next to him and draped her arms over his back, running her hands through the hair on the far side of his head. He began to cry louder, shifting his head until it was lying in her lap, and she held him there, rocking side to side while Margot and Dorian went in search of an open drive-through.

Neither Joy nor Elliot had moved an inch by the time they got back with three of the strongest coffees on the menu, a chocolate milkshake and a burger, by way of bribery munchies, in an attempt to get the stoned 16-year-old to talk.

It worked. The smell of the burger being enough to get Elliot to lift his head long enough that Joy could make eye contact. His face was red and swollen, his eyes barely able to hold themselves open under the weight of tears.

"I'm so sorry," he croaked.

"What are you doing smoking that shit?" she said, brushing her hands across his cheeks, "Have I taught you nothing."

Elliot shrugged. "Is it bad?"

"The house, yeah, it's bad. But it's only a house."

"I didn't ..... " he began, but Joy quickly shushed him.

"You didn't think, did you? But sometimes we don't because thinking isn't easy, especially when the consequence of thinking is counterproductive to what we want to do. So, we just do it instead. But then we have to accept the consequences of not thinking. It's all part of learning to be a grown-up, Buddy." She said, dipping her head so that her eyes followed his. "But there's a lot of grown-ups who still haven't figured it out yet, so I guess you're already one step ahead of them, so long as you learn to think in the future."

He nodded, rubbing his eyes as he took the milkshake from Margot before spotting Dorian, who was mooching around behind a hedge.

"What's he doing here?" he spat.

Joy watched as her sons' eyes narrowed. She hadn't expected any of them to accept Dorian with open arms. She hadn't really expected to have to introduce them at all. Reaching over, she gripped his fingers in her own. They were shaking. Scared? Stoned? Cold? Maybe a bit of all three.

"He's my friend," she said. "When Mischa called, he brought me home, to you. But that doesn't matter. Wanna tell me what you were arguing with dad about?"

"He wouldn't let us watch you." Said Elliot, "We wanted to see you on stage winning an award, and he wouldn't let us. He cut the plug off Mischa's telly."

Joy glanced over to Dorian and back to Elliot. "You could have just respected that. I wouldn't have minded. You could have watched the repeat with me tomorrow. I would have liked that."

"It wasn't about the show. He was looking for an argument all day, picking little fights. He wouldn't take Zach to the park. He was raging over you. And him." he said, shooting a dagger towards Dorian.

Joy moistened her lips, "Yes, well, your dad didn't think either, and now *he's* facing the consequences. But that's his dumpster fire, not yours."

"Where are we going to live?" asked Elliot.

Joy sighed, "We'll figure something out. I was thinking about moving anyway. We can afford it now, somewhere bigger, maybe a bigger garden. We can finally get you those football goal posts you've been begging for every Christmas."

Joy had been thinking about moving for a while, she'd only put it off because of Zachary, but she didn't have much choice now. Even if the insurance paid out, it could take months.

Elliot sniffled loudly, nodding, he dropped his head onto Joy's shoulder, as she squeezed his hand just that little bit tighter.

Chapter 41

He's done what?" hissed Joy into the phone, her face switching from grimace to cringe and back again, as she listened on in horror.

"Ok, thanks, I'll speak to him *again*. I'm so sorry," she said.

The line cut dead, and Joy shoved her phone into her pocket and pushed her way back through the double doors of the little café and re-joined her friends at the table.

"What is it?" asked Meryl, shovelling carrot cake into her mouth from a tiny spoon.

"Trouble in paradise? asked Margot.

"No, it's the school, again," she said, picking up her cappuccino, taking a sip from the wide rim and then licking the chocolatey froth from her top lip. "Zach isn't coping. On Monday, he smacked his teacher, yesterday, he dropped his trousers in assembly and tried to pee on an artificial sunflower, and now he's bitten another child. In the face."

"He's gone through a lot this year. It'll settle down," said Carlee, draining the last of her latte and scooping chocolate syrup from the bottom with her finger.

"But he's fine at home," protested Joy.

"Because *you're* there," said Meryl, "You're his comfort blanket."

"And he seems to like the new house," added Joy.

This wasn't strictly true. He had taken a week or two to come to terms with the move. Joy had tried to make it as much like their old house as she could, but their furniture had been so old, it was impossible to get new, and while she'd managed to replace most, if not all, of his toys, and bribed the landlord into letting them decorate his bedroom like it was at home, it was just so much bigger, and she had woken most morning to find him in her bed because his was soaking wet.

Joy, on the other hand, loved it. It was all she had ever dreamed of. Built on the new estate on the opposite side of the village, she finally had a kitchen big enough for a full-size table and with enough space to have gadgets, a washer and a drier, *and* a dishwasher. She loved that dishwasher more than anything else. The whole house was bright and airy and clean, and with five bedrooms, no one had to share. Mischa finally had a full sized room, which had now been designated the nursery.

Yet even she still didn't feel completely at home there, but Zachary had seemed to settle after the first couple of weeks and had even stopped hiding under the side table. But she couldn't say for sure if that was just because it was a different table. She had spoken to him often, explained how there was nothing she could do, that their house wasn't safe, and she knew he understood, but she also knew that where Zachary was concerned, there was a world of difference between understanding and accepting.

"Maybe it's just burnout," said Carlee.

"Half term is coming up, my class have turned into little shits this week, and they're all neurotypical," added Meryl.

"Enough negative," said Margot, swooping back in from the toilets, "You were telling us about Dr Luurve."

Joy rolled her eyes, "He's fine, as far as I know."

"You having second thoughts?" asked Carlee.

Joy sighed, "Not really. Things have just been *different* since we went public."

Margot shuffled her chair a little closer. "Different how?"

"I don't know," said Joy, shrugging. "I tried to call him twice this week, and he didn't answer."

"Does he normally answer?" asked Meryl.

"I dunno, I've never called him in the week before. I'd just show up on a Friday, like tah'dah. But we just don't spend as much alone time anymore. Before, we were always alone, and it was just us. I liked being alone. But now he wants to go out or lunch, and dinner, or to the park, and he's obsessed with talking to "fans."

"Ah, but that's because before," said Meryl, "you were sneaking around like naughty teenagers, and now, you're behaving like adults. Adulting is boring."

"But the sex is still good, right?" asked Margot.

"Yeah, amazing, but again different. Whenever I stay at his he gets up straight after and goes for a workout, says he needs to make the most of the testosterone surge or some shit."

"But that's his territory," said Carlee, "It's not neutral ground like a hotel. At a hotel, there's nothing else to do but shag, but if you're in his space, you have to fall into his routine."

Joy took another long sip of cappuccino, "But he's the one that pushed for this. I was happy with how things were?"

"Because," said Carlee, "before, it wasn't real. Now it is and real comes with expectations that never meet up to the fantasy. You'll adjust, eventually."

Joy's nose wrinkled as her top lip shrugged. "Is it the same with Marco?" she asked.

"God no," spluttered Margot, nearly choking on her chai latte, "There is nothing boring about that boy. He's like a calculator,"

"A what?" chimed Meryl, Joy and Carlee in unison.

"A calculator," she replied, holding her arms up either side of her head as if it was self-explanatory. "You know, like if you keep pressing the right button, the numbers just keep going up and up and up until your brain fogs and your eyes cross. It's the Portuguese apparently they're all like that, i things don't work out with lover boy, we should move," she said, nodding directly at Joy.

Joy groaned as she heard her phone start to ring again "She picked it up without looking. "What?"

Joy heard the line connect, followed by "Joy, is that you it's Cheryl, from the studio."

"Fuck?" said Joy, covering the mouthpiece with her other hand. She cleared her throat, "Hi Cheryl, sorry about that . . ."

Cheryl cut her off, "Can you come in a little earlier tomorrow, Joy? The producer wants a word."

"The producer, have I done something wrong." She asked.

"No, it's all good. See you tomorrow." The line cut dead before she could say anything else.

Meryl, Margot and Carlee, all leaned forward across the table.

"I've been summoned to the headmaster's office," she said, dropping her phone back into her bag.

"Why?" asked Meryl, still chewing on her last mouthful o carrot cake.

"I guess I'll find out tomorrow." She replied.

Chapter 42

The following morning, Joy left as soon as she'd dropped Zachary off at school, instead of going home to shower first. Swanning onto the empty set, she followed the sound of voices backstage until she found Jacquie with two of the producers in a conference room behind the coffee machine.

Grabbing a flat white on the way past, she knocked at the door and was quickly called inside. She was about to sit down at the table when the door opened again, and Dorian rushed into the room, taking a seat beside her. He leaned into her and running his hand down her back. He tucked his littlest two fingers into her waistband.

"Sorry I've missed your calls. I've been in endless meetings. It's been relentless," he whispered into her ear between planting soft kisses on her neck. "I'll make it up to you after the show."

"Wasn't important," she replied flatly. "Have you been called in early too?"

"No, I was already in the building, I saw you arrive. What's going on?"

Joy shrugged, as the taller of the two men, the one with a bulbous nose and bright white hair, slat a large green folder down on the table and turned to face her. The other shorter man, who looked a lot like Penfold from Dangermouse never so much as lifted his nose from his folder.

"Right, Joy, we have a situation." He said sternly.

Joy gulped. She had never met these producers before Jacquie was the executive producer together with her husband, and Joy didn't really understand the different functions and why the show needed more than one or why there needed to be three of them now staring at her.

"Michaela, our weekend workout girl, has broken her leg in a riding accident," he said solemnly, "Horse threw her, the poor thing, but we have a show to run."

"And we need someone to step in and take her place," added Jacquie, who was clearly just as eager to get this over and done with as Joy was.

It took Joy a moment to work out exactly what it was they were asking her, or as it turned out, telling her that she needed to do, and as it sunk in, she broke out into nervous laughter until she realised that no one else was laughing. And then she wanted to cry. "Wait, you want me to exercise. What, are you hoping I might have another heart attack live